FLATLINED 2:

RESUSCITATED

KS OLIVER

Cover Designed by Aija Monique of AMB Branding

Published by Diamante' Publications, LLC

www.diamantepublications.com

ACKNOWLEDGEMENTS

I want to first thank God for keeping me and Blessing me with the ability to tell and write my story. I'm claiming my healing in advance. Thank you for my faith and my strength. I've been through it all and some, but it has only humbled me and made me even stronger. I am made of bricks now.

To my babies, Sha'Kwan and K'Shaun. We did it again. I can't thank the two of you enough for teaching me every day about what it is to truly love unconditionally. Thank you for picking me of all people to be your mom. I am truly blessed.

B. here we are again. Thank you for everything, especially being a part of this journey with me. It has been a great lesson on life. Thank you for being different and for riding with me no matter what.

To my parents (Clarine & C.O) and my grandparents (Mary & Woody Oliver), my mother in law Rose Abby, my step dad Leroy White and my step mom Desiree Thornton-Oliver. Last but not least my mother from another Sharyn Whitfield. Thank you for everything. You have supported me in everything I have set out to do. I appreciate each of you and the unique things that you bring out of me.

S/O to ALL of my siblings and
nieces /nephews.

Thank You China "MUA" Smith of Unique Faces Makeup and Deasha Phillips, my stylist for my gorgeous cover picture.

A Huge thank you to Aija Butler for a great cover once again. I appreciate you as a designer and a friend.

Thank you to my day 1's Racquel Williams, LeTorri Mitchell, Sakiyna Washington,Reynica Young, Kim Stone, Latrice Burns, Nadia Brown, Karen Cabret, Chaun Tucker, Dominique Watson, Karessa Martin and Aunt Minnie (Leigh McKnight).

My sister in law Claudette Davis. Thank you for being the big sister I always wanted but never had.

To my brothers from another Jacorey Oneal and Rashad Bligen. I love yall both down. Time flies and the sky is the limit. Hold your head up and keep going.

Markini Smith my brother and best friend we are at the end of our race. Thank you for not crossing the finish line without me.

Mickey Jermaine (MJB), thank you for always being there. You have been a great person and a listening ear for years and I appreciate you more than you know. I can never have enough prayers.

S/O to the Literary Ladies of the ATL Kenni York, Kierra Petty, and Nika Michelle. Thank you for helping me to tell my story and for always being there when I needed you and when I didn't. My sisters in Lit and boy do we act the part. We don't always get along, but you are there when I need you always.

Last but not least my readers and supporters I couldn't do this without you. I appreciate you all. Dr. Gladue, Dr Leslie, Dr. Staton, Mita Rhodes, Marco Andujar, Tiffani Andujar, Jacqueline Bradsher, Khayree Acklin, Dominee Tillman, Dorothy Abby, Karen Fields, Cristana Smith, Todd Simmons Jr, Tina Williams, Roberta Wilson,

Angelina Concepcion, Erka Diggs, Tory Lowe, Polow Don, Kendra Graves, Crystal Alexis, Ebonee Jones-Dunbar, Jina Love, JeaNida Luckie-Weatherall, Marissa Palmer, Imani Acklin, Tacara Wilson, Wendy Scriven, Joyce Dickerson, Chico, Alexis Goodwyn, Juanesia Faulks, Priscilla Murray, Mary Glover, Morticia Gray, Monica Alexander, Donna Merz, Cash Alexander,Kim Jones, Laquanda Mack, Meldamion Huguley, Krystal Moon, Ilka Natal, James Bonds,Patrice Prayer, Quinitra Johnson, Yaasiyn Andujar, Shameka Reynolds, Rasheeda Reynolds, Angel Taylor, Kendra Littleton, Bridget Harvey, Spenecia Flemming, Cryshonda Kiser, Chauncey Hairston, Linda Hairston, Jessica Champion, Bev Uter, Anthony Francis, Kenyetta Hall, Iyona Mack , Jamora Johnson, GiGi Gilbert, Flora Edwards, Shy Misses, Charlmayne Settles, Charlecia Martin, Kathleen Lucus, Marilyn Simmons, Anita Wiley, Cherelle LaBove, Evelyn McKnight, Marquette Pitts, Derelle Hamilton Kisha McRae, T'Shsean Harris, Kim Swanagan, Audrey White, Qiana Drennon, Stacey Thibodeaux, Rashaun Whitson, Alba Henderson, Selena Dabbs, Tara Waters, Robin Waters, Majestic Cruz, Jamerrick Brown, Linnea, NeNe Capri, Nasia Stalutti, Terri C Ross, Flora Edwards, Juanesia Edwards, Felicia Henderson, Shanae Acklin, Tiffany Lide, Erica Walton, Sherita Walton, Ms Jeanette, Anttelicia Daniels, Crystal Andujar ,John Brandon, Felicia Doss- Curtis, Renee Wallace, Lola Bandz, Erma J Batemon, Nickie Batemon, Melverna Monroe, Reesie and many more….

DEDICATION

I dedicate this book to all of the people who have had a hand in molding me into the woman I am today, but especially to those who didn't physically make it to see me rise above all of life's challenges. RIP Edna Mae Andujar. RIP Ruben Andujar. RIP Mark Watkins. RIP De'Andre Muckelvaney. Rip Jarvis Jones.

In Loving Memory of my brother Ajmal "Red" Acklin and my Aunt Lisa Lee. I watched you too fight and it makes me even more determined to WIN. Each and every time I feel like it's gotten too hard, I think of you both and your willingness to fight back. It is then that I am reminded of the type of family I come from. We don't give up. Though you aren't here, I know that God just had other plans. As long as I continue to fight this battle, we all WIN.

A Special Dedication to those Lives that Lupus Stole

Rest in Peace

Patricia Ann Swanagan
February 1961- July 2013

Kamisha S Fenner-Lowe
March 1977- November 2006

Herminia Beltran
September 1953- November 2013

~ PROLOGUE ~

The breeze of the cool, tropical air brushed past the stray locks that managed to escape the wrap that held Kai's curls back away from her face and nape. She inhaled a quick breath to not disrupt her breathing and tightly grasped the railing as she gazed out across the ocean. It was the clearest blue she'd ever seen in all of her 30 years of existence. It was so pure, so crystal, and so majestic in color and calmness that she couldn't help but compare it to her life. Although the waves were moving at a rhythmic pace with the occasional crashing of tides here and there, Kai couldn't think of a better metaphor for her life than the presence of the ocean. Just like it, she'd experienced what was once a steady pace followed by unexpected crashes, or incidents, yet things had managed to settle back down into a rhythm that wasn't exactly like its start, but was soothing just the same.

Closing her eyes, Kai envisioned the dress hanging from the closet door in her double-sized, top deck, ocean view cabin. She didn't need to look at it because she knew its details by heart. She could just about feel the thin, satin fabric against her flesh. The crispness of the white was symbolic. This time was pure and true; this time was going to be the happily ever after that she deserved. She smiled to herself. Even beyond this day she knew that she'd keep that dress forever, though she'd probably never wear it again. It wasn't just because of the significance it held pertaining to the change that she was about to experience in the next couple of hours. It was because HE had chose it for her.

Kai wanted to scream across the deck with joy as she took in the entire view. Paradise lay before her and just beyond its horizon stood the beginning of her forever. If she could bottle up the view and the nostalgia of the moment to keep it forever also, she certainly would have because it was all something else that HE was responsible for. It felt great to have someone who understood her and was in-tune with her so precisely that he could pull off such an elaborate magnitude of surprise that left Kai completely speechless. Truth be told, it was a state of being that Kai hadn't been in for over a year since regaining her grasp on who she truly was. Others would surely marvel over the fact that the outspoken Kai was rendered speechless as HE dominated her heart. She was nothing short of willing to follow his lead knowing that he had only innocent intentions and objectives that were developed from a loving place.

"Are you ready?" A gentle, feminine voice asked from the doorway behind her.

Kai didn't need to turn around to see that Sissy was looking at her with eyes of adoration. While Sissy marveled over Kai's strength, Kai marveled over Sissy's insight. It had been Sissy who was determined that this day would come. But, even Sissy had no idea that it would be this grand and this phenomenal. There was something about the sentimentality of it all that just made them both feel a renewed confidence in the power of love.

With her back still to the older woman, Kai nodded her head. "As ready as I'll ever be."

Sissy moved forward and stood beside Kai at the railing. Slowly, she reached for Kai's hand and gave it a reassuring squeeze. Even in the warmth of the tropical land that they were blessed to be visiting, Kai's palm was ice cold. Sissy felt the young beauty tremble and smiled at her. "Cold hands make for a warm heart."

Kai smiled as she continued to glance out over the water.

"You're nervous?"

Kai considered the question. In the last few years she'd been through more than any one person could ever bear and still remained sane, yet there she was; still living and breathing and able to tell about it all. She'd had enough ups and downs to know when something was right or wrong. That calming peace reminiscent of her ocean view rested inside of her. "No," she replied shaking her head ever so slightly. "I'm not nervous. I'm ready."

Sissy looked over her shoulder toward the open door and caught a glimpse of the shadow of Kai's dress. "That dress tho!"

"I know right! I'm telling you, day after day that man doesn't cease to amaze me. I'm telling you, honey that dress is the perfect contrast to that dang orange jumpsuit I was wearing half a year ago." She cringed at the thought, but forgetting it simply wasn't possibly. It was a part of her story now; a part of her truth.

"Ooh no, girl. Orange is not your color."

"No girl, my color is red as in I was seeing nothing but red to land me there." She grasped the railing and leaned over laughing. The memory was comical now, but the actual incident had been tragically emotional at the time. "I was out for blood, honey."

Sissy chuckled. "I betcha nobody's gonna press your buttons again. That was a true testament to how crazy you can get, girl. Truth be told, I was scared for brother's life."

They shared a laugh, both fully knowing how dire the circumstances had been and how passionate Kai could be when something actually touched her heart and pulled at her emotions.

"I can almost still smell it," Kai said, breaking their moment of amusement.

"What? The stankness of that cell?"

"That and the mix of blood and sweat," Kai whispered. "And I can almost recall that heated feeling that was ripping through me, nearly blinding me. I couldn't do anything but swing, girl. I was swinging for my life, for my sanity, for my family back, for my health back, for my peace of mind back, for my heart back…All that anger…all that frustration…Honestly, I didn't realize that I had such physical strength, but I was determined to end dude's life with the blow of my fist." She balled her hand up at the memory and her diamond caught the glare of the sun, creating a sparkle effect that neither she nor Sissy missed.

Sissy grabbed her hand. "Yeah, he got what he deserved and that whole thing is behind you now. You can move on. It's okay Kai."

Tears welled in the pockets of Kai's eyes as she turned to the woman who was like her big sister.

"It's okay to let it go and revel in your happily ever after, Baby Girl," Sissy told her. "You deserve it. The past is in the past. Satan didn't win this one, Baby Girl."

Kai nodded and turned her head to focus her eyes back on the flow of the beautiful waters before her. She did so just in time for a lone tear to roll down her cheek. A lot had transpired; some things she'd never forget and some things she wished she very well could. But, even that most damning, fatal memory wasn't going to taint the beauty of today. Sissy was right. Satan hadn't won this one and nothing or no one was about to rob her of the happily ever after she'd been through turmoil and frustration to finally get to; not even the thought of what she'd done.

Part 1:

Struggling to Breathe

Resuscitated

~ Chapter 1 ~

"What did he say?" Mz. C asked.

Kai sucked in her breath and waved her hand mindlessly as if her mother could see it through the phone. "I couldn't really care less. All I know is that I better have my money on time because I don't have a problem catching a flight back to England. But he better think twice about messing with me like that because he knows that with me taking that long flight I'll have plenty of time to plan out how I'm going to deal with his butt and he don't want none of this."

"You're not flying to no England," her mother responded exasperatedly. "Last thing you need to be doing is taking a trip anywhere and getting yourself all stressed out over this mess. Hopefully he'll just sign the papers and it can all be over and done with."

Kai paused at her position in front her glass coffee table overlooking the set of candles she was customizing for a wedding that she was planning. She stepped back and took a seat on her black leather couch, shaking her head at the pile of rhinestones she still had to hot-glue to the candles. The task itself wasn't strenuous, but considering the two trips she'd taken back and forth to the laundry room downstairs, the quick trip she'd taken for her treatment that morning, and the bending and lifting she'd been doing in the process of packing a couple of boxes filled with stuff for this event, she was beginning to feel a little winded. But, for Kai it wasn't unusual. That was the kind of thing that she'd learned to deal with since learning that she was living with Lupus.

In May of 2010, following a series of misdiagnoses and horrid declines in her health, Kai Davis was diagnosed with Lupus. The entire ordeal had been life altering, not to mention heartbreaking. Her proverbial plate was overfilled with depressing news as diagnosis after diagnosis found its way to her doorstep. As if trying to regain some level of acceptable health wasn't taxing enough, Kai was hit with a double-whammy: as her health was fading so was her marriage. At a time when she needed him the most, her husband, DeWayne Davis, had decided to withdraw his compassion and support. She got that it was all a bit much to deal with and perhaps at times she herself was hard to take, but that in sickness and in health, 'til death do us part portion of their vows resonated loudly in her mind and spirit. Maybe it was hard for DeWayne to cope, but at the end of the day he wasn't the one suffering; he wasn't the one who didn't know which breath would be his last. It was she who had to face the world with Satan utilizing several illnesses to try to hinder her from enjoying life. If anything, she was the one in need of assistance with coping. For that reason, she'd decided enough was enough and left DeWayne there in England to figure out how he was going to cope while she focused on what she deemed was most important: Surviving for the sake of her children. The hardships leading up to the Lupus diagnosis had been nothing short of dramatic and exhausting, but the emotional shift in her life following it seemed like a greater burden than her actual illnesses.

Now, as Kai clutched her chest and tried to regulate her breathing so that she could press on with her work, she listened as her mother discussed her pending divorce. Kai had long since filled out the paperwork necessary to file for divorce, but needed DeWayne's signature. She'd mailed the forms to him and had been waiting three months for him to return them with his signature. Not only had he failed to do so whenever she mentioned it to him via phone, but he'd given her a whole spiel on how they needed to try again and how she was acting out of emotion rather than actually thinking it through. He could believe whatever he wanted to believe, but Kai was done. Now more than ever she realized how precious life was and didn't want to waste another moment in a failing marriage with a man that didn't support her in her darkest hours.

"Okay, ma. I gotta go," Kai said, cutting her mother off partly because she didn't want to discuss it anymore and partly because she needed a minute to regroup.

"You okay?" Mz. C asked with concern lacing her tongue.

Kai knew better than to alert her mother. The last thing she wanted was to get her mother riled up and running over to rescue her. Over time Kai had learned how to manage these types of moments. She was resilient if nothing else and was determined to not let it get the best of her. It had taken her some time to come to terms with everything and now that she was on a path to moving out of her depression and reclaiming some parts of her life, Kai couldn't allow herself to backslide, or let others see any bit of weakness in her.

"Yeah, I'm okay." She told a half-truth, but it wouldn't be the first time, nor would it be the last. She was flaring and she knew it, but she could deal with it. She would be okay.

"You sure? 'Cause honey, you sound like—"

"No, Ma. I'm okay. I'm gonna call you later."

"What time is that wedding you're doing?"

"Two o'clock tomorrow."

"Okay, 'cause if you need me to come then I'll—"

Kai cut her mother short again. "Mz. C, what did I tell you? I'm fine, honey. Go parent Khy or something," she joked.

Mz. C gave a faint chuckle and reserved her concern. She knew her daughter, but she also knew not to press the issue. "Uh-huh. You make sure you dial this phone later."

"Yes ma'am. Love ya'."

"I love you too."

Kai disconnected the call and tossed her cell phone onto the sofa next to her. Her body was telling her that the time would soon come for her to throw in her white towel and go in to be seen about. Shaking her head, she dismissed the idea. She had work to do. When it was time to tend to herself she would. She felt weak as she kneeled down in front of the glass table, picked up her tweezers and began to assemble the rhinestones once more.

Her company, Kai's Soirées, was beginning to pick up clientele and her reputation in the Atlanta area was stellar. By no means was she going to let this little lapse she felt coming on hamper her from providing her current client with quality as promised. Coordinating and designing gave her pleasure and relief. It allowed her to step outside of the depressing reality she was living and gave her a chance to continuously create something beautiful and great. The fact that it brought in a considerable profit was icing on the cake. She needed to be able to do something to keep her sanity and supplement her income. Although DeWayne was sending money home to support their family during the separation, she still couldn't rely on him alone. It wasn't in her nature to do so. Kai was a go-getter, always had been and would ultimately continue to be so. Since she was 17 she'd fended for herself, and owned her own home and car while maintaining a decent job. Now, given her diagnosis, she was unable to take a regular nine to five desk job, or any job that would be considered strenuous. Her medical team simply wouldn't allow it. Truthfully and most importantly, she knew that her body wouldn't go for it either. With a business degree, a criminal justice background, and a certificate in medical billing, there was no way that Kai could just sit there and do nothing to provide for herself and her children. Being a business owner was the next best thing. It afforded her the opportunity to generate her own income and it gave her a sense of accomplishment. She wasn't offering up that milestone in her life to Lupus no matter what.

***

Kai turned onto her right side and stared out of the tiny slit between the panels of her curtains. She didn't have to look at the clock on her dresser to know that it was still the middle of the night. For hours she'd been lying there attempting to go to sleep despite the agonizing pain that was consuming her body. She'd been telling herself all day that it was mind over matter, that she could press on and work through it, but in this moment she wasn't sure how much longer she could be strong. At times like this she missed having someone next to her; someone to comfort her, get her whatever she needed, or in this case someone to escort her to the emergency room, which was the one place she dreaded going. The thought of the long waits, the stuffy waiting room, rude hospital staff, and hours wasted doing nothing but waiting. Steps of the whole emergency room experience made Kai want to just shut her eyes and block out the pain. Unfortunately, it wasn't that simple and even more unfortunate was the fact that there was no one there to endure it all with her.

Screw DeWayne and his lack of support, she thought to herself as she winced at the relentless aching sensation that was claiming her body. Her thoughts quickly shifted to doing what was necessary now. Who was there, or not was of no consequence. Slowly, she managed to sit upright in bed and take a look at the clock. 3 A.M. was a perfect time to visit DeKalb Medical in the middle of the week. Perhaps it'll be empty, she prayed as she reached for her cell phone. Luckily, her brother Morris was temporarily living with her. She would have to rely on him to keep an eye on her house and her sleeping children and even possibly get them ready for school if she didn't return home in time for whatever reason. Scrolling through the call log alone gave her great difficulty as she tried to find her brother's cell number. A sigh of relief escaped her lips as she finally hit the call button.

"Yeah," he answered groggily after four rings.

Another sigh found its way out of Kai's mouth. She'd been afraid that he was sleeping so hard that he'd miss her call. There was no way she would be able to make it down two flights of stairs to reach his room in her basement in order to let him know that she was leaving. "I gotta go to the emergency room," she told him.

"Huh?"

"Wake up, boy! I need you to watch out for the kids and make sure they get up in time for the bus. I have to go to the emergency room."

A rustling sound occurred as she listened and envisioned him sitting up in bed, pulling himself into a more alert state. "You aight? What's wrong?"

No, I'm not alright, she thought. "I'll be okay. Just some pain. Go back to sleep, but you know, keep your eye out for the kids and when I hang up set your alarm for 6:15 to get them up from school."

"You need anything?" The concern building in his voice was apparent.

"Just for you to tend to the kids," she reiterated as she began to slide out of her bed.

"You don't need me to go with you?"

"For what? To watch them give me a shot? Just get the kids to school. I'll call you when I'm on the way back."

Morris was reluctantly acquiesced to his sister's request. "Alright. 6:15." A yawn echoed through the line.

Kai slightly shook her head and hoped that he actually remembered to set the alarm before dozing back off to sleep. "A'ight, bye," she said before disconnecting the call.

It took her longer than usual to pull on a pair of gray sweat pants and a black tank-top that she often referred to as one of her uniforms. Very rarely did she deviate from the simple outfit when doing routine things, such as visiting a medical facility. She had to have enough black and white tank tops as well as t-shirts of varying cuts to start her own black and white boutique. The ease of it was perfect for her. She never knew when she would have to pull something on right quick and could never really go wrong with a simple, classic black or white top. You could never be tacky in those standard colors. She may have been going to the ER, but just because she wasn't feeling her best didn't mean that she had to look a hot mess.

Kai took her time slipping into her shoes before she grabbed her purse, and made her way out of the house. Really, she had no other choice. Her body wouldn't allow her to make certain movements, or move above a certain speed without threatening to pull her to the ground in agony. She knew that her family hated it when she transported herself to the emergency room. To them it was an emergent situation of the worse kind whenever she deemed it necessary to go in. Memories of the two times that she'd flatlined while in an emergency didn't sit well with them. Kai understood it, but she'd gone through enough of the visits and flare-ups alone to know the procedure like the back of her hand. She also knew that she really didn't need an entourage.

The thought of DeWayne resurfaced as she put her white Ford Explorer into reverse and backed out of her driveway into the silence of the early morning. Although she never wanted to alarm her family unnecessarily, it would have been nice to have the man who had pledged forever to her by her side. The streets were empty as she made her way through the city of Decatur in pursuit of DeKalb Medical Center's emergency room. It took her nearly 25 minutes to get there due to the strenuousness of gripping the steering wheel and the discomfort of sitting upright in the driver's seat.

Finally she reached the facility, parked, and walked in through the automatic glass doors to sign in at the triage desk. To her surprise, she wasn't mandated to sit in the waiting room before being ushered back to the small triage room.

"What brings you in this morning?" The male nurse asked.

"I'm having severe pain in my joints," she said. "Arms, legs, neck. Stiffness. I have Lupus, so I'm flaring."

The nurse keyed some stuff into the computer system and without looking at her, pointed to a chart on the wall. "Rate your pain from a 0 to a 10."

Was he serious? Kai didn't look at that chart. She knew it like she knew her social security number. Cutting her eyes and chalking it up to the nurse being unfamiliar with Lupus flares and the pain associated with it. "It's a nine," she replied.

He tapped the keys some more and asked her a series of health related questions before coming over to her with his thermometer and blood pressure cuff in tow. "Open your mouth and stick this under your tongue," he recited robotically.

Kai followed his instructions. As he placed the stick inside of her mouth she noticed him taking in her appearance. She'd gained a little weight over the course of the past couple of years, but it looked good on her. People often marveled over the ebony beauty and she was used to it. It wasn't a conceited notion, yet a truthful observation.

Kai was starting to take pride in the fact that she was regaining the unyielding confidence she once had before the diagnosis. The problem now with walking in her grace was that most didn't associate beauty with illnesses. The prejudice and ignorant comments and behaviors perturbed her to no end, and the expression on the nurse's face indicated that he was thinking exactly what she was used to people thinking.

The nurse pointed to her left arm and she lifted it slightly so that he could put the blood pressure cuff on. They operated in silence as he pressed the corresponding buttons to get the cuff to tighten. Seconds later the contraption dangling from her lips beeped and the nurse removed it, still without saying a word. A few more seconds passed and the monitor attached to the blood pressure cuff beeped and reflected its reading. Only then did the nurse disrupt the verbal silence.

"Ninety over sixty!" He exclaimed as he stared at the monitor. His eyes darted over to Kai's and she returned his stare without blinking. "How long have you been experiencing this body pain?" He asked as he removed the cuff.

"A week."

"How long has it been since you've been diagnosed with Lupus?" He stood in front of her with a scolding expression on his face.

Kai smirked. She knew where this was going. "Nearly two years ago."

"You know with pain for that long you should really have been to your rheumatologist by now. With your blood pressure this low it's a pretty dangerous situation."

Kai squinted to get a good look at his badge which was awkwardly turned as it dangled from the lancet and string around his neck. "Let me tell you, Daniel, I've been dealing with this for a minute and I'm pretty good at maintaining. The last thing I'm about to do is be constantly complaining about a condition that there is no cure for and running back and forth from the doctor's office knowing that they're limited in what they can do for me. I've just about learned had to manage this thing and let me tell you, mama makes being sick look easy." That last remark was to let him know that she knew he'd originally assumed that much of nothing was wrong with her based on her appearance. He could eat dog poop for all she cared. Kai was over people, their narrow-mindedness, and their misconception on how life was for every Lupie.

Daniel, the nurse, took the hint and turned away from Kai to tap his computer keys once more. "We're gonna go ahead and get you into a room and get some blood work done before the doctor comes in to chat with you, okay?"

Kai nodded and pulled out her phone. "I know the drill," she told him, no longer concerned with engaging in even the idlest of conversation with him.

Daniel led her to an exam room and instructed her to get undressed while pointing to a gown that she should change in to. Kai simply pursed her lips and nodded. Moments after getting changed there was a tap on the door. She prayed that it wasn't Daniel returning to get her blood. She'd had enough of his smugness. "Come in," she called out hoarsely.

The door popped open and a round, dark skinned woman with a huge smile entered with her supply cart filled with tubes, syringes, and colorful rubber bands. “Good morning sweetie.” Her energy was a little too upbeat for Kai, but it was a welcomed change from the dry attitude turned condescending reaction she’d received from Daniel.

“I’ve had better mornings,” Kai replied honestly. Then she thought about some of the worse mornings of her life when she hadn’t been able to move at all, let alone drive herself to the hospital. “Hmm, but I’m blessed all the same,” she followed up.

The phlebotomist smiled as she sat her cart on the counter and washed her hands. “That’s what I like to hear,” she said. “I’m Roberta, but everyone calls me Robbie. We’re just gonna rob you of some of your crimson spirit so we can get it down to the lab and see what’s going on with you.”

Kai chuckled. “I’m sure it’s the same ole – same ole.”

The cheerful woman snapped on her plastic gloves and walked over to inspect Kai’s veins. “Uh-oh, that sounds not so good.”

“It is what it is,” Kai responded.

Robbie retrieved a blue band and tied it snuggly around Kai’s right arm. “Any trouble getting your red river to flow before?”

Her terminology made Kai grin a little as she shook her head.

“Alrighty.” Robbie selected a needle and gave Kai a reassuring smile. “You’ll feel a little prick and then lickety-split we’ll have spillage.”

True to her statement, Kai felt a very slight prick and together the women watched as her blood began to flow through the narrow suction tube and down into the myriad of plastic vales that the woman soon capped off with colored tops. The process lasted six minutes tops and before Kai knew it she was once again alone. The chart on the wall indicated that the approximate wait time to receive the results of her blood work back was 45 minutes. She rolled her eyes and pulled out her cellphone once more. Without a special person by her side to at least keep her entertained while she continued to sit in pain, she decided to focus her attention on Facebook.

Wondering if anyone else was up at that time of the morning, Kai posted a simple status.

I'm just about sick and tired of being sick and tired! – at DeKalb Medical Center

She scrolled through her timeline mindlessly as the seconds turned into minutes. Trying to ignore her thoughts and feelings was becoming an even greater task than trying to ignore the pain that was assaulting her body. Her eyes watered up and Kai wasn't sure how much longer she could sit there waiting for someone to do something to provide her with even an ounce of relief. Just as the thought entered her mind the beep of her text message indicator became drowned out by the sound of another tap at the door.

"Come in," she said once again as she placed the phone beside her on the exam bed.

"It's me again sweetie," Robbie called out gleefully as she teeter-totted back into the room. She held up a syringe that was labeled and smiled. "The candy lady's here for ya'."

Kai's prayers had been answered. *Finally something for my pain*, she thought. "What is it?" She asked. She had her assumptions, but with everything that she'd been through over the years she needed to know exactly what was happening and what was being given to her.

"It's a little Toradol shot to numb that pesky pain you're experiencing," Robbie replied as she scrubbed her hands and put on a fresh pair of gloves. She walked over to Kai and smiled.

"Arm or tushy?"

The thought of getting up and attempting to bend over, or even slightly leaning over to give the tech access to her behind made Kai want to throw her hands up in defeat. It simply wasn't going to happen. Her eyes darted down to her left arm and Robbie instantly shuffled over to her left side to administer the shot. In just a few quick movements it was over and done.

"Those results should be back soon, but someone from radiology is going to come zip you down for an x-ray and then zip you right back," Robbie advised.

"X-ray?" Kai asked.

"Yes, ma'am. With the Fibrosis we wanna get a peek at those lungs girlie."

Kai nodded. "Ah. Of course." In her mind she'd skipped over that step, simply wanting to be freed of the pain that was tormenting her and released to go rest in the comfort of her own bed.

"Sit tight for me." Robbie patted Kai's legs and exited the room.

The blinking light on her cell reminded Kai that she had an incoming text. 'Who would be texting me at this hour', she wondered. But she didn't have to wonder long as she picked up the phone and clicked the icon for her texts to see what awaited her. The message was from Adrian,

Billy's godfather. He also happened to be the cousin of Bill, Billy's father. A smile found its way to her lips as she read his words.

Don't give up, Kai. I'm waiting for you. We're crossing the finish line together. When one of us wins, we both win.

The message was short and sweet, but it touched her heart tremendously. The tears that she'd been holding back for what seemed like forever could no longer stay pressed behind the invisible dam she'd been holding up. They flooded from her eyes as her heart ached for the love and comfort of the man that promised her the moon and stars. How Adrian's message brought her back to thoughts of DeWayne was beyond her. After a while, she figured that his sincerity and support from a distance reflected what she wished she could get from her husband.

It touched her that Adrian knew exactly what to say to bring her the slightest bit of comfort. It touched her even more that although he was going through his own medical and health ordeal, he found the time and the heart to reach out to her so that she could feel encouraged. Adrian had recently been shot and was dealing with the aftermath of a series of multiple surgeries. Kai admired Adrian's strength and perseverance. Out of all the people she knew, only Adrian shared that bond with her of knowing what it was like to be at heaven's front door. The empathy she received from him was genuine and greatly appreciated. His message was perhaps the written and electronically received push that she needed to grin and bear this trip to the hospital as well as her unresolved feelings for DeWayne and keep pressing forward.

With a refined belief in her ability to overcome the current obstacles before her, Kai returned to her Facebook app. It wasn't like her to post such a telling and defeated status as the one she'd made just minutes ago, so it was only fitting to her that she follow it up with something to reflect the growth she'd experienced via Adrian's text. Often times, she'd pick up a pen and scribble out a verse or two as a way of sorting through her feelings. With no pen or paper in sight, her Facebook wall was the next best thing. She wrote the words 'Who do you think you are' and then pondered on it before diving right in without hesitation, expelling her thoughts and feelings through key strokes of her phone's keyboard.

Who do you think you are coming in trying to take over my life?

Constant test and countless times under the knife.

I remember all of the days you tried to just take me.

I have seen way too many people praying for healing, did you miss the memo? Can't you see?

You messed with my white counts and cause me extreme amounts of pain.

I'm a child of God, you can't claim my life so what's the point? What do you have to gain?

So when pain didn't work you decided to hit me where it hurts: my self-esteem;

Taking away my pretty girl defense when my skin was clear and clean.

Then a few months later putting the shortness of breath to test; A mass on the lungs shown with an X-ray of the chest.

In a major flare for the next 122 days.

Trying to break my faith in several ways.

Another go 'round with the constant nerve ache

So excruciating, the best actress couldn't fake.

One more try, you sent my body into shock.

It came and went with no explanation, not even from the ER doc.

So let me tell you Satan, once more...stay under my feet where you need to be.

I promise you will have no victories with me.

Without hesitation she posted it. The raw emotions that occurred when remembering all she'd been through, thinking of all she was currently dealing with, and wondering what she had to look forward to made her shake with tears. Kai clutched the phone to her chest and tried with all her might to keep herself from aggravating the pattern of her breathing worse than what it was, but it couldn't be helped. She was in a bubble all alone with no one within physical reach who could possibly understand. The fight to remain strong for herself, her children, and the rest of her family often times felt as tiring as the fight she was battling against the Lupus. Kai was tired; resilient, but tired. She kept up a great front about being okay and she continued to keep it moving, but on the inside she was dying and aching from something much greater than the effects of all of her illnesses combined. That broken heart phenomenon was a killer.

Over the past couple of years she and DeWayne had fallen into a pattern that was becoming more tiresome than anything. After leaving him and returning to America to raise her children alone, Kai had managed to deal with her health issues, tend to the children, and create her own source of income without the immediate moral support of her spouse. DeWayne called periodically to check in, but even those calls were becoming more distant by way of their regard for one another. When they spoke, it was typically only about Landon and his wellbeing. Consumed with so much contempt for his nonchalant behavior and inability to comprehend all that she went through to care for their family on a day to day basis, Kai could barely even get through those phone calls. Inevitably an argument would ensue, resulting in her exploding over the line and hanging up on him.

Very rarely did he ever inquire about her specifically. It killed her that the man who was supposed to be her better half didn't appear to be the least bit concerned about her health. Since he felt unobligated to inquire, Kai didn't feel compelled to share the details of her ongoing health issues. The truth was that she was getting worse by the day and the more depressed she became over the reality of her condition and her marriage, the sicker her body seemed to become. Still, Kai refused to succumb to it. She also refused to give him any power by letting him know just how much his attitude and lack of support was affecting her.

A knock at the door pulled her out of her thoughts and caused her eyes to avert upward. A short young guy pushed the exam room door open and entered with a wheel chair. "Last name Davis?" He questioned.

Kai nodded, her eyes were large with tears glazing over her pupils.

"I'm Kalem from Radiology," the young man advised. "Taking you down for X-ray."

Kalem helped her down from the exam room table without her asking. Kai wasn't accustomed to special treatment.

"I got it," she told him as she headed for the door with her cell phone and purse in her hands.

"Here, ma'am." Kalem pointed to the wheel chair. "Gotta take you in the wheel chair."

Kai huffed. "What I need that for?" She asked between struggled breaths. "I'm capable of walking."

"Hospital policy," he advised. "And with the way you're breathing we wouldn't want you to fall out in the hall on the way down. We can't be liable for that kind of mishap."

Her eyebrow rose, but Kai eased her frame into the red wheel chair. She was silent as the man wheeled her out of the room and down the hall. Her incoming message alert sounded and she glanced down at the screen as it lit up in her hand. There was a Facebook notification from Author Jenae M. Robinson. Kai's eyebrow went up. Kai had always been an avid reader and had befriended quite a few author friends on social media, however very rarely did she actually converse with any of them. Intrigued by the receipt of the message in her inbox, Kai tapped her screen to read the other woman's words.

Hey, I know you don't know me, but I read your poem. You are very talented and strong. I will keep you in my prayers, but aside from that...have you ever thought of writing a book?

As Kalem wheeled her into a dim room with lots of machinery, Kai considered Janae's question. *Writing a book*, she thought. *What do I know about writing a book?*

The thought had never before occurred to her although she frequently wrote in journals as a way of dealing with her many emotions. Still, the notion of putting together a body of work like reminiscent of any of the numerous novels she'd fallen in love with over the years seemed like a complex task for more than one reason. She wasn't a writer. How was she supposed to just up and put together a book with no previous writing experience? It was clear to Kai that Janae was suggesting that she write a book about her life, but the thought of exposing her inner most thoughts and fears for all of the world to see and scrutinize disturbed her. *Could I really put myself out on front street like that*, she wondered.

"You can leave your things in the chair and come over to this table," Kalem stated as he moved over the get his film ready for the X-ray.

Kai rose from her seat and placed her purse in the chair, but couldn't tear her eyes away from the message she'd read several times. Quickly, she sent a response.

I can't write a book...I would have to tell people every embarrassing detail of my life. I don't know if I can really be that naked or how I'd even go about it.

Before she could finish viewing her wall and take stock of the number of people who had liked the poem she'd recently posted, Jenae sent a reply.

It's okay. You can always get somebody to help you...whether it's walking you through writing it or writing it for you...whatever.

"Ma'am," Kalem called out to her.

"I'm coming," Kai assured him as she tossed her phone into her bag and approached the table.

"Are you pregnant, or could you possibly be pregnant?"

The question was preposterous to her, but routine to him. "Ha! No man around to plant seeds so there's no possibility of anything growing in this body. With everything that I've been going through the last thing I want to add to my list of concerns is a pregnancy, honey."

Kalem's eyebrows rose in response to her answer and he pointed to the table. "Slide onto the table for me and you can use this blanket to cover up your lower half."

Kai followed instructions.

"Place your arms up above your head for me. I'm just going to take a couple of quick shots. Before each flash I'll ask you to take a deep breath in for me and then between flashes you'll exhale. Are you comfortable?"

"Not really, but yeah," Kai responded, not at all happy with the feel of the cool table beneath her thin hospital gown.

The entire process took all of ten minutes and before Kai knew it she was settling back into the red wheelchair and waiting patiently for the radiologist to wheel her back to her room. She picked up her phone to re-read the message from Janae. *She's really serious about this*, Kai thought. Her fingers wasted no time in replying.

Kai: I mean, honestly I have no doubt that I can do anything I put my mind to. It's just a matter of getting started and learning how to do it correctly.

Janae: Girl, the first thing to do is actually get something down on paper. As for getting it edited, formatted, and published…I can help you figure all that out. You're not by yourself, Girl. You have resources available to you.

Kai: See, I knew I liked you. LOL

Janae: LOL. But seriously, if you tell your story it could possibly help someone else that's feeling some of the same type of emotions. I think you were destined to inspire, Girl 'cause you definitely got me over here feeling inspired. You testimony was meant to be shared boo.

Kai: Hmm. I'll consider it.

Janae: Oh no ma'am. That wasn't an option. You gon' do this thing.

Kai: LOL. You volunteering me huh? Okay, so you know that you're in this with me now, right.

Janae: I got you sis. I'm gonna stay on you about this until you're finished writing. And then we're gonna get this story out even if I have to show you how to self-publish it myself.

Kai: Just like that, huh?

Janae: Just like that!

"All done," Kalem said as he pushed down the brake on the wheel chair and disrupted the flow of her Facebook banter. "Your doctor should be in shortly to discuss your results with you. Hope you get to feeling better."

Whether she believed his words to be sincere or not, Kai gave the radiologist a smirk as she transitioned back to her position on the exam table. "Oh, I'm gonna be okay, trust. This is just another go around the track for me."

Kalem exited the room without another word and Kai laid back to contemplate her options. She was all for helping other Lupies through the turmoil that she knew so well and the thought of possibly educating others who were unfamiliar with the silent disease actually excited her. She thought back to the presumptuous looks Daniel, the triage nurse, had given her earlier. If she could teach people like him, and the other folks she'd encountered over the years who swore her up and down that nothing was wrong with her; perhaps she'd be doing the world a courtesy. Only the Lord knew how tired she was of others underestimating the struggle.

With just that short conversation over the course of this unexpected hospital visit a new era had begun for her; a new venture had been settled upon. She was going to write a book of poetry and with God's blessing she prayed that it would be of some inspiration to others.

"Ms. Davis? Ms. Davis?" A voice was calling for her in the quiet of the hospital room.

Kai's eyes fluttered and she moved to sit up noticing that the pain meds she'd been given earlier had managed to subdue her discomfort a bit. At some point she'd obviously fallen asleep and was now being awakened by an Arabic physician whose name she couldn't pronounce. Kai pursed her lips and focused on the doctor.

"Hello, how are you?" He asked.

Her throat was dry and burning as she swallowed hard before responding. "Wish I was home in my own bed."

"Yes, yes. We're going to get you to your bed, Ms. Davis. I'm Dr. Sayegh. So you came in this morning for your joint pains and body aches associated with the Lupus...and your difficulty in breathing. We gave you the pain medication, the Toradol, for your discomfort. Have you experienced any relief?"

She nodded slightly. "Mmmhmm. Some."

Dr. Sayegh shuffled through a few papers and he too nodded his head. "Good, good. We're going to give you an injection. Uh, a 60 milligram steroid shot…um, Triamcinolone, that should help with the inflammation. I'm going to have the nurse check your vitals again and if everything is stable, uh especially your blood pressure…it was considerably low when you came in. If everything is stable we will, uh, give you a referral to follow up with your doctor and get you on home to your bed. Sounds good?"

"Sounds about right," Kai replied. The visit was pretty much routine to her and all she wanted was for it to be over. With the pain medication and the addition of the steroids in her system, Kai knew she'd be just fine. It was something she'd grown accustomed to yet hated the rigmarole of having to endure an emergency room visit.

Looking at the time on her cell phone, she perked up. Although tedious, the visit really hadn't taken that long, and if they hurried up and discharged her she'd be able to make it home in time to put her boys on the bus for school. The upside of things brought a tiny smile to her full lips.

~ CHAPTER 2 ~

Beyonce's "Resentment" overpowered the clicking sound of her keys and vibrated against the stained oak desk situated in the far corner of her bedroom. The moment she heard the first three bars of the ringtone she immediately wanted to throw her cellphone across the room. Sitting in front of her desktop computer, she stared over the jumbled document that contained various poems not in the mood to deal with his foolishness from overseas. Her fingers ached as she tried to type the words that were fading on the various sheets of folder paper and journal entries she'd compiled overtime. Her frustration from trying to work through the discomfort only intensified as she pondered over what it was he could possibly want.

Taking a deep breath, she leaned back in the black, leather office chair and reluctantly pressed the TALK button. "Hello," she greeted dryly without meaning to. The annoyance in her tone escaped naturally without force.

"Yeah, what you doing?" He asked causally as if they'd just spoken yesterday.

"Working," she replied, hoping he'd forego any small talk and simply get to the point.

"Oh, you not in the bed? You not in pain today?"

Not appreciating his condescending tone and smart-aleck remark, Kai turned her attitude up a notch and proceeded to give him the business. "Contrary to what you may think this household doesn't run itself. The only time I'm in bed is when my body completely shuts down and it's just physically impossible for me to do anything at all. You should know me better than that, honey. I'ma work if I don't do nothing else."

"No need to catch an attitude."

"Oh no, I'm just telling you. As if you haven't been married to me long enough to know me, but just for your knowledge I'm making it known that Kai's no stranger to work. Lupus or not, I'm gon' always do for me and mine."

"Okay, I didn't call for all that."

She laughed dryly. "I bet. What did you call for? Can we go ahead and get to the point so I can get back to more important things?"

"I was just calling to check on Landon and to make sure that everything was good."

Her eyebrow rose. "Well Landon is at school, honey. You should know what his schedule is like by now and be well aware of the time difference. Everything is great over this way."

"Yeah?"

He was fishing for something, but Kai wasn't sure what nor did she care.

"Oh, okay. Anything else going on, Fat Girl?"

"Like what? Aside from me working and tending to these kids, ain't nothing."

"Hmmm, so nobody's hanging on your shoulder?"

"Hanging on my shoulder?" Kai's eyebrow rose yet again. "Really? You calling me for this? Why you worried about who's over here checking for me? Be concerned about sending me back those papers signed. Be concerned about making sure I get my money on time. I'm not calling you asking which skank you got laying next to you these days. You're focused on the wrong thing." Her temper was flaring and she knew that the best possible thing to do at the moment was simply to hang up.

"Why you getting all defensive? You're still my wife. I have a right to ask—"

He'd really gone and done it now. Kai pushed away from her keyboard feeling her temples pounding. Her vision became blurred as she tried to keep her tone and volume in check. He had a way of pressing her buttons as only he could and yet she hadn't yet mastered the art of not giving in to his probing.

"Now you wanna pull the husband card? What? The thought of someone being here giving me attention makes you wanna be a better husband?" She taunted him. "It's none of ya' business who I'm keeping company with. You lost your right to stake any kinda claim on me. So if you wanna keep sitting over there concentrating on what's happening here, be my guess."

Although her words insinuated that she was seeing someone, it couldn't have been any further from the truth. She knew that he was only assuming, but she also knew that her response would eat at him and lead him to believe that his assumptions were correct. Kai envisioned the way DeWayne bit the inside of his jaw when he was angry or deeply contemplating. At the very moment she was certain that he was doing both. *Serves him right*, she thought. *Ain't nobody got time for him to be playing with their feelings. I'm over this mess.*

"Yeah, so if you're done trying to get up in my business I gotta get back to work." Feeling that her job of handing him back his feelings was done, Kai pressed the

END button on her cell and rolled her chair back up to her computer.

She took a deep breath and tried to regain some composure so that she cold refocus on piecing together the makings of her book. *My book*, she thought as her fingers lightly touched the pages of a journal that lie open on her desk. *I can't believe I'm really doing this*. She repositioned her fingers over the home row keys of her keyboard and completed the typed version of a poem she'd written nearly a year prior, during a time when she was completely engulfed in misery and despair without the comfort that she desired – craved- from the one person who should have been willing to walk to the edge of the earth for her. As her finger tips gave typographical life to the emotions penned before her, Kai's face became flushed and her eyes watered over the very vivid and still prevalent feelings that pulled at her heartstrings.

The words of physical and emotional struggle that constituted her memories made Kai shutter. It was as if she was reliving the original moment that had led to the birth of that very poem. Only, it was a memory revisited time and time again because of the relentless ailment that seemed to frequently torment her body. Shaking off the euphoria, Kai pressed the last punctuation denoting the end of that piece and stared at the screen. After hitting save, she mindlessly scrolled up through the pages in awe of the fact that she'd compiled her darkest thoughts into one document with the intent to share it with the world. *But what would I call it*, she wondered as the pages flew upward on the screen.

Kai looked at the time and figured it was cool to give her newfound mentor and friend a call. She grabbed the cell and scrolled her contacts in search of the number Jenae had previously inboxed her. It took only a matter of seconds before the line was connected and Jenae's voice boomed inside of Kai's ear, bursting with positivity.

"Hey gorgeous! What's going on?"

"Girl, nothing much. Sitting over here working on this project you done put me up to," Kai said, feeling comfortable with the relationship that she and Jenae had developed since their first Facebook conversation.

"That's what's up! You better get it in, girl. We gotta get this best seller popping."

Kai gave a nervous laugh. "I don't know about that. Shoot, I'm calling you now because I don't even know what to call this mess. You know, this isn't my realm. I don't know nothing about this."

"Stop saying that! You're creative, girl. We can come up with a banging title. I wouldn't even be worried about it if you haven't finished the actual manuscript. You know how long I've left work untitled? Sometimes I wait 'til it's all done and go back to reflect over what all has happened in the book and my title derives from that."

"Well, it's basically done," Kai advised. "I typed up all my poems that I wanted to include…I'm not sure if maybe I included too few or too many. I don't know. But, they're here in this one document now. I just gotta find a title."

"Okay, so what would you say your focus is? Think of it that way," Jenae guided her.

"Really it's like a glimpse back over how I was feeling when I was first diagnosed. The physical pain, the frustration of people not understanding, doctors not knowing what was wrong and trying to make me out to be crazy, and the battle I had to fight with myself over whether or not I was going to let this thing consume me."

"Uh-huh, and praise God that you didn't, honey, because you are too talented and gifted and have too much to offer the world to succumb to any of that. Plus I'm not just gon' let you do it."

They shared a laugh and it warmed Kai's heart to feel connected to someone whose genuineness and sincerity was reminiscent of her best friend, Nikki Love.

"Yeah, girl. I got these kids watching me and I know that if for no other reason I gotta be the strength they need, you know what I mean? Shoot, I'm amazed going through this pile of memories…amazed at how I managed to pull through those times when so much as sitting up in bed was a challenge for me. Girl, they done handed me down every diagnosis in the book it feels like. I'm like, how much can a person take?"

"Yeah, but it's given you a mighty testimony and plus you're still standing despite it all."

A light bulb went off inside of Kai's head. "Girl, that's it."

"What?"

Kai cradled her cell between her left ear and her shoulder as she scrolled up to the very beginning of her Word document and hit the insert title page command. "That's my title, boo. Still Standing," she replied as her fingers eagerly typed out the words.

"I like it!" Jenae beamed through the phone. "See there, all you needed to do was talk that thing out girl."

Kai's cursor blinked just behind the word '*by*'. "Do I use my real name or a pen name?"

"What do you want to do?"

"I think I'd rather use a pen name…something meaningful," Kai rationalized.

"Hmmm." Jenae considered the dilemma for a moment. "Well, you just said that the boys are pretty much your motivation. Can't get much more meaningful than that."

"Okay…" Kai wasn't sure where her friend was going with her statements. "I can't use both of their names. That's too masculine sounding."

"Shorten it then. Use just their initials as you own and then your last name."

"So what? B.L. Davis or L.B. Davis?"

"You like that?"

"No," Kai laughed. "I'd rather not use my married name since I'm not even going to be married for much longer."

"Well, what's your maiden name then?"

"Oliver. I can use that name and give homage to my family for all they've done for me and how they've been there for me. So that's kinda like a tribute to everyone who is most important to me."

"Okay then so—"

"And I think I'd rather use the children's middle names."

"Okay…so what's that?"

"Well Landon's middle name is K'Shaun and Billy's middle name is Sha'Kwan …so…K.S. Oliver."

"K.S. Oliver." Jenae considered it. "I like it. It has a ring to it."

Kai smiled as she typed out the name, *K.S. Oliver*. Seeing her new identity boldly staring at her on the screen made her heart rate quicken. "Still Standing by K.S. Oliver," she read aloud. "It's real."

Jenae giggled. "It's gonna be even more real when you get that first paperback in your hand."

Kai wasn't ready to move on to the particulars of publishing. She was still reeling over the fact that there was a book before her, penned completely by her that focused on her emotions and struggles. It was surreal. The feeling of accomplishment surpassed the anguish she'd just experienced moments ago with DeWayne on the line. Even the bitter taste he left in her mouth couldn't taint the awesome feeling brewing inside of her. She was about to become an author, a goal she'd never considered before Jenae put the idea in her head. *I'm so blessed*, she thought. *So very blessed.*

"Okay," Kai said shaking her head and hitting the save button once more. "Put me up on this publishing game."

~ *Chapter 3* ~

The stiffness made it impossible for her to do anything but lie straight as a board while she stared at the ceiling. The tears trickled down the sides of her face and into her ears. The thought of lifting her hand to gently wipe them away was dismissed immediately. It wasn't a possibility. Her cell phone rested only inches away from her on the bed, but reaching out for it would constitute more of a struggle and more pain than she was capable of dealing with. Judging by the way the sun was peeking through the closed blinds; Kai knew that it was morning. The sounds down the hall gave evidence to the fact that her children were up and about preparing for school. Maybe natural instinct had awakened them. Maybe her brother, Morris, had gotten them up. Surely her absence during this daily routine would be noticed soon and some relief would find its way to her doorway.

As her eyes closed, sealed by her liquid anguish, Kai tried to mentally remove herself from the room, her body, and the moment. She was oblivious to the hint of energy in the room as Billy peered through her partially opened door. From his position he could see the distress in her face, the rigid tenseness of her body's position, and the cell phone that lay useless to her right, just beyond her grasp. He didn't dare go inside and ask a series of questions that he already knew the answers to. This wasn't new to him. This wasn't rocket science. It was simple reasoning; an algebraic equation in and of itself: x=a+b. In his mind, 'a' was the demeanor that his mother was exhibiting and b was the fact that she was unable to contact anyone. It wasn't hard for him to solve for x, concluding that his mother was having a Lupus flare that was impairing her ability to so much as call for help.

Billy backed out of the room and headed to the kitchen. His younger brother, Landon exited his own bedroom and followed closely behind him.

"Wha you do?" Landon asked in his broken English and incorrect grammar. "Billy, wha you do?"

"I gotta take care of Mom," Billy answered without looking back at his sibling. "Go put your pants and shirt on and I'll give you a cereal bar, okay?"

"Want my mama."

"No, don't go in there, okay? Just go put your clothes on like I told you." This time Billy turned and gave him a stern look as he reached into the pantry to grab a packet of brown sugar and maple syrup oatmeal. "Go!" He barked when Landon acted as if he wasn't going to obey.

Quickly, Landon ran off and Billy busied himself with preparing warm oatmeal in the microwave and pouring up a glass of orange juice. He grabbed a chair from the kitchen table and pushed it over to the refrigerator. His eyes glanced over at the time on the oven and he shook his head, hoping that he wouldn't miss his school bus. Climbing up in the chair, he stood on his toes and reached for the myriad of pill bottles that were all prescribed to his mother. He wasn't sure which one was going to take her out of her misery, but he was devoted to taking them all. Inside of one of the lower cabinets he retrieved a bed tray which he'd often used for these types of occasions. Placing the breakfast and the medicine on the tray, Billy hurried down the hall to his mother's room and used his foot to kick the door the rest of the way open.

"Mom," he called out as he sat the tray on the floor beside the bed. "I'm here. I'm going to help you."

Kai's eyes fluttered as her attempt to morph out of the situation was aborted due to the distraction that Billy created. She moved her eyes to look at him, daring not to move her neck. Her lips parted, but her mouth was so dry that speaking was a chore. "Go to school," she stated hoarsely and weakly.

Billy reached under her head and adjusted all of her pillows before taking his mother's hand and staring her in the eyes. He was silently encouraging her to place herself in an upright position. At first her eyes pleaded with him to just let her be. She wanted to avoid the excruciating pain at all costs, but there was more determination in her son's glare and his grasp than she could muster up for herself. This morning, he was the pillar of strength that she passionately tried to present herself as for him and his brother.

Taking a deep breath that could never truly prepare her for the aggravation of her ailment, Kai allowed Billy to help reposition her body until she was seated with her back against the pillows, although awkwardly.

Satisfied with his work, Billy quickly retrieved the bed tray from the floor and placed it over his mother's lap. "I got your medicines mom. I didn't know which one was the right one so I got them all." He held up the bottles in her direct line of vision. "Tell me which one." He went through each until she signaled that it was the right one to help ease her pain at the moment. Billy wasted no time pouring out a capsule, slipping it past his mother's dry lips, and holding the straw from her orange juice to her mouth so that she could wash the pill down. If he could have helped ease the swallow of the medication somehow, he definitely would have given it a shot.

After she'd taken another couple of sips, Billy placed the juice back on the tray and picked up a spoonful of oatmeal. He airplaned the spoon towards his mother's mouth and ignored the tears that leaked from them. He knew that she was feeling some kind of way, but it was of no consequence. There was nothing he wouldn't do for her no matter what. Weakly, Kai parted her lips to allow the oatmeal to grace her pallet. Billy watched her struggle to get it down as he scooped up another spoonful.

"School!" Landon called out from the doorway. "Mama! Mama!"

"Shhh!" Billy hissed over his shoulder. "Mom's resting. You gotta be quiet. Go to the door with your book bag. I'm coming."

Landon stared for a few moments and then followed his brother's directions. Seeing his mother lying still and not responding to his calls startled him. The only action he could think to perform in the wake of his disturbance was obedience.

"You gotta eat something since you took your medicine mom," Billy told his mom as he tried to get her to take one more bite before he had to go.

Her tears were unceasing but she managed to take that spoonful of warm sweetness. As she got it down, Billy wiped the corners of her eyes with his tiny fingers. He leaned forward and kissed her forehead gently. "***You're a chocolate something amazing mom," he told her. "You're gonna feel better soon. Okay?" He stared into her eyes.

There was nothing she could say. Her heart was heavy with a mix of emotions as she watched her oldest scamper from her bedroom in order to throw on the rest of his uniform and get out to the bus stop.

Billy grabbed his book bag on his way down the stairs to the front door. Hesitating at the door, he turned and headed to the basement where his uncle's room was located. "Uncle Morris!" he called out. "Check on mom! She's sick." He waited until he heard the rustling of sheets and the thud of Morris's feet assaulting the floor as he made his way out of his room. Only then did he hurry back to the front door to usher his brother out. They had only seconds to make it to the bus stop.

Kai heard the open and close of the door followed by the sound of movement down the hall. Her lips smiled despite her pain. Not only had Billy set her up with food and meds, but he'd also made certain that she had someone there to help her. As Morris entered the room and took in the scene, Kai closed her eyes and thanked God for blessing her with her angels.

***

Before she knew it a week had passed and Kai was feeling only slightly better at the tail end of her most recent flare up. It was time to get back on the grind; she'd been down long enough.

"You sure you ready to do some work girl?" Nikki Love entered the room with a glass filled with fresh lemonade. Upon hearing that her bestie wasn't well, she'd dropped everything to make her way to Decatur to be with Kai.

Kai reached for the glass that was being handed to her just as she settled into her computer chair for the first time in a long time. "Girl, yes. I can't just sit around here doing nothing. That's not going to work out."

"I'm not saying do nothing. I'm saying take it easy."

Kai sipped the bitter sweet beverage and then pursed her lips, giving her friend a sour expression. "You know me better than that. I gotta keep it moving." Kai focused her attention on her computer screen as she logged into her email account.

"Well, don't overdo it superwoman. Here, I got your mail." Nikki handed Kai the small pile of sales papers and envelopes that she'd pulled out of the mailbox earlier.

"Last thing I wanna do is go through some bills," Kai stated, shuffling through the mail as she waited for her account to load.

Nikki took a seat on the edge of the bed and turned the channel on the television. She stopped upon seeing an episode of *Maury*. "Ooh, let's see who gon' be the daddy today." She laughed at her own humor and folded her legs Indian-style on the bed.

"In the case of two year old Julian," Maury spoke through the surround sound. "We tested Marcus, Adrian's current fiancé of three years, and his best friend Michael."

"Oh, what a skank," Nikki commented. "Who does that?"

"Marcus..." Maury paused for dramatic effect. "You are *not* the father!"

"Oh my God!" Adrian, the seemingly surprised mother exclaimed from the television set.

"Oh my God!" Kai also cried out.

Nikki laughed. "Girl, please. You had to know that was gon' happen. It's almost never the current boo's baby. I think they purposely go out and find all of the unscrupulousness, classless, tacky, gutter chicks they can find to drag on this show and air all their dirty laundry like some idiots. If I'm sleeping with every dude in the trailer park there's no way in the world I'm about to go put my business on front street, letting the world know I'm community property basically, and then have the audacity to fall out and act surprised when the paternity test comes back negative."

Kai's hand was over her mouth and her ears were deaf to Nikki's rambling. Her eyes were fixated on the words that nearly jumped from her computer screen. Her heart was pounding. She couldn't believe how quickly things were moving. "Unbelievable."

Nikki shook her head. "It's not really that surprising Baby Mama. It's the same ole' mess every time."

"What?" Kai looked at her friend perplexedly and then followed her gaze to the buffoonery being displayed on her flat screen. "No, not that mess. I'm not even paying attention to that crap. I got my acceptance letter today."

It was now Nikki's turn to look confused. "Acceptance for what?"

"A publisher wants to publish Still Standing," Kai advised in awe, re-reading the email from Written Word Publications.

"Are you serious?" Nikki asked excitedly.

Kai's head bobbed up and down. "Dead serious. I wasn't playing about getting this done." From the time she'd finished compiling the manuscript, condensing her 150 poems down to a select group that truly spoke to her health struggle, she'd soaked up all of the information possible from Jenae about the publishing industry. She'd submitted inquires and the first couple of poems from her manuscript to several different companies. Seeing a positive reply after hearing the horror stories of multiple denials from various other authors, Kai felt that she was truly tapping into a new era of her destiny.

"I'm so proud of you," Nikki said, getting up to squeeze her bestie lovingly. "That's really awesome! So what's the next step?"

"I have to go over the contract and sign it and then they'll send it to edit and cover design," Kai explained, having read the email several times by this point.

"Girl, this is phenomenal. You're my shero."

Kai grabbed an envelope from the stack of mail and laughed while looking at Nikki. "Really, silly? That's how you feel?"

"Yes, girl!" Nikki's smile shined brightly as she returned to perch upon the edge of the bed with her head cocked to the side. "We're going to have to celebrate, boo! It's not every day that you get a book published. My famous friend."

"Girl please, ain't nobody famous. One book does not a famous person make."

"Look at you speaking all philosophical and stuff." Nikki laughed. "We're gonna celebrate," she said, adamant about her idea. "Even if I have to order you a strip-a-gram and have him come to your house dressed like a book."

"Oh my God!" Kai cried out.

Nikki burst out laughing and fell back on the bed. "Calm down Baby Mama! I was only playing. Dang! You over there about to have a stroke or something. Like you ain't never seen any—"

"I can't believe this freckle-nackle b.s.! Who does this?" Kai declared, tossing an envelope onto the desk and pushing back her chair to re-read the letter in her hand one more time.

Nikki sat up. "Girl, I said I was just playing."

Kai shook her head slowly and covered her hand with her mouth in an attempt to hamper the obscenities dancing at the tip of her tongue from escaping out.

Nikki realized that her friend's outburst had nothing to do with her outrageous joke. Concerned, she planted both feet firmly on the ground and stared at the back of Kai's head. "What happened? Something with the contract?" Nikki was trying to put two and two together because just a second ago they'd both been overjoyed about Kai's good news. Now, something had seriously altered that, pushing Kai clear across the spectrum from happy to completely dismay.

"This joker ain't been paying the car note," she managed to say, verbally tripping over the venom she desperately wanted to spew. "All these months and he just failed to pay the dang car note. What was he thinking?"

"Was that part of y'all's agreement? That he'd pay it while y'all are separated?"

Kai snatched the paper away from her eyes and slightly turned her head in her friend's direction. "Of course, why else do you think I'm pissed like this? I mean true, he gives me the child support monthly, but that money only goes so far. Considering that I'm not working a steady job and getting a steady income, I rely on him to do the responsible thing…to do what he said he would do."

Nikki shook her head. "Times have changed, Kai."

"What does that mean?" Kai's scowl was now directed at Nikki verses the vision of DeWayne that had previously been floating in her mind as she poured over the letter from the auto lender.

"If y'all are really getting divorced then you're gonna have to get accustomed to handling financial matters on your own."

"He still has a family. No matter what, we got these responsibilities together, so he's equally responsible for tending to them if not more," Kai stated matter-of-factly.

"Yeah, logically that sounds all fine and well, but the realism of it is honey that you're like a single mother now. You gotta have single mother survival thoughts here, babe."

Kai turned away. "If it's one thing I know how to do it's survive."

"Yeah, well take that feistiness and figure out how you're going to handle this situation that you got popping because it's clear that you're not going to be able to rely on him to do the responsible thing, Kai. At the end of the day it's you and these babies here. Not you, them, and him."

Nikki's words were only adding fuel to the blazing fire that was growing inside of Kai's body. Sorry joker, she thought. He's doing this to spite me…to prove to me that I'll need him before he needs me. Doesn't he know that I'm a fighter? She stared down at the letter and rolled her eyes before reaching for her cell.

"Whoa, what you 'bout to do?" Nikki asked. She knew her friend well enough to know that the conversation she was about to initiate wasn't going to be anything pretty.

"Oh, he 'bout to hear about this," Kai replied, scrolling through her contacts for DeWayne's number with no regards for the time of day and the time difference overseas.

"You sure you don't wanna wait until you've calmed down a little bit?"

"Absolutely not!"

"Okay, Girl…don't get yourself all riled up and stuff. Don't let that man make you sick."

"Oh, I'm good, but he's gon' hear about this here." Kai listened as the line rung in a broken fashion in her ear. Four rings in and just as she thought the voice mail would greet her, igniting her anger to a more intense level, she heard a rustling sound and the crackle of DeWayne clearing his voice. Before he could utter the words hello in what she knew would be a sleepy tone of voice, Kai went right in. "DeWayne, was there something you forgot to tell me?"

He cleared his throat once more as he tried to focus on what her sharp tone was confronting him with. "Wh-what?"

"Did you forget to tell me something?" She repeated herself.

"Huh?" He was disoriented and was in no mood to decipher his estranged wife's attitude.

"If you can huh you can hear. I got a forwarded letter in the mail talking about they've been trying to contact you regarding the loan for the truck. I'm sure you know why that is."

"I'm gonna have to call you back."

"No! You're gonna talk to me now. What, you thought you could renege on our agreement? Somehow you thought that was acceptable? Now what you gon' do if they repossess the freakin' truck, De? What you gon' do? How do you expect me to get our kids around and get back and forth to these doctor appointments?"

"You so smart and independent, so I'm sure you can figure something out," he shot back boldly.

The retort nearly knocked Kai out of her seat. She hadn't expected him to be so cocky about the ordeal, but there was also no way she was about to back down. He was flailing her buttons again and was about to get more than he bargained for in return. "Oh, that's how you wanna play it now De? You wanna be a butthole about it?"

"You can always ask your new dude to help you out a little bit. Isn't that what a man's supposed to do for his woman? Take care of her? Help her out when she needs it?"

Where was he getting his information, she wondered and then decidedly realized that she didn't really care. His insecurity was his own problem and his assumptions would eat him alive sooner or later. Kai had done a lot of things, such as shut him out after his lack of support and proceeding to prepare for a life without him, but she had yet to go so far as to get with another man when she hadn't yet successfully ended their relationship. In her eyes, they were separated and he had no right to be dipping and dabbing in her business, but she was still married separated or not. As long as she still harbored his last name it just didn't feel right to cozy up to someone new despite the number of men who repeatedly showed interest in her.

"You know what? You're absolutely right," Kai spat into the phone. "I will most definitely figure it out. I was doing it on my own before you so please don't think anything will be different after you."

"Yeah, I bet."

"You'd bet right. And trust, what you won't do the next brother very well will. Believe that. The one thing I'll never be hurting for is a man that wants to tend to my needs, boo. Don't worry about it. Just send my papers back!" She disconnected the call before he could offer up a snappy reply. Whatever he had to say, he could save it. She wasn't in the mood to listen to anything else he had to say. With the overdue notice resting on her desk and the out of line comments he'd made during their short call, Kai had learned all that she needed to about her husband. He was being petty and she wasn't about to let him gain the upper hand. "Ugh!" She exclaimed as she dropped her cell phone onto the desk.

"Too much," Nikki commented. Having only heard Kai's end of the conversation, she already knew that the outcome hadn't turned out well. Seeing her friend tormented by her finances at a time when she should be jumping for joy over her accomplishments made Nikki wanna hop a flight to England and give DeWayne the business. She didn't like it when anyone messed with her bestie. It disturbed her spirit. "Don't you do it," she told Kai.

Kai took a deep breath, yet failed to turn around. "Do what?"

"Don't let him knock you off your square. Just a minute ago you were happy. You have so much to look forward to. That hasn't changed just 'cause you read that letter and he pissed you off. Maybe he'll get his stuff together; maybe he won't. You have to be strong for you and these boys and be prepared to do you either way."

Kai didn't respond. Nikki knew her well enough to know that she was affected by DeWayne's insensitive behavior despite the front she put up. She'd meant it when she told him that another man would be honored to take care of her, but she also felt crushed each and every time he pulled one of his stunts. It was getting old. She was ready for him to just sign the papers already and put them both out of their misery.

"You know what you need?" Nikki asked as she walked over and threw her arms around her friend lovingly.

Kai shook her head. "Girl, how I'm feeling I need a drink."

"Mmm-mmm. You needa go out."

Kai looked over at the time on her clock. "Not today boo. Billy has wrestling practice and—

Nikki playfully mushed Kai's head. "Not with me, silly. With some fine, sexy, yummy something. You need to be wined and dined, boo-boo."

"What?" *Was she serious?* With all of the drama going on in her marriage alone what made Nikki think that she had time or any interest in putting up with another dude, even if only as temporarily as a three hour date? "Girl, stop."

"You stop." Nikki's tone was now serious. "You're too fly of a woman, a good woman at that, to be sitting around the house brooding over what your estranged husband has and hasn't done, will or won't do. Life goes on, honey, and there's more to it than just work and taking your medicine every day. Believe me."

Kai glanced at the notice from the lender lying on her desk. She did need to get out and live a little. She harbored a lot of stress between trying to make ends meet, staying on top of her health issues, and dealing with her obviously irreparable marriage. Perhaps a little male attention wouldn't be so out of line. She chuckled to herself. Even with the weight gain from the steroids that were frequently pumped into her body, she was still pulling interest left and right. She often times avoided her inbox due to the myriads of messages from guys she knew and contacts she didn't know personally all wanting a little of her time. She'd never given any of them the time of day beyond cordial conversation via inbox, but maybe it was time to spread her wings a little bit.

Kai looked up into the beautiful brown eyes of her fair complexioned friend. Nikki's grin ran from ear to ear. She was excited about the prospect of Kai moving on and as pissed as Kai was, she wanted to be at least a tenth excited as well. However, something inside of her just wouldn't allow her to cross that bridge yet. It was like beginning the final chapter of her marital disaster and Kai wasn't certain that she could cope. "I don't know," she said slowly, almost feeling bad for verbally wiping the smile off of her bestie's face. "I just don't know girl."

"You don't know?" Nikki's eyes bulged, but only for a second. She knew Kai. There was no point in trying to persuade her to do anything that she wasn't open to doing. If ever she'd met a headstrong, stubbornly determined individual it was most definitely Kai. Nikki sighed. "All these brothers out here checking for yo' chocolate self. They're gonna be lining up to turn in their applications once you say go," she joked. She squeezed Kai once more with the complete understanding that once her friend was ready she'd make the decision to get herself back out in the game. It wasn't an easy call given how long Kai and DeWayne had been married. Nikki didn't expect her to abandon her feelings for the man; that was unrealistic. It was simply her desire to see the sparkle return to Kai's eyes and hear of her getting the attention and royal treatment that she deserved.

Kai nodded her head in acknowledgement that Nikki was letting up on the situation. She steepled her finger tips just above the bridge of her nose, closed her eyes and paused for a moment. It was too much. With her book venture on the brink of coming to complete fruition and everyday life struggles, she didn't want to focus on her emotions and personal life. It was an area of her life that was so bleak that she wasn't prepared to deal with it. Depression was real. She could feel her spirit plummeting at the thought of how far gone her relationship with DeWayne had gone. *Why would he put me in this jacked up position at this point in my life, she wondered. God, what is the point of it all? Whatever happened to love and that whole 'til death do us part bit? What happened to the happily ever after I was supposed to have with the man who once swept me off my feet and made me do the one thing I thought I'd never do: commit?* Kai felt the tears building and knew that she had to pull herself out of it. There was no way she was going to pull out the anti-depressants. She was downing enough medication to service a basketball team. She feared that the inclusion of one more substance would certainly send her over the edge.

"Ugh!" she exclaimed following a deep breath in and a long exhale. "Moving on," she stated out loud as if convincing Nikki that she was over and done with the thoughts that were plaguing her. The truth was that if anyone needed to be convinced that she was actually shrugging it off it was her. Kai made a mental note to hit up her homie MJB later to discuss things. She loved Nikki to pieces, but sometimes she needed a softer touch and a male's point of view. MJB understood her on a more personal, border-line intimate, nearly spiritual level and right about now she needed all the guidance and compassion she knew he'd have to offer. The thought of him and their history made her smile through the hurt she was experiencing. Theirs was a love-story so pure and touching and she valued the bond that they had developed over the last couple of years. Staring at the black screen of her desktop, the memories felt like just yesterday.

FLASHBACK, MAY 2011

Billy was gone with his dad and being the ever so thoughtful parental figure that he was, Bill had also taken

Landon along with them for the weekend. The house was devoid of any signs of life aside from the uneven breathing that was escaping Kai's lips and the sound of her ceiling fan twirling overhead. Even Morris was away for the weekend, booed up with his girlfriend Sarah at her place. Kai was completely alone and in a considerable amount of pain. She'd taken her medication, but it appeared to be working slower than usual on that day. It was just her luck. The radiating spurts of tension that flowed through her body weren't severe enough to lure her to the emergency room, but it was torturing enough to bring her to tears as she laid on the side of her bed. Laying there was the only thing she could manage to do without causing herself any further discomfort. At times like this, she hated being alone.

Kai contemplated calling her mother or one of her siblings but like usual she dismissed the idea. She never wanted to get them upset or frightened over her condition. No one wanted to admit it, but every time she so much as sniffled or had a headache all her family could remember or envision was her flatlining. She understood their trepidation, but she needed someone who wasn't going to be frightened right now. She was scared enough and certainly in way too much discomfort to have the energy to comfort an ill-at-ease family member.

Kai grimaced a bit as she toyed with her phone, going through her contact list to see who she could possibly get to give her a little encouragement. She considered hitting up Nikki, but decided against it as well. She loved Nikki to pieces and she was the kind of friend that would drop everything she was doing and run right to Kai's side. You couldn't find anyone more down for you than that. The problem with that though was that Kai knew that Nikki wasn't in a position to just come right over. She was overseas and there was no way she could hop a plane or jet that would get her there fast enough to wipe Kai's tears away and stroke her now disarrayed locs until she was sound asleep.

Scrolling through her contacts for a second time, Kai's eyes fell upon her brother Blacc's number. She felt a flutter in her heart as she pressed the CALL button. Blacc was her sister Terri's ex-boyfriend, but despite their failed relationship Blacc and Kai still kept in touch. He was like a brother to her, during and after his dealings with Terri, so much so that Kai actually referred to him as her brother. He was always a very sympathetic ear whenever she had issues, be it health or personal. Blacc never passed judgment and despite his street-tailored methodical approach to things, he was a very insightful guy with a gentle spirit that most wouldn't believe existed beyond his hardened exterior. He reminded Kai a little bit of herself: so strong and seemingly unbreakable to the outside world, but sensitive and nearly broken on the inside.

Blacc was the type of guy that was stubborn in his own right and was married to the streets. It was what caused the demise of he and Terri's relationship. It was also what had landed him in the Lowndes County Jail. Despite his location, Blacc was still available to her by phone. Kai marveled over how the jail officials were so lax in their confinement of the prisoners either turning a blind eye, or just not realizing that the inmates had personal cells.

"Hello?"

The voice that answered the phone was unfamiliar to Kai. She had to look down at her screen to be sure that she'd dialed the correct number. "Um...hello?" Was her unsure reply.

"What's good beautiful?"

Even through her tears Kai was taken aback for the familiarity in which the man on the other end spoke to her. "Um, is Blacc around?"

"Oh naw, that nigga done got caught slippin' and been put in the hole," the voice explained.

"And you are?"

"My bad. I'm Jermaine, Blacc's cellmate. You know he can't have the cellie in the hole, so he left it here with me. He told me all about you though. You know, whenever you write to him and stuff...he let me read some of them poems you sent to him. It's all so deep and stuff. Ma, I'm telling you...you got a nigga in love with you on paper over here."

Kai chuckled and felt the ripple of pain assaulting her body in massive directions to the point where she couldn't make out the origins of the original bout of discomfort. Her tears fell freely, some landing on her phone and others spilling across her nose due to the position in which she was laying. "It's nice to meet you, Jermaine," she managed to get out. She hadn't expected to actually hold a conversation, much less with a complete stranger. Whenever she broke down and called Jermaine during these trying times he basically did all of the talking. He provided her with the encouragement she needed to press out without having to so much as utter a syllable. Clearly, that wasn't going to happen during this particular flare up.

"What's wrong ma?" Jermaine asked. The sincerity in his voice nearly shocked Kai seeing as though they had no connection.

"Nothing," she muttered. "So can you—"

"Come on ma. Don't do that," Jermaine pleaded with her, cutting her off midsentence before she could cut their conversation short. "You sound like you over there crying."

Kai sniffled. "I'm in a little pain," she admitted although downplaying what she was feeling.

"Yeah, I knew something wasn't right baby. I could hear it all in your voice. Blacc told me 'bout how you be suffering all the time. He showed me some pictures of you. You know you fine as hell right? I'm like, man that's messed up how such a beautiful creature could be enduring so much pain and ain't nothing nobody can do to stop it. I'm so sorry you got to go through all that. Man, when he told me 'bout some of the things you've been through, he had a nigga 'bout to cry in here. And I ain't no punk nigga like that, but baby, my heart goes out to you. For real."

She felt that his words were genuine and it touched her that a complete stranger would feel so emotional about her personal struggle. "Thank you," she whispered. "That's sweet. It's all good though...this ain't nothing. I've experienced worse than what I'm going through now."

"Hmmm. I believe you judging by what I've heard, but listening to the tears and the sadness in your voice baby, I'm here for you either way."

"You're here for me?" Kai questioned. "You don't even know me."

"Shoot, I feel like I know you. Done read your words, seen your pictures over and over, heard your story, now I'm finally hearing your beautiful voice. You don't know it yet ma, but I know you real well and you gon' get to know me well too."

"Oh I am?"

"Yessir!"

"What's your last name?"

"Um...Bradley."

"Um? You had to think about what your name was?"

Jermaine laughed off his nervousness. "Naw, was just surprised at the question. What you ask that for? You the man trying to get me caught up? Shoot, I'm already locked up. Ain't much else can happen to me."

"Calm ya' nerves. Paranoid much? I just like to know who I'm talking to," Kai explained as she wiped her eyes free from the tears that had gathered in the inner corners. "You said I was gon' get to know you well didn't you?"

"True, true."

"So JB, what makes you think we're gonna get all cozied up like that?"

"Nothing wrong with having a good friend on ya' team is it?"

"I have good friends."

"Nothing wrong with having another good friend with a good listening ear who happens to think that you're the best thing since chicken and waffles ma."

Kai couldn't stifle her laughter although the rattle of her body only aggravated the uneasiness. "Chicken and waffles, huh?"

"You know it."

"Hmmm. Okay. I'll take that." She chuckled lightly. "So, since you know so much about me you know I'm also married."

"Yeah, yo' boy said you were separated."

"That's true. Been separated a short while."

"Messed up. No way you should be dealing with all this drama and stuff by yourself. You need a man there to take care of you ma."

"I can take care of myself."

"Yeah, I get all that independent woman ish. That's cool and all. I respect that. That's sexy. But, still...at the end of the day a man is supposed to make sure his woman is good, especially if she's a good woman that's been holding him down. If your wifey ain't good, how you gon' be good? No real man's gon' turn his back on his woman when she's down, man. If you were my woman I swear I'd be giving you all that moral support and love and affection that you need."

"You running game on me JB?"

"Ma, I'on run game. I spit facts. I'm just telling you what it is."

"Mmmhmm. And how would you do all of that for me while your behind over there locked up with Blacc."

"Semantics, Ma. Semantics. They ain't built no cell or jail that can keep a man's heart locked away from a woman that's touched his spirit. I ain't necessarily gotta be with you in the flesh for you to feel my support, my love, and my encouragement. There's other ways to be intimate with someone...other ways to be there with and for them."

Kai had to admit that he was saying all the right things at a time when she was lost and so far gone that she could really use his verbal anchor to hold her steady. But she was no fool. Jermaine could spit out all the sweet nothings in the world, yet she wasn't adept to just fall for anything. After everything she'd gone through with DeWayne while overseas her eyes were open wide. Never again would she allow a man to weasel his way into her spirit only to disappoint her in the end.

"You still there, ma?" Jermaine asked sweetly in her ear with his enticing southern drawl.

Kai hadn't realized that her eyes had closed and she'd gone silent listening to him express himself. Suddenly she felt soothed and comforted. "I'm here. Just listening to you."

"You okay over there?"

"Mmmhmmm. I think my meds are starting to kick in."

"That's a good thing. You want me to let you go on to sleep then? Ain't no telling when that nigga Blacc coming back. He got into a fight with some dudes during recess from two blocks down. Man, they be wildin' in here. You know yo' boy. He don't hold his tongue or his fists for nobody."

"Yeah. He better calm himself down."

"Gotta stand your ground, you know? Anyway, I'ma let you get some sleep. You need to rest."

"You can keep talking," she said in a rushed manner that surprised even her. "I mean, listening to you is kinda helping me relax so..." Her words trailed off. She was unsure of where to go with it seeing as though she was unsure as to where they were going with the course of the discussion in the first place. She hadn't really been doing the telephone thing with any dude since the split with

DeWayne and she certainly wasn't looking for a fling, especially not with a guy she'd probably never get to lay eyes on anyway. But, it felt good to hear his admiration and although their newfound friendship was based upon a sight-unseen situation, Kai felt he was sincere in his words and sincerity went a long way with her considering all that she'd endured.

"Uh-huh. I knew you was gon' be hooked on a brother," Jermaine joked with her. "Naw, it's cool ma. I'm here for you. We can talk about anything you want or you can just close your pretty little eyes and listen to me talk if it's gon' help you. It's whatever you wanna do."

"Talk to me," she instructed him, snuggling down into her covers and finally feeling more relaxed than she had for hours. "Tell me about you."

"Aight. Anything you want."

And it went like that for the duration of their friendship. That five hour conversation was the genesis of a unique relationship that she could never explain to anyone without them assuming that it was much more to it than she disclosed. Jermaine respected and admired her. When he told her that she was beautiful she knew it wasn't just on some superficial level. He'd met her via her words as she penned them to Blacc before Blacc had ever given him a glimpse at her physical being. He'd said it himself that he was in love with her on paper and the more they talked the more she believed that they truly had a connection that was unexplainable. He frequently told her how much he cared for her and how much he wanted to make her his woman and kiss away the pain. She never once gave him the indication that she was going to turn her heart over to him.

She was too tattered from her recent heartbreak courtesy of DeWayne to lightly tread into the waters of a relationship with Jermaine or any other man for that matter. In addition, she was still married; separated in the physical and legal sense, but still married all the same.

For almost a year they continued to correspond via text, phone, calls, and the occasional letter. Every heart felt thing he ever put in writing to her would turn out to the highlight of her day as she struggled through the depressive state she'd spiraled into. She almost lived for his written pick me ups and sporadic, yet endearing phone calls. He was her perfect contrast to the strained encounters often had with the man who should have been melting her heart. But, as with all things good all of that came to shattering end the day she'd received a letter from him with news that changed her complete outlook on what they shared.

The letter started off normal; inquiries about her health, declarations of his love for her, details about the mess going on behind the prison walls, and thanking her for the last couple of poems she'd penned just for him. That was all fine, but it was the last bit of information that rocked her. His whole spiel about wanting to come clean to her put her on high alert; Jermaine was married. In his letter he explained that he valued their connection and never wanted to be anything short of honest with her. Although he and his wife, Jillian, were legally separated and had been for nearly seven years at that time, Jermaine claimed that it was on his conscience to share that information with Kai so that it would never come up later as a surprise.

By the time this information reached her, Kai had already meant Jermaine's mother, Ms. Peggy, who lived in Atlanta just minutes away from her. He'd pretty much pulled her into his family and she'd built a relationship with them. Ms. Peggy loved her and treated her as if she was one of her very own offspring. Never once had the 75 year-old diva uttered a word about her son's wife, estranged or not. But, Kai wasn't upset with Ms. Peggy. It truly wasn't her place to disclose that information to her. In fact, she wouldn't have been surprised if Ms. Peggy had assumed that her son had already made Kai aware of Jillian's existence.

Kai had waited three days for him to contact her. By no means was she going to write him back after he'd dropped that bomb, or reach out to him via phone. She was hurt. It felt silly feeling that way since she'd already expressed to him that she wasn't ready to tinker with the idea of being coupled up with another man until she was done with the one whose last name she shared. But, for months they'd developed something special and it had taken him all that time to divulge that piece of his life. It was beyond her how the man could profess to love her, yet feel it was okay to never once mention his poor, unsuspecting wife.

Tired of waiting to hear from her, he'd finally called acting and sounding as if nothing was wrong. "What's up beautiful?" He greeted her.

"Nothing," Kai said sourly. She wasn't exactly the kind of person who could mask her emotions even over the phone.

"What's the matter?" He asked, knowing full well that things weren't right.

"Nothing's wrong. Everything's peachy keen," she replied sarcastically.

"Come on ma! This me you talking to. Don't do that?"

"Don't do what?" She asked coyly.

"Don't play games with me. Don't keep secrets."

"Oh, you mean like the secret you been keeping all this time about your wife?"

Jermaine was silent for a minute. "You got my letter," he stated rather than asked.

"Mmmhmm."

"So why didn't you call or write me back if you felt some kind of way about it? We should be able to discuss anything, right?"

"Oh really now? That's the kind of relationship we have."

"You know this."

"Obviously I don't because if it really was the kinda relationship we have then you shoulda been came out your mouth to tell me about wifey way before now JB. And dropping that mess in a letter? Are you serious? You knew I was gon' have a problem with that off bat and that's why you wrote it instead of telling it to me verbally... 'cause you knew there was no way in all things holy that I was gonna just accept that bomb and not have something to say."

"It's not really that big of a deal Kai. I mean, we been separated forever so..."

She couldn't believe his nerve. "Not that big of a deal? Are you serious? It musta been that big of a deal because you purposely didn't say anything. Even when we talk about my marriage and my separation. Those were golden opportunities for you to say something, but you chose to sit on it and guess what! You chose wrong."

"So you mad now?"

Kai considered it. "Naw. What I'm gon' be mad for? I'm used to dudes being on some foolish mess. Difference is, in this case you aren't my dude so this doesn't really affect me."

"Kai...I'm separated. Sep-a-ra-ted. So why the 'tude?"

"No tude. I'm just being real."

"You know I love you. Like I said, I told you because I didn't want it to seem like I was keeping secrets."

"Which you were."

He sucked his teeth. "Kai, come on, man. I love you, girl. And my intention is to make you Mrs. Bradley."

Kai laughed dryly although all she wanted to do was cry. She wondered if DeWayne was somewhere telling some foreign skank the same lie. "Yeah, problem with that is there's already a Mrs. Bradley."

"Until I get my divorce finalized. It's about you, Kai. Everything I feel and everything in me screams that I'm supposed to be with you. You are like the epitome of what a woman should be and I can't let that slip from my grasp."

"So what? You expect me to sit around and wait for you to decide to so much as initiate a divorce in hopes that when you get out, whenever that is, that you'll wife me? I can't begin to tell you how much of that is wrong and just ain't gon' happen, but I'll tell you this. Kai Davis doesn't play second best to no one. If I can't be number one, I'm not on the team at all, boo."

"You are number one."

"Jillian Bradley's number one."

"Ugh, come on!"

"Stating facts. Look, I gotta go." She couldn't bring herself to carry on with the conversation. Her hurt made her tongue slick and she didn't want to start spewing out stuff that she knew she'd never be able to take back. Some of it he'd deserve and some of it he'd have to take on DeWayne's behalf. But before it got to that point, she felt it was best to just end it all then and there.

"You just gon' jump fly with me and then bounce?" Jermaine challenged. "That's how we handle things now Kai? We're adults! Let's talk about this."

"What's there to talk about? You're married. You haven't attempted to get a divorce in how long now? And I'm not gon' be anybody's side chick ever. That about sums all that up. So, either you can say goodbye or I can just hang up now. Your choice."

"That's cold. You being real hypocritical right now."

Kai opened her mouth to respond but her finger was quicker than her vocal chords as she hit the END button on her phone. She wasn't about to allow him to hear her emotional response to the way he'd managed to shatter and tarnish her image of their special, yet border-line forbidden, relationship. Disappointment seemed plentiful in her life and at that point she felt like it was best to just add Jermaine to the list as yet another one.

Resuscitated

Current Day

Kai blinked away tears that she hadn't realized were threatening to drip. Remembering her and Jermaine's loving beginning and unexpected halt made her emotional all over again. Time had passed, nearly a year, without them having any communication. With the DeWayne drama and being sick, Kai just hadn't felt compelled to rekindle the connection she and Jermaine had established. That was up until she'd gotten a message from another incarcerated buddy of his via Facebook asking for her number on Jermaine's behalf. She'd hesitated. By that time she'd sent DeWayne the divorce papers to sign and was adamant that the marriage needed to end. Truthfully, she missed the long phone calls, the heartwarming letters, and the tender moments she and Jermaine had once shared. On impulse, she'd given the buddy her number and it hadn't taken long for Jermaine to hit her up. Since that day, he remained her someone special; her sounding board and shoulder to lean on. Kai knew that she could tell Jermaine just about anything and he'd offer her an honest opinion laced with compassion. She needed that right about now.

~ CHAPTER 4 ~

"Man that's that bull," Jermaine said, his calm and collected tone filling Kai's ear. "But ain't nothing but a thang, Ma. I'ma help you."

Kai had told him about the past due car note and DeWayne's nonchalant attitude. Jermaine didn't like the fact that she'd spoken to her ex in the first place, but Kai had to explain to him over and over again that their interaction didn't extend beyond financial matters and children updates. "How you gon' help me?" Kai inquired.

"I'ma shoot you some bread towards that bill. I know you gotta get back and forth to your appointments and stuff. And the kids gotta get where they go so…I'ma have something sent to you, aight? I'ma get my mama to put some money into your account. Who you bank with?"

Kai laughed. "I know you not about to have your mama handing over her money like that."

"Get outta here. I wouldn't take bread from my own mother. I'm the kinda man that takes care of his women…wifey and mama."

The statement made Kai think of Jillian, his wife, but she kept her comments to herself. Jermaine was about to lace her pockets, so who was she to come at him about some dramatic stuff? "Well, it's Wells Fargo since you wanna know."

"Bet. Run me the account number and you'll have that in like two days."

"How much you sending?"

"Lil something. You'll see. You trust me?"

Again she remembered his previous marital secret, but quickly pushed the thought out of her mind. "Yeah," she simply replied.

"Then believe me when I say I got you."

"Well, alright then." Kai appreciated the gesture and if he really did manage to get the money into her account she'd be most appreciative, but at the end of the day she wasn't going to bank on it. More and more she was learning the hard way that she needed to rely on herself and herself alone. "I can't even believe that he'd do this mess," she muttered in reference to DeWayne.

"Man, don't even think about it. You're my wifey, I got this. Don't be giving him the satisfaction of thinking that you need him for anything. I don't even understand why you would call dude."

Kai's eyebrow rose. "Because it needed to be addressed."

"Something goes wrong you call your man."

"I just wanna point out that you're not my man JB." Her words were cutting, but Kai only knew how to shoot straight. His lovey-dovey talk was endearing, but she never wanted him to get it mistaken that they were a couple.

"Get outta here," he said in an attempt to brush off her statement.

Kai laughed. "Okay, don't be over there fooling yourself. You know I love you down, but I refuse to play the side chick." It was a proclamation she'd made to him a million times, yet somehow Kai never could get Jermaine to truly understand that she wasn't relenting in her decision to not pretend that they were in some fairy tale romance.

The truth remained that he had a wife and estranged or not, Kai respected that.

"You can't be my side chick when you're my number one," Jermaine replied, giving his standard rebuttal. "Man, you let De know I'm sitting on him, man. I'm telling you. Give your heart to me completely woman, forget all that other mess, and I'll treat you like royalty. I only need one chance to show you how much of a queen you are."

Although she was flattered, Kai was already over their ongoing debate. "So, let me get back to what I was doing over here."

"Yeah, so I'ma get that money to you."

"Thank you, sir."

"No problem beautiful. I wish you'd come see me."

That was something else she wasn't down to do— visit a man in jail, much less someone else's husband. "You already know how that goes."

"Man, when I get outta here…" Jermaine didn't bother to finish his sentence. They both knew where his thoughts were. "I love me some you girl. I'ma call you back soon. Focus on that book thing. I know you gon' be like a best seller or something. I'm proud of you."

Kai loved the interest that Jermaine took in the things that she had going on. Her spirits were instantly lifted by the mere fact that there was a man who was willing to give her what was probably a great sum of the money resting on his prison books and cared enough to give her a pat on the back with regards to her endeavor. Secretly she wished that DeWayne would read a page from whatever book Jermaine had gotten his morals and chivalric behavior from.

"Thanks babe," she replied to Jermaine with a smile in her voice. "Be good."

"No doubt. You too. You know you precious cargo. Make sure you take care of yourself. And text me that account number!"

"Will do!" She hung up and stared at the phone shaking her head. She'd told DeWayne that any man would be willing to treat her the way she deserved. Jermaine was living proof of her statement.

***

Kai and Nikki sat side by side in the doctor's office as Kai waited to be seen by the pulmonologist at Emory Medical Center. It wasn't a visit that Kai was looking forward to, but it was yet another one of those things she had to endure because of her illnesses. Kai suffered from Lupus induced Pulmonary Fibrosis, which warranted these visits every six to eight months. It was tedious and unpleasant, but not a necessarily horrible experience. She'd only carted Nikki along because they had plans to hit the mall and do lunch right after in celebration of her book deal.

Kai's phone buzzed while they waited, indicating that she had a Facebook notification. She went to the app to see who had tagged her in what. Her eyes browsed over an advertisement that she knew nothing about, but was immediately interested in. "Hmm," she said as she read.

"What?" Nikki asked between texts she was sending on her on cell.

"I just got tagged in this post about a poetry event in North Carolina in honor of Lupus."

"That's cool. You going?"

Kai shrugged. "I don't even know who this is." Looking at the event page, Kai saw the name of the host – The Princess of Poetry. Her interest was piqued. Kai took it upon herself to reach out to the woman via inbox.

Hi there! I was just tagged about your Late Night Poetry post and wanted to inquire about the event. I am a Lupus survivor and coincidentally I'm also a poet.

Kai laid the phone on her lap and looked up at the receptionist with attitude etched in her expression. She was ready to get the appointment over with and didn't feel inclined to waste her day away in the waiting room.

"What's the matter, boo?" Nikki asked, taking note of her friend's demeanor.

"I'm ready to go! Nobody has time to just be sitting here all day. Truth be told I don't even want to be here." Kai felt her phone buzz and looked down to see that a reply had been sent to her inbox.

Yes, yes. A colleague of mine tagged you. I've heard about you and your upcoming book right? A poetry book. I'd be honored if you'd come out and do a few pieces. You can set up a table and sell some books while you're here. But we'd love to have you.

"Yasss!" Kai let out.

"Hmmm," came Nikki's half interested reply.

"See, I just sat here and booked my first signing. I have other things I could be doing rather than spending my day waiting to be tortured." As her lips moved so did her fingers in an effort to respond to the Princess of Poetry.

I'd be honored to. I have the date and time from the flyer and will put it on my calendar. Make sure to forward me any other promo material for the event and I'll see you there.

Nikki watched as Kai sent her message. "Where's the signing? How'd you do that?"

"Somebody tagged me on a flyer for this event in North Carolina. A poetry event for Lupus."

"Oh, that's perfect for you girl."

"Yeah and it's right on time because it falls right after the release of my book so I can promote and sell it there. The coordinator said that someone referred her to me so I'm gonna be one of their featured poets that night."

"Look at my little celebrity friend," Nikki gushed. "Get it girl. You doing the dang thing."

"Shoot, I'm trying," Kai said making a mental note to hit Jermaine up later to share her good news. She knew that he loved to hear about her accomplishments and was the only male figure in her life at that point.

"Mrs. Davis." The physician assistant was standing in the open doorway calling for her.

Kai looked up and sucked her teeth. "Finally," she stated as she grabbed her belongings and headed toward the door with Nikki in tow.

"Um...patients only," the P.A. stated.

Kai frowned up. "She's okay. She's my moral support just in case I get out of hand in here while y'all poking and jabbing and giving me a hard time. Trust me, you're gonna want her to keep me grounded especially considering I'm all kinds of moody right about now."

The young P.A., whose name tag read Patrice, shrugged and led the way to the exam room. She was used to Kai's feistiness and had grown rather fond of her personality over the course of her last few visits. Kai was unfazed either way. She was simply ready to get it all over with. The woman commenced to getting Kai's vitals. "Anything of concern for you today, Mrs. Davis?" she asked.

Kai turned up her lips and shook her head. "Nothing really. Just the same thing. Occasional trouble with breathing from so much as climbing the steps in my home. Sporadic shortness of breath."

"Any recent Lupus flares?"

"Yes ma'am. Just a couple of weeks ago."

"And did you have to go into the hospital for that or did you call our emergency line?" Patrice asked as she wrote down the results of Kai's temperature, which she'd taken with a forehead rolling device, and blood pressure.

"Neither. Took my meds and rode it out."

"So it wasn't that severe?"

"Not enough for me to endure the pain it would have caused just to make it to the hospital, no," Kai responded.

"Okay." Patrice looked over some notes in Kai's chart before giving her a comforting smile. She knew that Kai was going to give her some resistance to the next task. "Okay. We need to perform the stress test now. I'm going to have you walk up and down the hall way—"

"Ten times each way in a brisk walk not a jog or run," Kai said completing the woman's sentence and rolling her eyes. She handed her stuff to Nikki and rose from her chair to head to the door. "Well come on. I've done this enough times to know the drill. Let's do it." She was all for speeding things along.

Patrice led her to a back hallway of the clinic which happened to be the longest hallway within the establishment. The routine was so familiar to Kai that she could pretty much orchestrate the entire visit on her own without the medical stuff and with her eyes closed. Patrice held up the wall on one end of the hall and used a finger probe to test the oxygen saturation of Kai's blood at a resting heart rate. Once the oximetry was done, Patrice signaled for Kai to begin when ready. "10 laps or up to six minutes. Whichever comes first," she advised.

Kai huffed and removed her light jacket before beginning the trek up and down the hall. By her fifth lap back in Patrice's direction she was ready to call it quits, feeling her breathing becoming slightly restricted. "This is for the birds," she told Patrice in no uncertain terms.

The P.A. simply gave her a reassuring smile and tried her best to be supportive. "Slow your pace. You're almost done. Take a break if and when you need to." The woman looked down at her watch to note the time they had left.

"Haven't you heard of almost doesn't count?" Kai countered between huffs. "I'm…ready…for this…to be over."

"Stop trying to speak while you're moving," Patrice instructed her. "It only applies more pressure on your lungs as it fights for the oxygen it needs."

Kai cut her eyes at the woman and bit her tongue. She wanted to tell the younger lady where she could go and how she could get there in response to politely telling her to shut up. But, Kai realized that the woman was only doing her job and that her advice was solid. Soon after Patrice called time and Kai only had one lap left to complete. A little breathless, Kai grabbed her jacket from the lone chair she'd placed it on and followed Patrice back to the exam room where she once again ran the oximetry test and then provided Kai with an oxygen mask.

"Slow, deep breaths," Patrice coached.

Kai nodded as she inhaled the oxygen and allowed it to fill her lungs.

Nikki patted her friend's leg. Watching her made Nikki's heart pound. She understood why Kai despised these visits. Who wanted to deal with these battery of tests for the rest of their lives. Though she didn't say it at the moment, not that she hadn't voiced it before, Nikki really admired Kai's physical and emotional strength. With everything the woman was going through in her personal life she still worked hard to hold it all together despite the health issues that were constantly creating barriers for her. That was the thing about Kai. No matter what hurdles presented themselves, she always found a way to jump them and move one.

Patrice made some notes, left the room, and returned with a small plastic cup filled with water. She removed Kai's oxygen mask and handed her the cup. "So you know we have to do the pulmonary functioning test and then go over to the imaging room real quick to do a chest x-ray."

Kai chugged the water and moaned. "Ugh! The chamber."

"Yes, yes, I know. The awful dreaded chamber."

Kai was perturbed. She knew the routine caused for the chamber test, but she hated it just as much that day as she did the first time she'd ever had to do it. The machine was like being in a bubble and she was forced to breathe into a tube to measure her lung capacity. It didn't help matters that she was a tad bit claustrophobic. Sitting in that glass box encased like a sardine was never a fun experience for Kai. Reluctantly she followed Patrice over to the machine that she resented. The testing procedure lasted all of ten minutes, but Kai felt like it was an hour by the time she was done working her lungs to the max.

Silently she followed Patrice to the imaging room where she took a chest x-ray. Their stay in the imaging room was quiet and quick. Soon after Kai was sitting in her chair once again, next to Nikki, awaiting the pulmonologist, Dr. Sears, who would come in and discuss the test results and the current condition of her lungs.

"My Superwoman," Nikki said, rubbing her friend's back.

"Girl, this ain't nothing nice," Kai responded while shaking her head. "I'd trade places with any other healthy person any day of the week.

"I know that's right. I wish there was some way that I could save you from all of this."

"Me too," Kai responded. She thought about the situation and then realized that she should not complain. It could definitely be worse. In fact, she'd been in a worse position upon being diagnosed than she was at that exact moment, so she had to thank God for the blessings that he'd bestowed upon her life. She waved off the feeling of nostalgia that lingered in the room between herself and Nikki. "Don't worry about me honey. I'm gon' be okay. I'm so used to this that I'm just about over and done with it."

A light tap occurred at the door.

"Come in," Kai responded in a raspy voice.

"Good morning Mrs. Davis," Dr. Sears replied jovially as he walked into the room with his hands filled with Kai's medical chart and what appeared to be a couple of x-ray films. "Everything going okay for you today?"

"Considering I waited half a century in the waiting room to be seen only to come back here and be tortured," Kai spat out. "Uh, yeah. Everything's beautiful."

"We certainly apologize for the wait, but we're gonna try to get you on outta here as soon as we go over these results. Fair enough?"

Kai pursed her lips. "Hmmm."

"You brought a friend with you today," Dr. Sears commented as he hung up the two X-ray films he'd walked in with.

"This is my best friend Nikki Love," Kai said in introduction.

"Nice to meet you," the doctor replied flashing a bright smile at the pretty woman.

Nikki returned the smile. "Nice to meet you as well."

"It's good of you to come out and support your friend here."

"I have to. It's my responsibility. I have to make sure that you all are taking the very best care of her because I can't replace her."

Nikki's words reminded Kai of the way Jermaine often referred to her as precious cargo. It meant so much to her to have people in her life who were truly for her in good and in bad times.

"Understandable," the doctor acknowledged Nikki's sincerity. "Okay, we're going to take a look at these two images, okay?" He flicked a light that made the images more visible in the brightness of the room. "This is a picture of your lungs two years ago when you first came to me," he said pointing to the picture on the left. "And this is a picture taken today," he stated, pointing to the image on the right. "There's a noticeable difference in the deterioration of the lungs and the scar tissue that's caused by the fibrosis."

Kai simply stared at the images. She could see the difference, but wanted the doctor to get to the point. She recalled a time when he'd shown her what a pair of healthy lungs looked like in comparison to her own. The difference was enough to shake her. What she was seeing today rattled her a bit, but it was a battle that she'd been fighting for a while, so she pretty much knew the odds. "Talk to me," she instructed.

"With the rate of deterioration we're looking at a prognosis of three years tops without the occurrence of a transplant," Dr. Sears stated.

Nikki gasped. Kai couldn't look at her. It was reasons like this that she often went to her appointments alone. Once people started hearing numbers with regards to life expectancy and the notion of a possible life threatening surgery they became fearful. No one knew everything as it pertained to her diagnoses simply because she didn't want anyone treating her differently or practically waiting on pins and needles for her to die. She wasn't waiting to die, as much as she often felt like she wanted to. Kai was doing her best to hold on to her reasons to live.

"So, how soon can that be done?" Nikki asked out of pure concern.

"We are not quite there yet for the transplant," Dr. Sears replied. "But I'm going to suggest that we begin traveling the road toward that option within the next year. Meanwhile, we'll keep an eye on your lung capacity and breathing. Make sure you continue to take the Prednisone that's been prescribed to you. I'm going to change the dosage slightly so Patrice will call it in to your pharmacy for you. Do you have any questions for me?"

Kai shook her head no although she could feel the heat from Nikki as a thousand questions burned through her mind.

"Alright," Dr. Sears flicked his light switch and removed his X-rays. "It was a pleasure seeing you again and we'll schedule you to come back in about six months, okay?"

Kai grabbed up her things and rose. "Wouldn't miss it," she said dryly. "Come on, Nikki. Thank you Dr. Sears."

"Anytime. Take care of yourself."

"Trying my best," Kai commented as she sped out of the door with a confused Nikki in tow.

In rapid time Kai checked out and led Nikki out of the clinic and back to her Explorer. As they got into the car Nikki stared at her friend. "So you don't have anything to say about what the doctor said?"

Kai put her key in the ignition. "Not really. I try not to get all caught up in what the doctors have to say about how long my time is on earth. That's a God thing, honey. If I focused on that then I'd be a complete wreck. I have enough mess to sort through and get gray hairs about instead of worrying about what year, month, or day I'm going to die."

It was a hard pill to swallow, but Nikki knew better than to press the issue. Kai talked a good game and she put on a very brave front, but deep down Nikki knew that the doctor's prognosis had to affect her friend on some level. How could it not? Instead of forcing her to discuss it, Nikki simply fastened her seatbelt and considered her own thoughts. In that moment, she said a quick and silent prayer for her friend's wellbeing. Little did she know, but Kai was saying her own prayer, thanking God for whatever time she had left in the world to spend with her kids and somehow make all of her hardships serve some higher purpose.

***

The time had come. After months of working with the layout, fighting with Written Words Publications over her cover art and promotional plan, the day that Kai had been waiting for ever since the initial inbox message from Jenae had finally arrived— release day for Still Standing. Her hands had shaken uncontrollably upon receipt of her proof copies, but now it was time for all of the hard work to come together for the world to see. Sitting at her computer screen on May 20, 2013 Kai nervously typed in the web address for Amazon. The kids were at school and the house was empty. Time seemed to drag on ever so slowly as she waited for the results of the search she'd entered under her name. Within minutes, Kai found herself gasping for air. It was there. Her book, her compilation of poetic thoughts, was live on Amazon and available for purchase.

"I can't believe this," she whispered into the silence of the room. Quickly she reached for her phone. There was only one person who readily came to mind when she thought about whom she wanted to share the moment with.

As her fingers found the number and pressed the CALL button, Kai had to tap back into reality. Hurriedly she disconnected the call before it could be answered. Times had changed and no matter how much she still felt a sense of connection, there was no way that she could allow herself to keep back peddling. Biting down on her lower lip, she made another choice and this time she let the call go through.

"Hello?" Her mother's voice greeted her over the line.

"What you doing?" Kai asked.

"Working. What are you doing?"

"You know it's my release day," Kai stated as she copied and pasted the link for her book onto her Facebook wall to share.

"Mmmhmm. I know. So it's out?"

"Yep. It's live on Amazon now and I should get my box of paperbacks before the end of the week."

"Well look at you," Mz. C commented. "My baby doing big things."

Kai grinned. "I'ma tag you in the link on Facebook so you can share it with your coworkers and stuff."

"Oh, you know I will. Everybody and their mama about to know that my baby is an author. I don't know anybody else that can say that. You done gave me some bragging rights."

"Ma, you so silly."

Mz. C laughed. "I'm for real."

Kai knew that she was. If nothing else, Mz. C loved to brag about all of her children. She was truly proud of the good things they did and the adults that they'd become.

"Alright, ma'am. I just wanted to let you know what was what. I've got some promoting to do."

"Promoting? What kind of promoting? Doesn't the publishing company do that?"

"Mmm, allegedly honey, but you know me. I'm not sitting around waiting for nobody to do anything for me, especially stuff that I can do myself."

"Well alright then, Ms. Author."

"Authoress," Kai corrected her.

"Yeah, I'ma let you go. You over there correcting me and stuff."

They shared a laugh.

"Alright ma."

"I'll talk to you later. I love you."

"Love you too."

Following the call Kai delved into her social media promotions. Jane had put her up on game during their many discussions, advising her to do as much networking as possible with others in the industry and of course anyone who could be deemed a potential reader. That last category pretty much included any and everybody that she'd ever met. Geared up with a little industry knowledge, her first signing already booked, and a list of ideas she wished to explore, Kai was ready to make Still Standing and K.S. Oliver household names.

~ CHAPTER 5 ~

The family was four hours into the six hour drive to North Carolina. Everyone was excited about Kai's first big signing and of course her opportunity to stand up as an official Lupus Awareness Advocate. Mz. C had helped Kai rent a van in order to haul the whole crew— Kai, Billy, Landon, Nikki, Morris and his two small children, Mz. C., Terri, and Sean. Kai had invited Sissy, DeWayne's sister, but she reluctantly had to decline because of a prescheduled business trip. Despite the fact that she and DeWayne were starting divorce proceedings in the face, Kai continued to foster a loving, sisterly relationship with Sissy. In fact, they spoke on a more constant basis than Sissy and DeWayne ever did.

Nikki was at the wheel and Kai was situated in the passenger seat beside her. She had a focused gaze which hadn't deterred from the reflection she saw in the window. Over the clatter of discussion between all of the children and the adults in the large van, her own thoughts rang out loud. *I should be happy. I should be smiling. This is my first event and I should be on top of the world.* But those emotions couldn't have been any further from the reality that was killing her as she sat unmoving in her seat.

"You okay?" Nikki asked glancing quickly at her as she moved to change lanes. She realized that Kai hadn't uttered a word in quite some time and she wanted to make sure that her friend wasn't experiencing any kind of jitters. "Kai?" Nikki's eyebrows rose in concern.

Nikki's tone caught Mz. C's concern. She was seated directly behind Nikki with a good view of her daughter's profile. She leaned forward and touched Kai's arm drawing back at the warmth that greeted her palm. "Kai? What's wrong, baby?"

Kai shook her head. It would do no good for her to complain to them about the agonizing feeling that was ripping through her body. She felt her mother jerk her hand in surprise when she'd touched her. Kai knew that she had a fever. She realized it about an hour and a half after they'd got on the road. She cursed the universe for doing this to her at such an important time in her newly found career. Fate just seemed to have it out for her.

"Kai, you're burning up girl," her mother stated as she reached into the small cooler just beside her feet and pulled out a bottle of water. She handed it to Kai. "Drink this. Here."

Kai nodded slightly and took the bottle from her mother without giving her eye contact.

"You've got a fever you need to—"

"I'm fine," Kai muttered, cutting off her mother as she screwed the top off of the bottled water. "I'm just hot." It was a lie, but it was a necessary lie. It was because of her and her endeavors that her entire family had dropped their lives for a weekend to travel to North Carolina for this event. There was no way that she was going to ruin their excitement, diminish the joy on their faces and in their spirits at the mere thought of her success, nor the pride they had as a unit by telling them that she was falling apart. It just wasn't going to happen.

"You sure?" Mz. C. asked with uncertainty in her voice.

Kai put on her game face, turned around, and then gave her mother a quick reassuring smile. "Sure." She turned back in a front facing position and fought the urge to cry from the simple movements she'd just made. She prayed that her mother would just let it go because she didn't really have the energy to put up a verbal front. She just wanted to sit there, endure the ride, and pray that God would bless her with a little bit of comfort so that she could get through unloading the van and getting to her hotel room.

"Kai, if you—"

"Ma, what was the name of that place you was telling Sarah about the other day? That place where you got all that chicken for cheap?" Mz. C. was cut off yet again, but this time by Morris.

Kai exhaled slightly and she could feel Nikki throwing looks over at her, but she wasn't about to acknowledge them. She was grateful to her brother for pulling their mother into the conversation that he and Terri were having. She had no idea what they were talking about nor did she care. She was now left once more to deal with her pain silently, taking one for the team. Gritting her teeth, she pulled her cell out of the cup holder and scrolled through until she found Bill's number. She needed someone to know what was really going on; someone who could give her the push she needed to make it through the remainder of the car ride as well as the weekend. She thought about shooting Jermaine at text and then decided against it. He'd want to call and there was no way that she was going to have a conversation with him in the presence of her entire family. He'd also end up telling her how beautiful she was and what he would do to make things better for her if she was truly his. While she remained flattered by his admiration, it wasn't exactly what the doctor ordered at that moment. So, she sent a text to Bill disclosing her truth.

I'm so nervous...I'm flaring badly and can barely make it through this drive.

She waited for his response and realized something important— she was truly a ball of nerves. The whole time she'd been going through the process of writing the book, getting it published, and promoting it she hadn't felt this kind of anxiety that was eating at the pit of her stomach. There was this unspoken pressure that seemed to loom over her, like greatness was imminent. But what if she got in front of the crowd and couldn't perform? What if the words wouldn't manage to escape her Lupus infected voice box? What if she couldn't manage to sell herself to the audience enough to move some of units she'd brought along with her for sale? The what if's were eating her alive by the time Bill's reply came through.

Kai, you're making yourself sick. You need to have some faith in yourself and relax. You're the strongest woman I know and a great mother to our son. You need to focus, but you don't need to over analyze this. You got this. Don't make me have to come out there.

His last sentence brought a smile to her face. She knew that if she didn't pull it together and kept sending him messages indicative of not adhering to his solid advice, he would most definitely hop a flight and be by her side to put her in line. She appreciated that about him and their relationship in general. He knew her like no one else did and he was one of her biggest supporters. Although their relationship was now that of friend and co-parent, she could still rely on him whenever she needed just about anything, be it for either of her sons or herself personally. Kai recalled the numerous times she'd called on him when she had yet to know what it was that she was truly suffering from. He'd never left her side where moral support was concerned and she loved him for that.

Bill was right. She knew that her worrying wasn't helping her health-wise. She took a deep breath, knowing that she had to pull it together. *I got this. I got this,* she thought. She shot him back a quick message thanking him for his support and leaned back in her seat with her eyes closed. She allowed the blur of sounds to carry her off into a fitful, uncomfortable slumber, but even that was better than fighting to keep her tears at bay while awake.

***

"No!" Kai exclaimed in a whisper. "No, no no!" She tossed her pink pump to the floor and stared at her feet. They were swollen like puff balls and there was no way that she was going to be able to force her carefully chosen heels onto them.

Dressed in a cute purple, pink, and white top and that accented her figure and coordinated purple pants, Kai had planned to pull her look together with the sassy pink pumps. Only now, given her flare up and swollen extremities, that wasn't going to happen. She hadn't brought any other shoe that could accommodate her ensemble, or her current condition aside from the flip flops she rode to North Carolina in. There was no way she was going to waltz up into this purple affair, her first big event, wearing flip flops.

Nikki walked out of the bathroom and over to her friend to get one more look at her hair and makeup. “Girl, you are going to be killing them,” she gushed. She saw a flicker of frustration in Kai’s eyes and that feeling of unrest returned to her from earlier. “You okay?” She asked softly to not pique the interest of the others in the room.

Kai shook her head. This was one thing that she couldn’t lie about. “I can’t wear the dang shoes because my feet are swollen and I didn’t think to bring another pair just in case.”

“Hmmm. I got you girl. It’s okay.” Nikki hurried over to bag and pulled out a pair of black thong sandals. “Here you go. They aren’t pink, but at least they’ll be comfortable.”

Kai took the sandals and slipped them on her feet. She was grateful to Nikki for her help, but she was feeling unnerved by the way the experience just didn’t seem to be turning out the way she wanted it to.

“Come on, girl. We gotta get you to the spot superstar!” Nikki urged.

The rest of the family was already on their way to the van. Reluctantly, Kai trailed behind them with an excited Nikki by her side. After the short drive the clan arrived at the event hall and Kai did her best to put on a happy face. She was ready for what the night had in store. Despite the small wardrobe malfunction, the apparent swelling of her feet, and the aching that was tormenting her on the inside, Kai was good. She glided through the doors of the venue with her support system surrounding her, smiling and shaking hands with ease until her eyes fell upon them.

Across the room stood her father Tony and Grandma Lucy. Kai felt her resolve weakening. The shock was overwhelming and as she fell into her grandmother's arms the flood gates she'd been working so hard to keep shut came crashing down. Her mascara, her foundation, her liner— none of it was of any consequence to her as it all smeared and ran as a result of the liquid expression of her meltdown.

"No you're not sitting up here messing up this pretty face," Grandma Lucy whispered in her ear over the buzz of the crowd. "Ladies don't show their emotions out in public like this. Pull it together."

Kai knew her grandmother was right. She was the epitome of a real woman and Kai admired and valued her in many ways, for many reasons. Since the entire health scare had begun, Grandma Lucy had been instrumental in praying for Kai and keeping her in good spirits when all she'd wanted to do was succumb to that which was claiming her body. Grandma Lucy probably didn't know it, but Kai felt that it was she who had single-handedly saved her life. She'd been at her lowest point when her grandmother had summoned her for a visit during an empowerment retreat that had worked to redirect Kai's focus, mindset, and emotional balance. Sure, she was still a bit depressed about her situation and her marriage, but she was nowhere near as suicidal and spiritually broken as she'd been at that time.

"Come on honey. God's brought you this far baby," Grandma Lucy stated as she rubbed Kai's back.

Instantly, Kai felt better. God had sent her angel to her to make certain that she pulled through the event despite how busy Satan seemed to be that day. Pulling away from her grandmother's embrace, Kai noticed that her other siblings on her father's side were also in attendance. It was good to see Toni B and Quinell standing there beaming at her proudly. Grandma Lucy squeezed Kai's hand and Kai knew that everything was going to be okay.

After getting herself cleaned up, finding seats for everyone, and sitting through a few other performances, Kai's name was finally called. The crowd, mainly the section that housed nearly her entire family, went wild with applause. It was a surreal feeling and Kai felt her head swoon a little as she made her way to the stage. The lighting was low in the audience's area, but the spotlights shined brightly on Kai. She was literally in the limelight—this was her moment.

"Hello," she greeted the room. Her voice cracked so noticeably that she was certain the entire banquet hall was privy to her nervousness. She took a deep breath and squinted her eyes through the bright lights in an attempt to get a good look at the angel who she felt was there to fly her through this moment. "I'm poet and author K.S. Oliver from Atlanta and I'm also a Lupus patient and awareness advocate."

A round of applause and hoots of support resounded in response to her introduction.

"First and foremost I have to admit something to you," Kai said, hoping that her family wouldn't feel discouraged for her or upset with her for holding out on the truth. "I'm standing here talking to y'all, but I don't know how I'm doing it because I'm in the middle of a full flare. Secondly…I'm so nervous."

"It's okay!" A voice shouted from the back.

"Do your thang baby girl!" Another faceless voice rang out in the darkness.

"We understand! We got you!" Someone declared out of empathy to her left.

Kai felt herself loosen up as she began to tell the story that was her life, her testimony. She disclosed to the room full of strangers, who really weren't strangers, how she'd struggled to find adequate healthcare and a doctor who cared enough to not dismiss her concerns as merely crazy notions in her head. She told them about the weight loss, the hair loss, the diminish in her confidence over time, and of course the tragic tale of nearly losing her life twice— all at the hands of Lupus, the silent disease that many of them in that room were extremely familiar with. It pained her to share the details of the decline in her relationship as a result of trying to become acclimated with her health issues, new life regimens, and of course the reeling emotions that came with it. By the time she made it to the end of her story, proudly explaining how she turned her private thoughts into a poetry book with the help of Jenae and the support of her family, she was in tears. Saying out loud all that she'd lived made her grateful for the strength that she had somehow managed to tap into. To bring her segment to a close, Kai chose one of her poems from Still Standing to read aloud— one that she thought every Lupie in the room could relate to.

The applause following her conclusion made the entire ordeal worth it. Attendees, her family included, rose to their feet with tears in their own eyes, commending her for overcoming and continuing to live her life with purpose. Kai felt as if she'd won an Academy Award with the way she was so graciously received and celebrated in that moment. A heavy weight seemed to lift from her chest. She'd made it through her first public speaking engagement. The initial fear and anxiety she'd felt was gone. The whole thing had been like simply having a conversation with another Lupie who understood the struggle, but most importantly she felt that a connection had been made between herself and every other Lupie in the room. The feeling was phenomenal.

As Kai returned to her table where her books were on display, she was greeted by several who simply wanted to shake her hand or hug her neck. The book sales began to pour in, but what mattered most to Kai was the sense that she'd actually made a difference that night.

"You inspire me," an older woman said to her as she waited for Kai to finish signing her book. "The courage you had to get up there and share so candidly…I've been diagnosed with Lupus for about a year now and I didn't know nothing about it until the doctor told me I had it. This hair is a wig," she said pointing to her head. "I done lost my hair, my skin is horrid, and most days I don't even know who I am…Sometimes I can't even do simple things for myself like lift a fork to my mouth to eat. I feel sorry for my children. I got three kids, they all grown, and I feel like now they have to take care of me verses live their own lives. I was ready to say forget this whole thing…these pills, these treatments…but I see how God is moving in you and I know…I know that this isn't the end for me."

Kai handed the woman her book and one of her business cards. "It's not," she agreed with the older lady. "I didn't know anything about Lupus until I was diagnosed with it, but you know at some point I had to make a decision to roll with the punches and not allow it to run my life. Shoot, I have Lupus, Lupus doesn't have me."

The woman reached down and hugged Kai tightly. Kai returned the vigor of her embrace.

"That's powerful, little sister," the woman said. "Thank you. Thank you for sharing."

Kai went on to sign more books and mingle with more attendees. Before long Nikki walked over to giver Kai her cell phone. "Girl, you been getting all kinda notifications."

Kai took the phone and smiled. "Thank you."

"Get back to it Superstar."

"What y'all over there doing?" Kai's glance veered past Nikki to take a peek in her family's direction.

"Eating and talking to some of the other poets."

"How my babies?"

"Girl, they good. We got them. You do you." Nikki gave Kai a reassuring hug and scurried back over to the family to assist with the children.

Kai looked down at her cell phone and checked the notifications. Most were from Facebook but there was one text. It baffled Kai to see that it was from DeWayne. Immediately she felt the shift in her mood. She'd been working through her flare up, actually enjoying the remainder of the event, and now here he came with whatever it was he had up his sleeve. She had half the mind to ignore his text until the next day, but her curiosity wouldn't allow her to do that. Quickly, she clicked on his text and covered and cocked her head to the side in shock.

Good luck, Kai! I'm so proud of you. You never cease to amaze me. Love, D

Was he serious? The whole time she'd been making mention of her book venture he hadn't shown one bit of interest or concern. The only thing he'd been focused on was who was or wasn't lying up in her bed or smiling in her face. Not to mention the crap he'd pulled with the car situation. Thinking about it reminded her of Jermaine who had indeed fronted her money on more than one occasion, which she used to make sure that she didn't lose the automobile that was in DeWayne's name. She'd tinkered with the idea of letting the SUV get repossessed verses working out payments just to mess with his credit and to get back at him. But, the idea was ridiculous because she needed the car and with no stable employment to verify that she was credit worthy, no agency was going to give her a car loan. So, she budgeted accordingly with the occasional help from her special friend.

She re-read DeWayne's message and didn't know how to feel. She had barely had two words to share with him so how on earth did he know about her literary engagement? Sissy, she thought. It would be just like Sissy to drop a bug in her brother's ear and let him know that he was messing up.

"Excuse me," a shrill voice called to Kai, disrupting her thoughts. "I'm sorry to bother you."

Kai shook her head and put her cell phone away. "Honey, no! You're not bothering me at all. I can check messages anytime." She had work to do. Whatever

DeWayne had going on she'd deal with it later. Tonight was about her and she wasn't about to let him affect that in any way.

~ CHAPTER 6 ~

"I miss you."

Those three words escaping his lips and the gentle way in which it vibrated off of his vocal chords into Kai's ear made her want to cry. Be it confusion or joy, the emotional flood gates were weakening. For months, years now, she'd wanted to hear sincerity from him in the form of anything positive, especially an apology. Although that didn't occur him merely uttering the words I miss you was a beginning, or at least she hoped that it would be. DeWayne was her husband and she had a natural yearning for him that was undeniable. However, as much as she wanted the fairy tale of a happily ever after with the man whose last name she shared, Kai was no fool. They'd been on this merry-go-round for long enough to know that her husband wasn't the most emotionally reliable person. She needed to tread lightly and not invest so much of herself into him, or their relationship, so she would not be shattered again in the event that the outcome was less than favorable.

"You miss having someone to wash your drawers and cater to you?" She retorted in an effort to not appear to be softening.

"That too." He laughed. "Nobody fluffs and folds like you baby."

Kai chuckled, but quickly covered her mouth. She took a breath before responding. "Uh-huh, I'm sure you can find a Susie-cookie over there somewhere who knows how to manage your delicates."

"Yeah, but she wouldn't be my wife and she definitely wouldn't have the ass that you have. And she wouldn't be able to burn in the kitchen like you can. I mean, she might burn some stuff, but not in a good way."

Kai couldn't stifle her laugh this time. DeWayne had that effect on her. He was so incredibly corny that it was hilarious to her.

"Seriously though, if I wanted anyone else I'd get someone else. I miss my wife. I miss you. Your cute, little pudgy face, your kisses, holding your hand. Tell me you don't miss me."

He was trying to bait her, but Kai was sure that she was ready to go for it. She didn't want to lie to him and tell him that she didn't miss him. It would be like lying to herself and she couldn't do that. But, telling him the truth would seemingly give him the upper hand and she didn't want him to have some emotional hold over her. She'd been working hard adjusting to life on her own and trying with all of her might to get over him. She hadn't dated anyone, but she'd entertained a couple likely suitors via social media and sometimes even phone. The truth of the matter was that she wasn't completely over him and it hampered her from being able to take Nikki's advice and move on. Let Jermaine tell it, she was his, and as much as she cared about him there was no way that she could surrender her heart to even him. The whole wife thing didn't help matters much where Jermaine was concerned either.

"Hello?" DeWayne called out into the phone hoping that she hadn't hung up on him.

"Yeah, I'm here."

"You just going to remain silent?"

"I don't know."

"You don't know if you're going to remain silent?"

"No crazy, I don't know if I miss you or not."

"Really?" He wasn't buying it.

"I mean, I don't know if that's really a healthy statement to make because the last time I checked you were supposed to be signing the divorce papers and moving us one step closer to getting this over and done with."

"I don't want that," he stated.

"Excuse me?" She'd heard him clearly, but she wanted him to be very specific in his declaration.

"I don't want to get divorced."

"I didn't want to feel like my husband wasn't supportive and that happened. I didn't want to believe that my husband was cheating on me, but that happened." It was a reality that Kai rarely disclosed to anyone because it cut her so deeply that he would feel inclined to seek affection from some chick overseas verses make things work with the woman he'd vowed forever to.

"I want to make up for all of that."

"Why?" She challenged him. She knew that she was being a hard ass, but it was the persona that he'd forced her to adopt over time.

"Because you're my wife and we made a commitment to one another. Because you're the beat of my heart…you can't live without a heartbeat, Kai."

She felt it the moment her guard sunk to the ground. His words were so poetic that she almost wondered if he'd read them somewhere. Kai licked her lips and took a seat on her sofa. She'd been staring out of the living room window watching her children at play, but now she was feeling a little light headed and needed to sit down. DeWayne had managed to verbally knock her off of her feet.

"So what? You're dying?"

"Yep. I need immediate assistance."

"What?"

"It's an emergency."

"The heck?" Kai was confused.

"I'm taking emergency leave. I'm coming home for a short visit."

Her heart began to beat through her chest like a drum. Never had he volunteered to use his time to come home. Even when she was sick and nearly dying. She remembered a time when her medical team had had to phone him to explain the severity of her condition in order to get him to take leave and fly over to attend to his wife. The fact that he was willing to take time off just for a social visit in the name of working on their relationship spoke volumes.

"When?" It was the only word she could manage to say.

"In two weeks."

She was quickly surprised by how quickly he'd be arriving. Obviously he'd thought about it for a while because she knew that it took a minute to get leave approved. A long time had elapsed between now and when they'd last been together. Kai didn't know what to say or what to expect. She looked around the living room as her mind began to run through the list of things she needed to do in preparation for his visit.

"You there?" DeWayne inquired.

"Yep. Just taking it all in."

"That excited, huh?"

"Whatever. So where are you staying when you come?"

"Is that a real question?" He asked with just a hint of annoyance.

"I'm just saying, we haven't been together in so long I wasn't sure if you wanted to stay here or not." She knew that her asking the question would lead him to wonder once more who had been in her home in his absence— whose space would he be seemingly invading by showing up for and taking up residence for a minute. "Okay, so let me know your itinerary," she told him, warding off any questions he may have been considering asking.

"Will do. I'll forward my flight info to your email. Make sure you wear something sexy when you come get me from the airport."

"You better hope I show up to get you from the airport point blank," she countered. "The way you be having me feeling I might leave your butt out there stranded and gotta call a cab."

"Stop playing."

Kai laughed to herself at the fact that he truly believed she was joking. "Yeah, okay."

"I love you Kai Davis."

Her ears began to ring. She hadn't heard him utter those words in quite some time. This complete about face he was doing was really starting to overwhelm her. Kai pinched her left arm to make sure that she wasn't dreaming. Here he was saying all of the things she wanted him to say, but after so long. Where was all the affection, support, and adoration prior to now?

"What's going on?" She heard herself ask the question that had been screaming in her mind since the start of their discussion.

"What you mean?"

"Nuh-uh, don't give me that innocent crap. What is going on with you? I mean you had plenty of opportunities to act like you cared about me…about us. So, what's got you wanting to do the right thing now?" She leaned back against the sofa cushions and awaited his response.

"I can't take back none of the stuff that's happened, Kai. All I can do is be a better husband ongoing. I gotta go, okay? I'll shoot you that email."

"Okay. Be safe."

They ended the call and Kai realized that she hadn't returned the sentiment he'd offered to her. She wasn't sure if she'd purposely not responded with an 'I love you' of her own, or what, but she wondered if he even noticed that she hadn't done so. Sure she still loved him, but voicing that at this point was a hardship. She was still on the fence about them and what was going to happen with their marriage. Right about now all she could do was give him the chance that he seemed to want in order to prove himself. A smile crept upon her lips.

"My husband's coming home," she said out loud to herself. She had to admit that the thought had her giddy.

***

Kai rushed about making sure that the boys hadn't forgotten anything. It was almost time for her to head to the airport to get DeWayne. Her mother was there to get the children because they would be spending the night with her. It would give her and DeWayne a chance to have a night alone together to figure out where they were headed during his visit. Kai's hands shook as she scrambled through Landon's bag for the third time.

"You act like they're staying for a month or something," Mz. C commented, noticing how anal Kai was being over the children's belongings. "It's just overnight and I'm sure they have some stuff at my house anyway."

"Yeah, I just want to be certain," Kai stated. "Don't wanna have to make no runs or nothing."

"Runs for what? You think I'd call and ask you to bring anything, or do anything knowing you over here booed up."

"I don't know about all that booed up business," Kai responded, handing her mother Landon's bag.

"Uh-huh."

"What?" She looked at her mother coyly.

"I've had plenty of children honey so I know what it's like to be shipping 'em off to get your groove back."

Kai laughed. "Ma, please! Don't share."

"I'm just saying. And it's been a while. You long overdue baby."

"Ma!" Kai held up her left hand to silence her mother and cradled her stomach with her right hand as she laughed uncontrollably. "You are a mess. I can't with you."

"Come on kids!" Mz. C. yelled out for the boys. At the sound of her voice they came running.

"Kiss your mother goodbye," Mz. C. instructed.

The boys complied and then hurried out of the house to hop into their grandmother's car.

"Are you sure about this?" Mz. C. asked her oldest daughter.

"What?"

"Him. Are you sure about DeWayne?"

Kai let out a long breath. "Honestly, I don't know. I'm just going to see what happens…see how this visit goes and try to see where his head is at."

"Well, let me say this…ultimately it's your decision. Whatever you wanna do…but baby, don't feel like you have to stay with him because of Landon or financial reasons. Life is too short to be unhappy. I know I don't have to tell you that."

"No, you don't, but I understand." Kai knew that her mother was giving her a warning based on her own experiences. For years her mother had stayed in a relationship that was physically and emotionally detrimental. Kai had never understood what made her mother stay put in the union for so long, especially given the effects that it had on her and her siblings. She'd long since vowed to never stay committed to a man that didn't honor her body and spirit. Though DeWayne had never placed a hand on her, he'd certainly crushed her heart and as a result she'd walked away.

Mz. C. looked into her daughter's eyes for a few moments before pulling her close in an embrace. "I love you."

"Love you too boo," Kai responded. She watched as her mother turned to leave and chose not to mention the tears she'd seen in her eyes. Looking at her watch she realized that she too needed to be heading out of the door.

In nearly an hour she'd be face to face with her estranged husband. She had no idea what to expect.

***

The reunion had been a little awkward. Kai wasn't sure exactly how to greet him when she saw DeWayne make his way to her at his fight's designated baggage claim ramp. He'd given her a one-arm hug as he held on to the handle of his large rolling luggage bag. The drive home had been even more awkward. Years before they'd hold hands while riding to their destination. That display of affection didn't exactly feel warranted. They'd made idle chat about the house, the boys, and his flight all the way up until the time that they'd pulled into the driveway. And then a new thought, a new worry, occurred to her. They hadn't been intimate in forever and now here he would be sharing her bed.

She'd watched quietly as he unpacked a few things from his bag and made himself comfortable in the space that she considered to be her own. It almost felt like an invasion but one couldn't exactly say that to their husband, especially not when they whole point of it all was to try to rekindle whatever was left of the flame that burned between them. She knew that that tension wasn't all in her head. She could see it in the way he held his jaw before he spoke, as if he was bracing himself for whatever it was that she'd come back with. She noticed it in the way he asked permission to do certain things, such as change her television channel or use her soap when he decided to take a shower, or if it was okay to drink a certain soda that was unopened in the refrigerator.

As Kai busied herself about in the kitchen putting the finishing touches on dinner, she welcomed the space that was between them. She couldn't quite put her finger on whatever it was that she was feeling, but she was appreciative for the chance to be alone with her thoughts. DeWayne was resting peacefully, nestled in the plushness of her Louis Vuitton comforter while watching random movies on cable. Every now and then she'd hear his hearty laugh fill the otherwise quiet house. It gave her a mixed emotion of both comfort and anxiety.

The house smelled divine as she plated his all-time favorite: fried chicken which she'd cooked to a golden brown, crispy perfection just the way he liked it. She was taking a chance on the angel hair pasta and the steamed broccoli because he was a simple guy and would have preferred the chicken all by itself. Sauntering into the living room she sat their plates down on the blanket that was strategically placed in front of the blazing fire she'd started about twenty minutes earlier. She was setting the scene for a romantic evening and she hoped that he appreciated her efforts.

Returning to the kitchen, she grabbed the bottle of Riesling that she had chilling in the freezer for just a bit, and two long-stemmed wine glasses. She sat them on the floor and poured them to mid-full. Looking around she took in the atmosphere to ascertain that she wasn't missing anything. This was it. The moment they'd see if there was still something there.

"De!" she called out. "Come on!" She could have gone to the room to get him, but there was something about being near, or in her bedroom with him in close proximity that made her stomach knot up.

He trotted down the hall and stopped just at the edge of the sofa to get a good look at the ambience. "You went all out huh?"

"Just a little something," she stated as she turned off the lights to give the room the full effect that she was going for. She eased herself onto her spot on the blanket and he joined her. Immediately she handed him his glass.

"What is it?" He asked. She knew he was particular about what he ingested.

"A really good wine," she explained. "It's smooth. You'll like it."

He took a swallow and gave a funny look indicating that he could take or leave the alcoholic beverage. "Thanks for this," he said, putting his glass down and reaching for his fork. "It looks good." He took a bite of his chicken and nodded his head in approval. "Tastes good too," he stated.

"So how does it feel to be home?"

"Feels a little weird," he admitted. "But it's good to be with you. I've missed this."

"So you say."

"That I do. How does it feel to have me back home?"

She considered the question for a minute before answering. Taking a sip of her wine, she looked at him wishing that she could tap into his intentions and somehow know for certain what it was that was running through his head. "I'm still trying to figure it out."

"What's to figure out?"

Kai didn't miss the hurt expression on his face, but honesty was the best she could give him. "I mean, I'm used to my space now. I'm used to doing as I please how I please with no regards to another adult. I'm not used to a man being around so—"

"A man, or your husband?" He shot back.

"Either way," she responded, taking a bite of her pasta. "I have to get re-acclimated to your presence."

"What about your boy?"

"Who?" Her brows knitted up in confusion.

"Whoever you've been with. Whoever you've been seeing."

"You're always so worried about the next dude, but you should focus more on your own responsibilities to me. Not that I owe you an explanation or an account of what I'm doing, or not doing, but I haven't been seeing anyone; believe it or not."

"Yeah?" A look of relief flickered in his eyes and he quickly lowered his face so that she wouldn't catch it.

She had. "But if I did date someone it wouldn't be any of your business since we were very much separated and on our way to divorce, sir."

"I don't want to get divorced," he told her. "I told you that before. I don't want that for us."

"How do you suppose that we keep that from being our reality?" She was all ears now as she looked him in the eyes and waited out his response.

He took a sip of his wine before speaking and placed his glass down to give her his full attention. "Well, I think it's important for us to refocus…concentrate more on our rebuilding the friendship aspect of our relationship. I think so much has transpired that you've developed your ill feelings and I've developed mine, causing us to not get along, or not like each other so much at times."

"Agreed."

"I think that if we focus on that and then draw on what made us fall in love to begin with…you know, what made us want to get married, then maybe we can patch up the weak areas and create a more solid foundation."

Kai nodded. Again she wondered if he had read any of that in a book or some Hallmark card. He was making plenty of sense. Perhaps it was the wine, the beauty of the ambience, the naivety of her heart, or the power of his words that made Kai want to erase the past couple of years and melt into the arms of the man she'd expediently exchanged I-do's with.

"You down?" He asked her, taking her hand into his and kissing the back of it gently.

A familiar surge shot up her body and Kai knew without a doubt exactly how the evening would end. She nodded her head. "Only if you're for real, De. I don't have time to go back and forth playing games."

"Do I look like I'm playing?" He asked. He picked up their half-eaten dinner plates and sat them on the coffee table nearby before pulling her over to him and situated her between his legs so that she was leaning against his chest. He leaned down and kissed her gently on her cheek. "I love you, Kai," he told her again. "I want us to work."

Again, she failed to return the sentiment. Instead, she remained quiet letting her thoughts consume her and the moment flow in whichever direction it was going to go. This was now DeWayne's show and she was just watching to see how it played out.

He nestled his nose against her hair, her cheek, and then her neck. She squirmed a little as he replaced his nose with his lips, kissing her neck gingerly at first, then more aggressively as he reached down and held her hand. It was an intimate moment like no other they'd ever shared. Kai felt a burst of multiple emotions. Her husband was home indeed.

***

Nearly twelve hours had passed following Kai returning DeWayne to the airport for his journey back to England. She'd wrapped her arms around his neck drawing him into an embrace that promised him that the affection she was displaying was for him and him alone. Their goodbye was nothing like the tension of their hello just two weeks before. Kai was grateful for the time they'd spent together, alone and with the children. It appeared that they were on the road to rebuilding their relationship.

"So you enjoyed the visit? It seemed like y'all ain't never come up for air long enough to call nobody back," Sissy stated over the phone.

Unable to sleep as she awaited confirmation via call or text from DeWayne to verify that he'd made it home safely, Kai had taken the opportunity to call her sister-in-law back. She was finally returning the three missed calls that she'd had from her over the course of the last two weeks. "You're a mess," Kai responded. "We came up for air, but it's just that everything was kind of compacted into those few weeks and you know—"

"Yeah, yeah. Y'all had to make up for lost time," Sissy said, finishing Kai's statement. "Lemme find out y'all was over there working on a little girl."

"Ha!" Kai exclaimed nearly choking on the soda she was sipping on. "You wish."

"I do, I do! I think y'all would make a cute little chocolate baby girl."

"Hmmm, the last thing on my mind is having any body's baby, honey. I got too much on my plate to be changing diapers, mixing formula, and staying up nights. No thank you."

Sissy laughed in Kai's ear. "You say that now!"

"Mmmmhmmm. So while we're on the subject of your brother, why do you think it is that he's had this sudden change of heart?"

"Huh?"

"If you can huh you can hear," Kai said, breaking out into a laugh. "With your guilty ass."

"I resent that," Sissy responded in an attempt to sound hurt.

"Sissy, really? You sitting up here trying to tell me that you didn't say nothing at all to De before he made plans to come home on leave?"

"I just told him that if he didn't act like he was hungry someone else was gon' be munching on his chocolate cake."

Kai was dumbfounded. "Not the chocolate cake!" She laughed heartily and had to cover her mouth to not wake up the kids who were peacefully tucked away in their rooms down the hall. "You're a mess! I can't with you."

Sissy fought hard to get over her own bout of laughter. "I'm just saying," she struggled to get out. "I want to see y'all work out. Too many families out here breaking up and for what? Ain't nothing out there in dem streets worthy of a man walking away from his family."

Kai heard a buzzing in her ear and pulled the phone away to see the text that had come in. Her assumption was that it was DeWayne letting her know that all was well, but when she clicked on the message she saw that it was from Jermaine. She'd placed him on ice over the last couple of weeks to focus on DeWayne and her family. Although Jermaine hadn't liked it there was really nothing that he could do about it aside from respect it and wait for her to contact him.

Thinking about you. Hoping that you're at peace.

His message was sweet, but it didn't move her to respond. If she responded he'd send a follow up reply, or better yet he would realize that she was alone and he'd take a chance on calling. She wasn't ready to speak with him, especially if DeWayne called soon. Kai didn't feel like hurrying Jermaine off the line and hearing him all in his feelings about her saying that she had to go because her husband was calling. To avoid the drama she decided to just call him the next day. He'd be okay until then.

"...so if he gets it together my prayers would have been answered," Sissy was saying as Kai returned the phone to her ear.

"Uh-huh, you so worried about the state of my relationship, how are you and Stephen doing?"

Sissy let out an exaggerated sigh. "Girl...we don't even wanna go there."

"Yes we do. What's the matter?" Kai's eyebrows knitted up in concern. She detected frustration and hurt in

Sissy voice—two emotions that she herself was greatly familiar with.

"I don't think I can keep going like this. I'm over it."

"Over it? How are you going to throw in the towel on your own relationship but sit up here and tell me that me and DeWayne needa stay together?"

"Two different situations."

"Is it really that bad?" Kai asked. She wasn't privy to whatever drama was occurring between Sissy and her husband Stephen.

"Girl, some chick called my house and boldly asked for my husband. At that point I was done."

"Oh, no ma'am! He woulda been dealt with."

"Oh, he was. Trust. I'm divorcing his behind, honey. These chicks out here in the streets can have his lazy butt. Ain't nothing cute about a cheating man. But know what? I'm not stupid…folks cheat, things happen. But girl, I have no patience for a cheating, lazy son of a—"

Beep, beep.

Kai heard the buzz of an incoming call and pulled the phone away to check the CALLER ID. Finally, DeWayne was calling her back. "Hold on, Sissy. De's on the other line."

"Oh, go on girl. You can just call me tomorrow. Y'all gon' and cake on the phone. Hugs and kisses baby girl." Sissy hung up.

Kai caught DeWayne's call. "Hey you."

"Hey…just wanted to let you know I'm home."

Kai smiled a little and snuggled down into the comfort of her covers. "I mean that felt like the longest flight across the world ever," she joked.

"Yeah," he replied despondently.

"How was the flight anyway?"

"Long…you know."

"Hmmmm. What you got on your agenda? You 'bout to go to bed for a while? When are you scheduled to go back to work?"

"Yeah…I'ma take a nap for a minute…hold on." The urgent sound of the pause he created in their conversation alerted Kai.

She listened intently at rumblings in his background wondering what was going on. The faint sound of a female's voice caused Kai to sit straight up in bed. She stared blankly at the muted television across from her, not recognizing the pictures that flickered across the screen.

Finally he returned to the line. "Yeah. Hello?"

"What are you doing?" she wanted to know.

"Just uh…just settling in."

"With company?"

"Naw…"

"You know I can hear your background, right?" Kai was heated now. Not only had he quickly reverted back to the bastard that had made her see him differently in the first place, but now he was trying to play her for stupid.

"Yeah…that's the uh…the TV."

"It's the TV.," she repeated, nodding her head. She wanted to cry. For two weeks this man had put on an act like their marriage was so important to him. It hadn't taken long for him to drop the act and pick up some skank along the way. Kai was so livid that she wanted to spit nails into his forehead and watch the blood seep out slowly from each piercing hole.

"Yeah. I'ma message you later when I get up," he said hurriedly. "Aight?"

There was no point in arguing with him over the phone. What would it change? The massive amount of hurt that was filling her body almost incapacitated her. She completely tensed up and even her eyes failed to blink, much less release any tears. "Uh-huh," she said with little to no feeling. "Yeah, you go and enjoy your nap. Tell your whore that I said hello." Before he could respond she disconnected the call.

Finally her eyes fluttered and a blur of the last two weeks flashed before her eyes—the romantic evening in front of the fireplace, outings with the children, snuggling together in bed, listening to him tell her how they were going to piece their marriage back together, the intimacy they'd experienced when saying their goodbyes. It was all a painful hoax. She'd wasted fourteen days falling for his crap like some naïve school girl lingering on the arm of the most popular boy in school. She could have been working on the compilation of her next poetry book, or promoting Still Standing more heavily instead of giving him her undivided attention like a good wife should have been while her husband was home on leave. She considered calling Jermaine to vent, but thought against it. He'd only remind her that she was meant to be with him. Although she appreciated his affection, right now she was feeling extremely broken over this new round of shenanigans that her husband had initiated. She gasped for air as she fought to keep her tears at bay. When was she going to learn to stop letting that man affect her, husband or not? It was clear that she couldn't continue to breathe easily in the stifling, unfulfilling relationship that they called their marriage.

PART 2:

A BREATH OF FRESH AIR AND THEN...

~ CHAPTER 7 ~

"Hey Kai with your fine self," Ms. Peggy said as she slid into the passenger seat of Kai's Explorer.

Ms. Peggy was Jermaine's mother. Over the course of their unique relationship Jermaine had long since introduced his mother to the woman he wanted to be with over phone. It hadn't struck Ms. Peggy as odd that her incarcerated son would call her up on three-way with a woman that wasn't his wife. It was like it was simply because he'd often mentioned to his mother how he'd encountered a woman who would someday have his last name and bear his children once he was done serving his time. Jermaine had often sent money to Kai via his mother and vice versa. Although Jermaine was locked up in Valdosta, his 72 year-old mother lived right there in Atlanta, not even a twenty minute drive southeast of Kai.

On this particular day Kai'd scooped Ms. Peggy to take her out to lunch for her birthday. It was the kind of outing they took every once in a while, special occasion or not, because each woman had taken an instant liking to the other. Ms. Peggy never missed an opportunity to marvel over Kai's beautiful clear, chocolate complexion since the very first time they'd met in person. Jermaine loved the way Kai got along with his mother. It only solidified his belief that the two of them were meant to me. His mother had never cared much for his wife, Jillian— not when they were first married and not during their less than cordial separation.

"Hey, Ms. Peggy. Look at you all sharp with ya' hat on." Kai smiled as the older woman settled into her seat and clicked her seatbelt.

Ms. Peggy was decked out in a red and black pant suit with a large red hat. She didn't go out often, but when she did the woman turned some heads and brought attention to herself. She was always saying that she never knew if or when she would snag herself up a man.

"You talk to 'Maine today?" Ms. Peggy asked Kai. It wasn't unusual for Kai to hear from her son more than she did. If ever she had a concern about his wellbeing she knew to call Kai because nine times out of ten the young beauty would be able to give her an update.

"Um, not today, but I can call him now." Kai pulled out her cell and quickly dialed Jermaine's number. The phone rung and rung and soon she was greeted by the voice mail. She shrugged at Ms. Peggy as she pulled out of the parking lot and waited for the beep. "JB, it's Kai. Mama's here and she wanted to talk to you. We're on our way to lunch so call me back. Love you down."

The duo headed to Red Lobster which was Ms. Peggy's choice. As they chattered over cheddar biscuits, endless shrimp, and pink lemonade, Ms. Peggy filled Kai in on the drama that was going on in her family. Kai listened as the woman talked about that and other things before once more asking her to give Jermaine a call. Kai complied, but once again there was no answer.

"They probably are out having rec time or something," Kai assumed in an effort to give some form of explanation to Ms. Peggy when the woman appeared disappointed about not being able to speak to her son.

"That boy always doing something."

Kai didn't question the statement, or elaborate on it, although she knew it wasn't much that Jermaine could be doing while still imprisoned. It wasn't until after she'd taken Ms. Peggy home that her cell phone finally rang back with Jermaine's name on her CALLER ID.

"Leave it to you to be all late calling back and stuff," she stated in lieu of a salutation.

"What's going on? You still with my mom?" He asked.

"Boy, no. I dropped her off about twenty minutes ago. I'm almost home now."

"Where y'all go?"

"Red Lobster. You know she likes them dang biscuits."

"Look at you, fitting right in with my family."

Kai chuckled. "You know your mom loves her some me."

"Me too," he chimed in. "I'm gonna marry you one day. Watch."

She sucked in her breath in full knowledge of how the conversation was about to flow from there. "You already know my position on that."

"You already know mine."

"Uh-huh and ain't no way I'm about to play anybody's side chick."

"I love you, woman."

Kai laughed.

"It's not funny! I'm completely serious. The way I feel about you is unparrallel to any other feeling I've ever had. You're the sun in my sky Kai. When I tell you I love you I say it with a full prayer of us working out in my heart and with as much conviction as one man can muster up. I love you in a way I've never loved anybody."

"Your message has been sent."

Kai stopped her truck in her driveway just as the automated voice made the announcement. Her hand flew to her chest and she stifled her gasp of surprise. "Ummm, JB, who did you call before you called me?"

"Jillian," he admitted. "I don't know, I must have merged the calls somehow by mistake."

"Uh, you think." Kai burst out laughing. "Everything we just said is on her voicemail. You know she's about to be hitting all kinds of flips off of this."

"I don't know how I did it," Jermaine said, fumbling with his phone.

"Well, she hasn't called to snap on you just yet, so maybe you can still erase it. You got the password code to her phone? We can call it back and erase the message before she hears it." Kai's brain was moving at rapid speeds to figure out a way to save her friend from having a pointless argument over a love affair that didn't really exist and quite possibly never would.

"Naw, I'm not about to go through all of that."

"I'm trying to keep you from dealing with some mess later honey."

"I mean, I didn't say anything she doesn't know already."

"Excuse me?" Kai asked as she exited her truck.

"I mean, she knows I'm feeling someone else…you…It's not like she has some misconception that we're going to get back together."

"But she's still your wife honey. Very much so. So I could understand her feeling some kind of way about you leaving messages like that on her voicemail. Woman to woman, she'd have every right to be pissed with you JB."

"Why? We're not together. I want you. You know that."

"And I'm not giving ya' wife no reason to be looking at me like no home wrecker. I'm not doing it."

"You keep tripping about me being legally married when it's really a non-issue. What? Do you forget that you're married too and I'm not tripping off that?"

Kai paused in the foyer after closing her front door. Did he really just try to pull her card like that? Kai dropped her purse on the bottom step of the staircase that led to the upper level of her tri-level home. "First of all, DeWayne isn't right here in the city with me. Continents and an ocean separate us honey, so it's not like there's any potential drama there. Your wife is right here in Georgia boo, in Atlanta, so you doing what you're doing by being careless with the phone and making statements to her about moving on before you've even signed some divorce papers doesn't compare in the least bit to my situation."

"Point is we're both married, but I don't love you any less. We just had to go through the wrong ones to get to the right ones…to get to one another."

"You going to call and erase the message or what?" Kai asked, ignoring his last statement and heading on up the stairs to make her way to her bedroom.

"Nope. Forget her. It was a mistake, but if she hears it so what. I'm not going through all that extra nonsense just to spare her feelings over something she already knows."

Kai was done with it. If Jermaine wasn't concerned with how his mishap would affect Jillian, she wasn't going to waste any more of her breath lobbying for the woman. As far as she was concerned she'd done nothing wrong and had made it clear to Jermaine that she wasn't creeping with him, so Jillian would have no reason to find fault with her. Even still, Kai didn't feel overly obligated to protect Jillian's feelings. If the woman felt compelled to check someone she'd have to deal with her estranged husband.

***

The kids were at school and Kai was situated in front of her computer elbows deep in poems that she had written about the different relationships she'd had in her lifetime. With Still Standing exceeding her expectations by being featured in the Lupus Magazine and Bronze magazine, as well as her direct online paperback sales having her sending out books by the caseloads weekly, Kai was ready to delve into her next project. The one thing she noticed from watching the plethora of authors she'd come to know via social media was that in order to stay relevant in the game you had to keep up momentum. She didn't want to be some one-hit literary wonder that vanished into the realm of un-thought of authors.

For this project she'd decided to go a lighter route. While Still Standing was truthful and relatable, it was also very sad and heartbreaking. This time she wanted her poetry to be a little more upbeat and even more widely relatable. What better topic to cover than that of love? It was a universal emotion that everyone understood and experienced in some form or fashion at some point in their lives. She figured it would be a great contrast to her darker body of work. Her publishing company was giving her strife as they worked together to create a cover that spoke to her and gave life to the project she'd passionately entitled Affectionately 360. So far nothing that Written Word Publication's on staff cover designer had come up with was sufficient enough to represent Kai's vision. But, they still had time to pull it together as she was just now assembling the final pieces to the anthology and would be submitting it to the publisher to be formatted.

Taking a break from working, Kai strolled through Facebook saying her general good mornings. After accepting new friend requests, she promptly forwarded the connects her little spiel about her life and her testimony. Before she could log off she received an inbox message from one of those new friends.

What a compelling testimony. God bless you and thank you for sharing.

It was a tiny message, but it provoked Kai to click on the Facebook user's name to explore her page. Kenni York appeared to live in the same city as her and was apparently a fellow author judging by the books she had constantly promoted on her page. Kai scrolled through the woman's timeline to get a feel for her personality. It was important to Kai to affiliate herself with people who were drama-free in this business and gave off a positive vibe. Everything on the woman's page was business related and some kind of positive affirmation, so Kai returned to her inbox to send her a reply.

Kai: Thank you! I see that you're an author too and I'm in Stone Mountain.

Kenni: Oh yeah, you're right around the corner from me. Beautiful pic by the way.

Kai: Thank you.

Kenni: I noticed a lot of similarities between us while reading your bio. You have all boys, so do I. You're a military family, so I'm I. And you're an author, so am I. Kinda scary. Lol.

Kai: That's very interesting. We should link up some time. I don't have a lot of family oriented friends and my kids love to meet new kids. As for the husband, we're separated right now…he's overseas.

Kenni: My husband's deployed in Afghanistan. What branch is your husband in?

Kai: Navy

Kenni: We're Army

Kai: Cool. Yeah, we should link up. You're welcome to come here or we can meet somewhere like the park or something for the kids to play. Send me links to your books too so I can check you out and help promote any way I can.

Kenni: Will do! Thank you….lemme ask you something. I know you don't know me from Adam, but I get a good vibe from you so I feel like this may work…

Kai raised an eyebrow, unsure of what to expect next. She didn't have to wait long to find out.

Kenni: I'm putting together a venture that's about female authors in Atlanta. I'd love to meet with you to discuss the particulars to see if it's something you'd be interested in participating in. We can do lunch and it would give us an opportunity to get to know one another as well.

Kai considered it. She was big on promoting herself in any way that she could. It seemed like Kenni had been in the game for a minute so perhaps whatever she had in mind would turn out to be a feasible and lucrative venture that would help Kai branch out.

Kai: Sounds good. Tell me the date, time, and location and I'm there.

Kai's cell phone rang. She looked at the CALLER ID to see that it was Ms. Peggy calling. She considered allowing it to go to voicemail and getting back to her because she assumed that the woman was calling to inquire about her son. But instead, she pressed the button to her Bluetooth and accepted the call. "Hello mother," she greeted the woman pleasantly as she saved the Microsoft Word document that housed her latest manuscript.

"Hey Kai, with your fine self," Ms. Peggy replied. "You busy?"

"Um, just finishing up some work before my doctor's appointment. What's going on?"

"Have you heard from 'Maine?"

Kai gave a smile at her own insightfulness. She'd known exactly what the deal was. "No, ma'am. Not today."

"Girl, lemme tell you. That hussy called here talking a bunch of mess."

"Wait, what hussy?" Kai couldn't control her laughter. "Not the hussy though, Ms. Peggy."

"You know who I'm talkin' bout. That woman he married."

"Ah! Jillian." Kai shook her head as she glanced at her inbox to see Kenni's reply of a date and time for their meeting. She quickly sent back a message to confirm the date and returned her attention to Ms. Peggy who was in her ear going off at an octave Kai had never heard the older woman's voice reach before.

"Callin' me talkin' bout my son messing around with some lil' young thang that ain't gon' do nothing but take his money and then leave him. You know she talkin' 'bout you. Gon' sit here and call you a hood rat like I don't know who she's talking about."

Kai had to take a minute to compose herself. This was exactly the type of drama she didn't want nor need in her life. She'd almost felt sorry for Jillian knowing that she was holding on to a man who obviously didn't want her, but the moment she heard that the woman was dragging her good name through the mud any compassion Kai felt vanished. "Me? A hood rat? Obviously, she doesn't know me."

"Nuh-uh, honey listen. Obviously she don't know me. I had to tell her that I knew exactly who she was referring to and I told her Kai got more class than you've experienced from going through elementary school and high school."

Kai chuckled at the woman's attempt to be witty.

"I told her not to be calling up my phone with that nonsense calling folks names and stuff trying to start some mess on my phone. Nuh-uh, I don't do that mess. I ain't never liked her to begin with so she's real lucky I haven't handed her back her little feelings before today. 'Maine better go ahead get her and put her in her place calling up here like that. He needa go ahead and be done with that crazy girl and free us all of the headache."

Kai laughed. "Well, I'm sorry Ms. Peggy, but she got the right one today. I ain't never did nothing for her to be throwing shots at me. If anything I advocated for him to make a decision and do something about the state of their marriage. Now, JB accidently left a message on her voicemail with a conversation he and I were having, but even then Ms. Peggy, I didn't say anything disrespectful or to indicate that I was involved with her husband. If she was listening to what was said she'd realize that."

"Kai listen, that child ain't got the sense God gave her. She was adamant that she wasn't gon' give him no divorce. That if he sent her the papers she wasn't gon' sign nothing. You tell me what kinda fool woman calls up a man's mama to tell on him and to tell her that she playin' games with the woman's son. Now, where they do that at?"

Kai shook her head at the foolery. "Mmm mmm. I'ma need her to have several seats. I'm glad I don't know her and she doesn't know me because had she called my phone with that freckle-nackle, she woulda got an ear full and then some."

"I don't know what 'Maine gon' do with her, but he better do something," Ms. Peggy went on. "Can't nothing good come out of him trying to keep on with her crazy tail. I told her she ain't gotta worry about you…I told her, Kai ain't thinking 'bout 'Maine like that, honey. You sitting up here worrying about the wrong thing, you needa be trying to figure out what you gon' do with yourself and how you and this man gon' deal with the mess y'all created. Don't be pulling other folks into your foolishness."

Kai nodded. She was pleased to hear that Ms. Peggy completely understood that she wasn't trying to hook up with Jermaine in that way especially considering that he still had to attend to Jillian's psychotic behind. This drama was far too much for Kai to digest. She rose from the desk and headed to her closet for her shoes. "Well, they can have all of that extra nonsense. I ain't got time for it. But you killed me talking about that hussy called you, Ms. Peggy."

Ms. Peggy chuckled a little. "I'm serious. You know I don't play when it comes to my children and you like my own daughter. Listening to that child talking crazy 'bout you made me wanna put a switch to her tail."

"Not the switch!" Kai was dying. "You kill me, Ms. Peggy. I gotta get ready to head out to the doctor. I'll tell JB to call you if he hits me up."

"Okay baby. Hope everything's okay."

"Yep, just a routine visit. No worries."

"Okay, Kai. Talk to you soon."

Kai clicked off of the call and grabbed her purse. She should have known that some kind of fall out would occur from Jermaine's fallacy. He should have listened to her and deleted the message. It would have avoided Ms. Peggy wanting to put a switch to his wife's behind.

~ CHAPTER 8 ~

It wasn't a regular doctor's visit. Following her last doctor's appointment, Kai was referred to the Emory Heart Center to inquire about a possible murmur. She hadn't mentioned it to a soul because after everything she'd been through over the years Kai figured it could turn out to really be nothing, or to be something major. Either way, she didn't want to alarm anyone unnecessarily, especially without having all of the facts.

"So, I hear what it is that your doctor noted here," Dr. Epson, the cardiologist stated following his initial assessment while looking at Kai's medical notes on his computer screen. "And I'm not greatly alarmed by it, however we want to be proactive in making certain that it's not something major."

Kai pursed her lips. "Okay, so when you say it, what exactly are you referring to? Can you be more specific?"

Dr. Epson looked away from his screen. "With the way that you struggle to breathe at times it puts your body in a panic…it puts your heart in a panic. The fight to endure the pains associated with the Lupus also does something to the rhythm of your heartbeat. With your blood pressure plummeting from time to time as it's been known to do it raises some concerns. The low bp is associated with failure of the cardiovascular system. Not enough blood circulates to the heart muscle. A potential effect of that would be the onset of a heart attack, so we want to make sure you're heart healthy. In addition, that slight murmur your doctor detected could possibly be an arrhythmia, which is simply an irregular beating of your heart."

Kai saw his lips moving and heard the words that were flowing from them, but her mind was stuck on processing the fact that yet another one of her vital organs could be failing her. The Lupus was doing its best to attack the rest of her body by inflicting her with fibrosis and now it was quite possibly playing a role in developing an issue with her heart. Kai gripped her purse tightly and noticeably. She didn't want to hear anymore. "So now what?" She asked pointedly, assuming that another prescription was in her future.

Dr. Epson could sense his patient's growing discomfort with the conversation. "Now we monitor you. We aren't going to just jump in and assume the worse, so I want you to relax. It could very well be nothing. The objective here is to be certain that everything is okay and to keep an eye on anything that could be potentially fatal in the long run. You have a team of professionals dedicated to making sure that you live a full, and healthy life."

"A full life maybe, but healthy I don't know," Kai responded skeptically. "Seems like every time I turn around y'all are throwing a new diagnosis at me. I mean, a person can only take so much."

"I understand your frustration."

"Do you?"

"I do. I'm sure it isn't easy having to deal with constant medical limitations and I know that just being here and considering all of the extreme possibilities can't be a walk in the park for you. I apologize for that, but think of it this way. We're taking preventive measures now to avoid anything serious occurring in the future."

Kai leaned back in her chair. He was right about one thing— she was considering the extreme possibilities. The way she saw it, Dr. Epson was on the brink of providing her with yet another possible way that she could die and leave her children motherless. The thought rocked her to the core, but she wasn't about to let her emotions get the best of her in front of the doctor. "So how do we monitor it?"

"I'm going to have you wear a heart monitor for 42 hours. It can't be removed under any circumstances, so you'll have to safeguard it when you take a tub bath. The monitor will pick up the pattern of your heart rhythm as well as detect the flow of blood to the heart."

"A heart monitor," Kai repeated.

"That's right. Sit tight for me." Dr. Espon left the room and returned only moments later with a nurse in tow and a box that reminded Kai of a battery pack. "Okay. We're going to have you remove your shirt so that we can attach the electrodes to your chest area."

Kai took notice of the many cords coming from the pack and wondered how on earth she would manage to comfortably carry the machine around on her body for the next two full days. "Somehow I thought that you were gonna give me some little wristband or something," she commented as she removed her blouse."

"Oh, you may be thinking of the contraptions athletes use to keep up with their heart rate," the doctor responded as he sat the pack down on the exam table next to Kai. "Those are good for that minimal use, but this is state of the art technology that gives us a good, constant reading of your heart activity. It's like a portal EKG."

The nurse busied about placing the sticky pads of the electrodes over Kai's chest and back as the doctor continued to speak.

"Okay, electrodes are connected to the machine here and sends the readings straight to the machine," he explained. "You don't have to do anything to it. Just assume your usual activities. This strap here—" he held it up for her to view—"you can carry it over your shoulder like a purse or tote bag or you can place it across your chest like some backpacks are carried. Whichever is most comfortable for you."

"Not wearing it at all is most comfortable for me," Kai remarked.

The nurse chuckled as she picked up the paper coverings she'd peeled off of the pads in order to discard them. With her work done, she exited the room.

"I know it's not very comfortable," Dr. Epson stated.

"Or attractive. This thing's gonna clash with everything. That's not cute."

The doctor laughed. "I'm sorry it isn't more fashionable, but it's a necessity. Remember, we're being proactive here." He handed her the pack.

Kai promptly threw the strap over her shoulder. "I mean, I'm okay with the unfashionable part…if it wasn't so bulky I'd be okay."

"It's only for 48 hours. You'll come back in two days to return the machine to the office."

"So, I won't need to see you when I come back?"

"Nope. You'll just drop it with the receptionist and then we'll go over the results and be in touch with you as well as your other physicians. It's important for everyone involved in your medical care to be on the same page and know what's going on."

Kai nodded. "Gotcha. Well alrighty. Two days it is." She huffed as she put on her blouse and slid from the exam table."

Dr. Epson patted her shoulder. "It'll be fine. We'll speak with you soon, Kai."

"Thanks," she responded as she followed him out of the room and toward the exit. She was glad to be leaving his office, but hadn't expected to be doing so feeling slightly heavier. *Two days isn't so bad*, she thought. *I'd rather get this over with now and rule out any other possible conditions verses fall over and die unknowingly later.* The pep talk got her to the car and by the time she pulled out of her parking spot she knew that she was in need of a glass of wine and some upbeat conversation. With the publishing company working her nerves, the drama Ms. Peggy had shared with her earlier, and now having to wear this heart monitored combined, Kai's day hadn't been so great. She pulled out her cell and placed a call to her bestie. Some girl time was in order.

***

Kai pulled up in the parking lot fifteen minutes late for her lunch date with her new Facebook friend. She wasn't feeling her best earlier in the morning and was trying not to succumb to the feeling that was threatening to knock her over. She really wanted to be in the bed being still and allowing herself to catch her breath. But she knew that even minimizing her activity wasn't going to help the difficulty and aching that she was experiencing. She could have canceled, but this was business. She'd vowed to herself that she wouldn't let her health challenges interfere with her newfound hustle.

As Kai walked through Panera Bread looking for the woman with brown locs her hand brushed against the strap of the heart monitor in route to touching her rhinestone necklace that read Boss. Instantly she became conscious of the box of the monitor pressed against her back due to the way that she had it positioned. This chick's gonna think I'm all kinds of broken coming up in here with this big ole' pack on, Kai thought. Finally, her eyes locked with Kenni's a table far to the right and she headed on over in her direction.

"Hey boo," Kai greeted her with a hug. "Sorry I'm late. It's been a super hectic day."

"You're good," Kenni said with a smile. "I'm glad you were able to make it."

"Me too, honey. With how I was feeling I had to pull myself together and make it do what it do." She sat her purse down on the table. "So how does this work?" She asked, looking around the establishment. "I've never been here before."

"Oh, we just go up to the counter and order and then when it's ready they'll call our names," Kenni explained.

"So you haven't ordered already?"

Kenni shook her head. "I was waiting on you."

Kai reached for her bag and moved to stand up. "Oh, well come on, 'cause honey I'm all kinds of hungry. I could probably eat everything in here right about now," she joked as they headed to the line. "Fat girl problems."

Kenni giggled. "Girl, what you know about fat girl problems?" She observed the slenderness of Kai's waistline and the size of her arms before rubbing her own belly. "Look at this. This is fat girl problems."

Kai cocked her head to the side. "Don't be fooled. Trust, I've learned the art of sucking it in. But yes, I've got a lot more meat than I started out with honey. I'm thinking about getting lipo though. I already got my breasts done now I just gotta get my midsection right and I'll be good."

"Really?" Kenni asked in reference to the breast enhancement.

"Girl, yes. After I had my second child I had to get these things filled out. Best $4000 my husband ever spent."

They shared a laugh just before ordering their meals. Once back at the table and after they each had their correct orders in front of them, the duo got down to business.

"Okay honey, so tell me about this idea you have," Kai said.

Kenni pulled out a note book, retrieved a sheet of paper, and handed it to Kai. "So here's what I've got…and you can follow along with me. I'm looking to venture over into film in the way of creating and producing a reality show based on the lives of female authors residing in the Atlanta area. I think there're a lot of misconceptions about what it takes to make it in this industry and what the life of a writer is really like. Also, I feel like there are so many negative images of black women, especially in Atlanta, portrayed on television these days. Basically, I want to depict an accurate assessment on the full life of a writer, not just them sitting at a computer screen all day, as well as give the media, or give the viewers, some positive female images in contrast to all of the rachetery they're already seeing."

Kai looked at the synopsis outlined on the paper that Kenni had handed her. Listed at the top were the names of two other authors that Kai had heard of. "So, you've already talked to these other two about this?"

"Well, I spoke with one, Tammi, and she respectfully declined so I'll have to replace her, but I'm not certain with who yet. I'm not really familiar with a lot of people. Like, honestly, I stay in my little bubble, work on my projects, mind my own business, and I don't fraternize too much. I'm not really social-able like that. You know what I mean? I mean, I interact with the readers, but I don't run in circles really with other authors. I'm just…busy in my own bubble."

"I know a few people. I can think of a few names that might be good prospects. You know, people that live here. I think that Constance Leery is a good choice and Nika Michelle. She's a great author. So you have or haven't talked to Emery E. yet?" Kai asked, referring to the other name on the list.

"Briefly," Kenni answered. "We'll most likely do a phone discussion because her schedule is so crazy that we couldn't come up with a time to connect."

"Well, if we're going to do this then she's gonna have to be able to figure out when she'll have some time. It's not going to work if everyone isn't on the same page. You might even consider asking my boo, Racquel. Oh, her pen game is sick," Kai said speaking of yet another close friend she'd come to know during her venture into the literary field. "Get everyone on one accord and it should be all good."

Kenni smiled. "So you're in?"

Kai looked down at the paper again. The thought of getting some television exposure to help build her brand was nothing short of appealing. "Hey, I'm down to try anything that's positive. Just be mindful that I can't be grouped with no sheisty chicks. I'm that one who doesn't have a filter and if someone comes out of pocket well, there's your drama. It might be a good thing that the Tammi chick declined because I've heard about her, tried to connect with her before too and um…yeah, I didn't get a good vibe from her. She's one of those people who gives the impression that she's on some plateau while you're allegedly down in a valley or something. No, Ma'am. I'ma need you to check your ego at the door."

Kenni laughed. "Okay, well maybe God's lining it up so that the right people are pieced together for this project because Lord knows we don't want any disharmony. I wanna show us all being able to work together and get along without all the B.S."

"I feel you. I'm cool honey. I can get along with just about anybody. As long as you respect me and don't come at me sideways, I'm gonna respect you."

Kenni smiled. "Cool. So my next thing is getting everyone together with the guy who's going to film for us so we can answer questions and go over everything together. And just get a feel for everyone."

"Sounds good to me. Just let me know."

Their meeting was coming to a close. Kai checked her phone and noticed that it was close to time to pick the boys up from school.

"It's almost that time," Kai said. "I gotta get back over to Stone Mountain to get these kids off the bus and follow up with my publisher on my project we're trying to get out."

"Oh, you about to release another book?"

"Yes, girl. Gotta keep it moving. Another poetry book, but we're still trying to get some things together. I'm strongly considering letting my publisher go and getting out of my contract. I'm learning this business and quite frankly, I'm not seeing what they're doing for me that I can't do for myself." She thought for a second before asking, "Who are you published with?"

"I'm self-published right now," Kenni answered. "Waiting for the right deal to come along, but I'm doing it for myself and keeping all my monies for myself."

"Girl, I know that's right. This extra headache from this company's not worth the trouble. I got enough stuff to be stressed out about with trying to stay healthy and take care of my family to be dealing with some company dragging their feet and trying to tell me how my project should be. Shoot, I'm walking around right now with this dang heart monitor on feeling all awkward and stuff so you can see I have bigger things to be concerned about."

Kenni took notice of the machine hanging from Kai's body for the first time as she stood up and showed it to her. "Aw man, that sucks."

Kai waved her off. "It's coming off soon. The worse part about it is I can't bathe how I want to, or take showers like I like to do, 'cause you know it can't get wet. So I gotta do the tub bath thing and be very meticulous about how I wash to keep the dang thing safe."

Kenni stood from the table and grabbed up her things. "Well, at least it'll be over soon, you said. I hope nothing's seriously the matter."

"Girl, who knows. My body is always up to something, but you know what? I figure that when God's ready for me, he's gon' come from me no matter what."

They headed out of the door together, each considering their own thoughts following Kai's last statement. Kenni marveled over how well Kai was managing her health issues and keeping a positive attitude while still handling her business. Kai wondered herself how she was feeling so empowered after the terrible start she'd had that morning. As they ventured further into the parking lot, the women discovered that they were parked right next to one another.

"Okay, boo," Kai said as she turned around to give Kenni a goodbye hug. "It was good getting up with you. Let me know when we're doing the group meeting and I'll be there."

"Yes, ma'am! I'll talk to you later."

Kai climbed into the driver's seat of her SUV and took a deep breath upon turning the ignition. She needed to rest and she knew it, but she had so much to do when she got home. During the drive she pondered over her meeting with Kenni. She got good vibes from her. Kai had a thing about feeling people out and was typically never wrong in her assessments. You can't just break bread and befriend just anybody, she thought. But her intuition was telling her that something good was going to come out of this new alliance.

~ CHAPTER 9 ~

"What's up?" His tone was nonchalant and immediately she could sense that he was withdrawn from the conversation before it even began.

Why'd I even bother calling him, she questioned her own actions. "Just calling to check in and see if you were still alive since you haven't said boo here lately."

"Yeah, been busy. Just working," DeWayne said quickly.

Yeah, right, Kai thought. "Would be nice if you called home to check in between all your busyness. Munchie asked about you, so I just thought I'd get a report for him and advise you to call him when he gets out of school."

"I'll call him. What's good with him? He good?"

"Of course he's good. Everything's flowing over this way. Kids going to school, doing well. I'm working on getting my next book out. I'm feeling like crap on the inside, but you know me, I gotta keep handling my business. I had to wear a heart monitor for a couple days because they heard a little murmur, or whatever. Most annoying thing ever, but I've dealt with worse."

Silence came from his end.

Kai rolled her eyes. "So yeah, nothing I can't handle. I didn't want anything though. Just checking in."

"Aight. I'll call later."

"Mmmhmm." She wasn't going to hold her breath.

"Okay. Gotta go."

"Yeah." She hung up without saying goodbye.

The complete feel of their conversations was different. Gone was the tenderness he'd displayed during his leave. That whole bit about refocusing on the friendship aspect of their relationship appeared to be a distant memory—mere words that he'd spoken just for the sake of it. Kai shook her head. They were spiraling right back to that place where they'd been stuck for years. The way he'd sounded so uncaring and disinterested in anything she was saying made Kai want to go back in time and erase the fact that she'd dialed his number in the first place. He hadn't even bothered to inquire about her experience with the heart monitor, or the results of the study.

"He just doesn't care," she said to herself. Memories of how he used to dismiss her complaints of pain and discomfort before getting her official Lupus diagnosis returned to her mind. Kai's heart filled with so much pain as she realized that history was repeating itself. He wasn't the least bit concerned about what was going on with her and she wasn't the least bit willing to keep going back and forth with him.

Thinking about the way she'd fallen for his charade made Kai want to throw up. She'd given herself to him and allowed him to reenter her heart, wanting nothing more than to make things work with her husband. The way they'd made love and the quality time they'd spent had been meaningless apparently. She wondered why he'd even bothered to use his leave time just to come home and pretend to be in love and willing to work on their relationship. What satisfaction did he get out of drawing her in only to retreat back to his normal level of uncaring and lack of concern?

She hated to admit it, but she'd been played. Her conscience was telling her that he was cheating on her. Her good sense told her that they were no longer in sync despite any of her good intentions. It wasn't in her to play the docile, submissive wife to a man who was giving her no reason to do so. Red filled her eyes as the anger consumed her. What a waste of the time it had been for him to make so many empty promises. She wasn't sure if she was more pissed at him for playing with her emotions or herself for falling for his game. Kai stared at the phone in her hand. If he thought that she was going to stay on this roller coaster ride with him, he had another thing coming. He was playing the nonchalant butt-hole role, but the one thing that Kai knew was that she could do it a whole lot better.

Immediately she logged into her Facebook account and updated her status.

Getting ready for a special lunch outing with a special someone.

Kai smirked as she placed a series of hearts behind her status and pressed the POST button for all of the world to see. She and DeWayne were connected via Facebook though neither of them ever really commented or posted on the other's wall. Despite his aloofness and his social media silence, she knew that he paid attention to her postings. She was banking on him receiving the notification and reading her post. She could imagine him staring at his cell phone trying to figure out who she was going to lunch with especially after they'd just gotten off of the phone and she hadn't uttered a word about a lunch date. Let him wonder, she thought as she strolled to the kitchen to fix herself a sandwich. The only lunch date she truly had was with her computer as she continued to promote Still Standing while sending correspondence to Written Word Publications about her upcoming release, but DeWayne didn't need to know that. As far as Kai was concerned he could choke on his assumptions. If he wanted his wife he should have behaved like it. The time had come for her to start working toward putting a definite end to their mockery of a relationship.

***

Mint 2 Thai was located in a crowded plaza off of Clairmont Road in Decatur. Kai rode past the plaza twice in an attempt to find it. Her frustration was mounting especially considering that she was hungry, irritable, and hot. The Friday rush hour traffic was doing nothing to help her mood as the cars in front of her moved at the pace of drunken tortoises. She wished at that moment that Kenni had chosen an earlier time for this group meeting.

As she pulled into the first free parking spot that she could find, she pulled out her cell phone to see that she was nearly twenty minutes late. It wasn't her fault that the place was so hard to find, so she wasn't sweating her delayed arrival. She shot Kenni a quick text letting her know that she was about to walk in and proceeded to put on her heels to compliment her jeans and black fitted tank top. She was excited about hanging out with Kenni again, but even more interested to see how this meeting would turn out. Kenni's concept for the reality show was awesome, but Kai knew that the blend of women had to be on point in order for it to really work.

Walking into the modest Thai and sushi restaurant, it wasn't hard for Kai to locate Kenni and the other woman sitting with her. The place was nearly empty aside from two other couples sitting in isolated tables away from where their group was meeting.

"Hey, boo," Kai said as she greeted Kenni with a hug.

Kenni gave Kai a squeeze and nodded towards the other woman. "Kai, I want you to meet author Emery E."

Kai looked at the woman and instantly recognized her from the few photos she'd seen on Facebook. Emery didn't crack a smile, but gave Kai a once over while parting her lips to say hello. Kai's eyebrow went up as she took a seat next to Kenni.

"We're Facebook friends," Kai told Emery E. "It's always good to put an actual person and body with the online persona."

Emery E. nodded. "What have you written?"

Is she challenging me, Kai thought? Dang, I just sat down and already she's sizing me up? From Emery's matter-of-fact demeanor and corporate appearance it was clear to Kai that most others probably found her intimidating. The notion was laughable to Kai. She hadn't met a chick yet who could make her feel intimidated for any reason and Emery E. certainly wasn't going to be the one today. "My poetry anthology Still Standing came out last year. Working on releasing my next one in the next couple of months. For it to be my first time out of the literary gate I'm almost surprised at how well my paperback sales are going." She turned her attention to Kenni. "Girl, I just sent off a big order today to this Lupus support group."

"Oh, your book's about Lupus?" Emery E. asked as she scanned her menu.

"It's about my emotions after discovering that I have Lupus, Fibrosis, Fibromyalgia, and a bunch of other stuff, honey. That book touches more lives every day and the funny thing is I never started out trying to be an author, or a poet. I was just using writing as an outlet to get out some of my frustrations with dealing with the doctors, the inability to care for myself at times, not being able to play with my kids, folks not understanding and thinking that I'm crazy or that it's all in my head…because mind you, for the longest no one could tell me what was wrong with me. I was misdiagnosed but I knew that something else was going on. You know? You just know when something's not right with your body."

"Right," Emery E. cosigned. "Nobody knows your body better than you."

"Exactly. So I knew that I wasn't crazy. I got my baby, my medical records and high-tailed my butt on a plane back over to England where my husband was deployed to so that I could go see some doctors that knew what the hell they were doing. But I'll be damn if by the time I got that far I was sicker than I've probably ever been. Got to the hospital honey and flatlined. Now if that's not a story to tell then I don't know what is."

"Really?" Kai had Emery E.'s full attention now.

"Yeah. Oh, but that wasn't the first time. I flatlined twice. Was nothing but the grace of God that they were able to get me back. I'm a walking testimony of what it is to just walk by faith because I certainly coulda been long gone from this Earth by now."

"An experience like that has got to be life changing," Emery E. stated. "I can imagine how it would make you more appreciative of like the little things in life."

"Absolutely. I find myself not giving a baby's butt about none of the stuff some people get caught up in. I'm focused on my kids because tomorrow isn't promised for sure. Focused on my writing career, my event planning business, and being happy while I'm still alive, you know? I say what I want and do what I want because I'm gonna live this life I've got to the fullest. I don't have time to be living with no regrets."

"Mmm. I hear that."

The waiter approached for their orders and Kai realized that she hadn't even so much as cracked open her menu in all the time that she'd been sitting there. She allowed the other two women to order first before putting in her order for teriyaki chicken and chicken fried rice. By the time their meals returned the trio was deep into discussion about the progression of the reality show idea.

"The guy that I originally chose to film for us just started tripping on me out of nowhere," Kenni stated. "He was a friend of mine and called me up this morning asking me to PayPal him gas money to get out here this evening. I'm like...are you kidding me? So I asked him if it was going to be a request each time we're scheduled to get together to film and he said he'd like to be given a per diem. Mind you, he and I had previously been discussing this project for quite some time and he has been sitting with the contract for weeks...told me the terms seemed reasonable to him and never mentioned anything about a per diem. The way he was going to be paid for his services was via advertisement spaces that we would have secured to have the show placed on his lil' independent network until we got picked up by a major network. He was working on getting exposure for his network and I was concerned about getting exposure for the show. We would have been helping each other. And as a friend I coulda spotted him money for gas, with his out of work behind. It was his attitude after my question that crunched my peanut butter."

Kai nearly choked on her chicken. "No you didn't say crunched your peanut butter! Oh my god, I can't with you!"

Emery E. just shook her head.

Kenni laughed and continued on. "He started bugging out talking about I'd be spending thousands to get someone with his experience and knowledge to support our project. Then he told me he wouldn't be coming tonight since it was a problem sending him the gas money and that he wouldn't be speaking to me directly anymore that I'd hear from his lawyer soon."

"Where you get this crazy person from?" Kai asked between bites.

"I met him earlier in the year during my benefit event for sexual assault awareness."

"Girl, bye. How tacky of him to wait until we have a meeting scheduled to start making those kinds of demands. He's not professional at all and quite frankly it's a good thing you see that now before moving any further with him or passed off any money to him. Don't nobody need all of that drama and strife."

"So how are you going to get the project filmed and produced?" Emery E. asked, getting to the point.

"There are plenty of options," Kai answered for Kenni. "I mean, we could always put out an ad and I know a few people I could ask. Finding somebody with a camera can't be that hard."

"Yeah, I put an ad out for a film intern offering a stipend so hopefully I'll hear something back soon. I promptly sent his butt an email letting him know that his services were no longer required and then I blocked him from being able to send a reply," Kenni stated. "He really put a sour taste in my mouth."

"So after you find someone else what's the time frame looking like?" Emery E. asked. "I mean, I have a full-time job and kids so my time is really stretched. It sounds like a good project and I want to participate I just need to know how much of my time I'm going to be required to dedicate to it."

Kenni bit her lower lip. "Well, I'm not really sure how it will turn out, but the intent is for the camera person to spend time with each of us individually and follow us around a couple of times to see what our lives are like. So, for that you'd have to tell me what's best for you time wise. And then of course I want us to do group gatherings. I really want to get through this whole thing over the course of the summer. Just to get the pilot done and a couple of episodes."

Emery E. nodded. "Okay. Okay. I guess first things first you gotta find a new cameraman. I know when we first spoke you said you'd asked Tammi to be a part of it. How'd that turn out?"

"Yeah...she declined so..."

"Were you going to replace her with someone else or is it just going to be us? I think you'll need more than just us for the sake of balance."

"I was telling her that when we first met," Kai jumped in. "It's important to have a good balance of personalities."

"Yeah, I just don't know who," Kenni stated.

"I told you the name of a few."

"There are quite a few female authors that live in Atlanta," Emery E. stated.

"My objective was to pick authors that were on different levels within the industry. You know what I mean?"

"Mmmhmm," Kai stated. "I still think Nika Michelle would be a good option. She's been in the game for a while."

"I've heard of her," Emery E. commented, nodding her head.

"Yeah, Nika's good people. I hit her up on Facebook from time to time."

"Yes, I think I've seen her on there," Emery E. replied. "It seems like she has a pretty good following, so I'd suggest her too."

Kenni smiled. "Well, I guess it's settled. I'll feel out Nika Michelle and see what she has to say and then I'll get back to you guys once I've solidified things with her and a new cameraperson. Fair enough?"

"Fair enough," Emery E. answered as she signaled the waiter for the check and a to-go box.

"That'll work," Kai stated, leaning back in her seat.

Kenni looked at Kai's plate in disbelief. "I can't believe you ate all of that."

"Girl, I told you I don't play when it comes to food," Kai replied. "You thought I was playing? I can eat up something."

"Yeah, but where does it go?" Kenni joked.

Kai's phone buzzed. She checked the screen and saw that it was Jermaine calling. She sent him to voicemail with the intention of hitting him up later. "Girl, my appetite ain't no joke. Just think, at times when I'm sick I don't eat anything. My weight fluctuates between that and the steroids that have me on. So I'm happy when my appetite is healthy like this."

"Alright ladies," Emery E. said, standing up and reaching for her purse and to-go box. "I have to run. Let me know what happens and when the next meeting is, okay?"

"Alright sweetie," Kenni said pleasantly. "Be safe."

"See you later," Kai said rather dryly.

Emery E. waved her hand in the air and disappeared through the maze of tables and out of the door. Kai turned to Kenni and gave her a funny look.

"What?" Kenni stated.

"Girl, I don't know about that one. I mean, I hope it works out and hopefully she'll find time in her overly complex and busy schedule to participate but I wouldn't be surprised if she and I bumped heads every once in a while."

"Awwww. Really? Why?"

Kai shrugged as she put a twenty dollar bill on the table to cover her check. "I'm just saying."

They exited the restaurant and Kai gave Kenni a quick hug. "Let me know if you need help with anything."

"Will do!"

Kai headed on to her truck wondering what she could get into for the remainder of her kid free Friday evening.

***

"Do you have any idea how beautiful you are?"

Kai turned around to see a familiar face smiling at her while standing in line at Wal-Mart. She hadn't seen Jayson Brown in years. His full muscular arms put him in the mind of her oldest son's father. His piercing eyes and the way his long locs framed his face like a lion's mane made Kai's heart beat speed up.

"Thank you, boo," she replied sweetly, trying to keep her facial expressions in check.

"How you doing?"

"No complaints. Working, trying to take care of my menfolk, and staying busy. You?"

"Same…working, taking care of my daughter."

The mention of the word daughter made Kai's smile disappear. Any premature ideas of a liaison with this guy had just flown out of the window. It was never Kai's intention to have any dealings with a man that had a baby's mama stashed away somewhere. No good could come of that. Kai wasn't the type to hold her tongue and she never wanted to place herself in a situation where she'd have to give some child's mama the business for being disrespectful, especially if the mother wasn't completely over the man. Sure, she had her own children's fathers not to mention the fact that she was still legally married to DeWayne, but her cases were different in her eyes. Bill would never disrespect whomever she ended up in a relationship with. Their co-parenting relationship was solid and peaceful. As for DeWayne, he was clear across the waters doing his own thing and couldn't pose as a problem for anyone as long as he stayed there.

"How old is your daughter?" Kai asked, moving up in the line and just trying to make polite conversation.

"Four," he replied with a smile.

She couldn't help but notice his beautiful, straight, movie-star bright-white teeth. The part of his lips was so inviting .Shaking her head clear of the caliber of thoughts she hadn't had about a man in quite some time, Kai looked away and started placing her items on the checkout belt.

"So, you gonna give me your number or you gonna make me beg for it?" Jayson asked her.

"You don't have to beg," she stated bluntly. "All you gotta do is ask."

He smiled at her again as he began to help her place the remainder of her items on the belt. "May I have your number?"

Kai couldn't help but smile back at the sight of the slight dimple etched in his right jaw as he looked at her with alluring eyes. She felt a tingle ripple through her and knew that there was something uniquely special about this guy. Out of all the men that had tried to woo her and come on to her, this was the first time she'd had a physical reaction to the flirting.

Kai rattled off her number and he put it in his cell phone. The moment she moved to pay for her purchases, he gently nudged her out of the way.

"I got this," he told her.

She could have covered her own bill but it felt good to have someone step in and take care of it for her. She missed the days of having a dominant male around to play the role of provider. “Thank you, boo,” she said after he handed her the receipt for her things.

“I’m going to call you later,” he told her.

She simply nodded before pushing her cart away. Secretly she hoped that he would and she looked forward to the pending call.

~ CHAPTER 10 ~

Kai's call log was starting to reflect the truth of her life. Over time she conversed more and more with Jayson, caught up in the rapture of fresh, pure attraction that he exhibited. Nothing tainted the bond they were building and Kai found herself looking forward to their telephone calls daily. The calls began to turn into visits which she wasn't particularly sure about at first. The only man that had ventured into her home since separating from DeWayne was Bill. But, let DeWayne tell it, she'd been entertaining company for quite some time. The first time Kai invited Jayson over she'd almost called him up and canceled the invitation.

She wasn't feeling well and all she wanted to do was lie in bed and watch movies until falling into a pain medicine induced sleep. The children were away with Bill for the weekend and Morris was peacefully doing his own thing downstairs in the basement with Sarah. Jayson's schedule was awkward and he wasn't free until late at night to begin with. There wasn't much that they could do by way of a date aside from eating up a late night restaurant, but Kai wasn't hungry or willing to leave her house. Jayson had been adamant about coming over to see about her when she'd mentioned not feeling her best earlier in the day. He knew all about the Lupus and felt sad for her due to all that she had to endure. Having a man actually listen when she discussed what was ailing her and in turn want to see about her was refreshing. Sure, Jermaine expressed interest and concern for her wellbeing, as did Blacc, but what good could either of them do for her from behind bars aside from sympathizing and trying to rid her mind of negative thoughts? Kai figured that even if she had told Jayson not to come, he wouldn't have listened. He was genuinely concerned about her.

Kai was drifting in and out of consciousness when she felt a hand touch her face. Her instinct was to swat away whatever it was, but the aching in her joints wouldn't allow that to happen. She opened her eyes and tried to focus on the face that was peering back at her.

"How'd you get in?" She asked, realizing that she hadn't heard her phone or the doorbell ringing.

"Your brother let me in," Jayson answered, taking a seat on her bed beside her.

"He just let you in now knowing you from Adam? I'ma kick his butt."

Jayson shrugged. "Maybe he sensed that I was good people and wasn't gon' hurt nobody."

Kai noticed the takeout bag that he was gripping in his left hand. "What's all that?"

"I brought you something to eat."

Kai's nose scrunched up and she closed her eyes. "Uhhhhhhh," she said in a groaning manner.

"Un-uh," Jayson interjected. "I don't want to hear it. You have to eat something. You can't just be putting your medicine in your body and nothing else. That'll make you sick man."

"I don't want anything," Kai said softly, thinking that would be the end of it. She felt him rise from the bed and didn't bother to question his movements.

Moments later he returned, this time climbing onto her bed on the right side. She felt his hands pull her upward and then he held her still with his right arm as he used his left hand to adjust her pillows. Next, he helped her get into a comfortable upright position.

"What are you doing?" She questioned, feeling herself beginning to get annoyed and wishing that she'd been strong enough to demand that he not come over.

Jayson didn't answer her question. Instead he reached over beside him and pulled a chicken sandwich out of the McDonald's bag that he'd brought in. He unwrapped it and then held it to Kai's lips. She looked at him as if he suddenly gone bald before her. Was he serious? She shook her head, but he refused to lower the sandwich away from her mouth.

"I told you I don't want anything," she said, matching the intensity of the stare he was boring into her eyes with a solid, unwavering look of her own.

"And I told you that you can't just lay around with nothing in your stomach Kai," he retorted. "Bite."

"I...don't...want...it," she said through clenched teeth. Where did he get off coming into her house and telling her what to do? Didn't he realize that she was a very headstrong woman who didn't take too well to some man trying to call the shots? She was used to calling the shots. This role reversal was not what she'd expected at all.

He refused to back down. His nose flared a little as he stared at her seemingly daring her to not follow his instructions. "Kai," his voice said in an authoritative tone. He didn't bother to say anything more as he gave her a 'do it now' look.

Kai's resolve broke and she felt her guard weaken. It was clear that he wasn't going to leave her alone until she took at least one bite of the sandwich that he'd brought her. Reluctantly, she opened her mouth indicating that he should place the sandwich between her lips. He did so and she took a modest bite. He watched her as she chewed it as if he thought there was a chance that she wouldn't swallow the food. Once he was satisfied that it had gone down he shoved the sandwich back towards her lips.

"Seriously?" Kai complained. Although her complaints gave the impression that she wasn't feeling the way he was catering to her, Kai was secretly turned on by his caring behavior. She complied with his instructions to take another bite.

As she chewed, he reached over and retrieved a drink that he'd also brought along. He held the straw up to her lips as she took her time sipping the ice cold Dr. Pepper. The way he was taking care of her reminded Kai a lot of the way her oldest son did his best to attend to her when she wasn't feeling well. The thought warmed her heart.

After making sure that she'd downed the entire chicken sandwich and a good bit of the soda, Jayson helped Kai into a comfortable laying position, turned out the lights, and flicked through the television channels to find a movie they both would enjoy. Settling upon *Friday After Next*, Jayson snuggled up to Kay and gently held her in his arms.

"Thank you," she said softly into the dimly lit room.

"For what?" he whispered into her ear.

"Taking care of me."

He kissed her cheek softly. "That's what a man's supposed to do."

Nothing else was said. As the movie played, Kai drifted off into a semi-comfortable slumber. Her body was aching and the slight pressure of Jayson's body pressed against hers as he too fell asleep didn't help matters. The fact that he was so loving and giving her the affection she'd been missing for so long made it that much easier for her to endure the discomfort. She appreciated the way he didn't attempt to take advantage of her. He also didn't appear to have any desire to push their friendship along a more intimate path at a time when he knew that she was still so unsure about where her life was headed relationship wise. It was the sweetest night she'd ever had with a man that wasn't her husband. For just a moment, before slipping into the land of unconsciousness, Kai remembered what it was like when DeWayne had loved her in that way.

***

This was there third meeting and Kai was running late again. She didn't live far from Kenni, but she'd gotten caught up in dealing with the C.E.O. of Written Word Publications with regards to her upcoming release. She was annoyed that it had taken them forever to get her cover together and even still she wasn't one hundred percent thrilled with the outcome. She'd promised her readers a release date and wasn't in the business of reneging once she put something out in the universe. Time was of the essence and she wanted to make sure that everything went smoothly for this release. She already had plans for her third book and was eager to start working on it.

"Mommy's whose house is this?" Landon asked as Kai blocked the drive way of a modest two story home.

Her children watched as a small group of boys chased a football in the front yard. Not only would this be Kai's first time meeting author Nika Michelle and the first official taping of the Literary Ladies of the ATL, it was also Billy and Landon' s first time meeting Kenni's sons.

"This is Mommy's friend Ms. Kenni's house," Kai explained as she turned off the car. "Remember your manners and let's go."

"We can play outside ma?" Billy asked.

"Yeah Pops. Just make sure you stay in the yard and don't go nowhere."

"Yes, ma'am."

The boys bolted from the car and eagerly approached the other kids to introduce themselves. As Kai made her way down the steep driveway to the front porch, Kenni's youngest son tailed her.

"What's you name?" He asked with his broken incorrect grammar sounding adorable for a three year old.

"Ms. Kai," she responded. "What's your name?" she asked, poking him in his protruding belly.

"Keylan."

"Keylan? That's a nice name."

"You coming to see my mommy?"

"Yes I am. Is that okay?"

He gave her a grin so wide she couldn't help but return it with a smile of her own.

"Uh-huh," he said.

Kai tapped on the door lightly before heading on inside. “Hello, hello!” She called out, walking into the empty living room.

“Hey, boo!” Kenni called out. “We’re in the dining room.”

Kai continued straight ahead, walking into the dining room where the taping had already begun and Kenni and Nika Michelle were completely engaged in conversation. “Hellos,” Kai said playfully.

“Hey, girl,” Kenni said from her seat to the far left.

Nika Michelle rose from her chair and greeted Kai with a warm embrace. “Hey, Ms. Kai. It’s good to finally meet you.”

“You too boo,” Kai stated. “Girl, you’re so short.”

“I know.” Nika laughed. “I’m height challenged.”

Kai took a seat in the empty chair at the head of the table. Already she got a good vibe from Nika. The other woman’s energy was refreshing and her personality was upbeat. “Where’s Emery E.?” Kai inquired.

Kenni shrugged. “She told me she was going to have to pull out. That she has a lot going on in her life right now and she wasn’t sure that she could commit. And honestly, out of the people that I’ve tried to bring together the most positive and solid responses I’ve gotten have been from the two of you.”

“Awww, Kenni Benni,” Nika stated. “Well, everything ain’t for everybody.”

“True,” Kai chimed in. “I wasn’t sure if I was going to be able to take her anyway.”

"Emery E.?" Nika inquired. She laughed at the sight of Kai's facial expression. "What was wrong? She had a bad attitude?"

"No, it wasn't that. It was just that, you know…you can just sense whether or not your personality will mesh well with someone else's and I wasn't too certain that ours would. That's all."

"It is what it is," Kenni stated. "So we're here and our new camera lady is here," she said looking over to Kierra, the recent film graduate who had agreed to assist with their project. "This is Kierra, our angel."

Kierra smiled shyly and waved at Kai. "Hi."

"Look at you," Kai said. "You a thick something over there. I bet you be killing 'em at your school."

Kierra laughed. "I do aight," she joked softly.

"Oops, my bad. Are we messing it up by having a conversation with you?" Kai asked.

"Naw, it's okay. I'll just cut that out when I go back and edit."

Kenni took that moment to pull out the contracts and get down to business. It took the ladies all of thirty minutes to get through all of the papers, sign, and get back to having a more lively discussion. Topics ranged from writing styles, to publishing company experiences, to future projects, and of course the fate of the literary ladies. By the time the sun began to set, the ladies were still fully engrossed in conversation.

"Oops," Kierra called out.

The trio looked over to her.

"What's the matter?" Kenni asked.

"The battery died on this camera. I mean, we still have that one," Kierra said pointing to the other camera that she had situated on a tripod to get another angle of the ladies.

"I guess that's our cue to wrap it up," Nika stated.

"I was enjoying listening to you, man," Kierra stated. "I'm learning a lot. I have goals of becoming published myself so listening to everything you've been saying has really opened my eyes to a lot."

"Look at that," Nika replied. "A future author in our presence."

"Hopefully anyway," Kierra commented.

"Anything's possible," Kenni said.

"Yep," Kai jumped in. "And you got the three of us to give you any tips, advice, coaching…you got an editor right here," she said pointing to Nika. "We got you, boo. You're family now."

"Awww," Kierra gushed. "I feel like an honorary little sister."

"Too cute," Nika commented.

Kai rose from her seat. "Alright, let me get on. Nik, you need a ride back home?"

"Oh yes, Ma'am. If you don't mind," Nika replied.

"Cool. Come on." Kai approached Kenni. "Thanks, boo. Call me tomorrow."

"Will do," Kenni said. "Good meeting, ladies. I feel good about this."

As Kai exited the house and hollered for her sons to file into the truck she had to admit that she too felt good about their connection. In the past, a majority of her friends had been males, with the exception of Nikki Love and a few isolated chicks over the years. It felt good to be able to be surrounded by positive women with no negative agenda or cattiness. No matter what happened with their project, Kai had a feeling that something greater was brewing between the three of them.

***

"Happy release day boo-boo!" Nika Michelle squealed via Kai's ear piece.

Kai was driving down I-20 headed towards Conyers. She beamed from ear to ear. Her second book, Affectionately 360, had officially dropped that morning and Kai was experiencing mixed emotions. She knew that readers were still gravitating to Still Standing and hoped that she'd get the same welcoming response for the new title.

"Thanks boo," Kai said, switching lanes as she moved closer to her exit. "It took forever to get everything just right. I'm just glad that it all came together."

"All things in time," Nika said reassuringly. "I shared your link on my page and you know that I got my copy already so…"

"Thank you. We're gonna have to get together soon. See what Kenni has going on. I'ma talk to her later. And thank you again for the blurb," Kai said, referring to the excerpt that Nika had provided her to go inside of the new release.

"Any time honey. You know I got you."

"Cool. I'll call you later, girl."

"Aright, honey. Bye-bye."

The call disconnected and Kai drove the rest of the way to her mother's house where she was planning to have a heart to heart with her youngest brother, Khy. Mz. C had called the day before telling Kai that she wanted her to come over and join them in a sit down discussion about Khy's future. When Kai had inquired as to why, initially Mz. C held out, thinking that Kai would demand that she put Khy on the phone and abruptly give him her two cents via phone. That wasn't the way Mz. C wanted it to go down and luckily she'd convinced her daughter to handle things her way.

It didn't strike Kai as odd that her mother would reach out to her with regards to her brother. For ever it had appeared that Kai was like a second mother to all of her siblings due to her being the oldest. At times she herself felt like Khy was more like her son than her brother. Whenever a crisis arose within the family Kai was always the one that everyone turned to. She was the most level-headed, sensible one, especially when it came to business matters.

It was late afternoon and Kai had gotten Morris to agree to get the children off of the bus and watch them until she returned home following this errand. She didn't anticipate it taking long and was determined to be out of there within the hour because of the online interview she had lined up a Facebook book club. Waltzing into her mother's house the smell of her mother's spaghetti sauce greeted her senses before she could so much as shout out hello. *No, she didn't get me over here with some food,* Kai thought as she headed straight for the kitchen.

"Hey," Mz. C greeted her oldest daughter. "Where the boys?"

"They should be home by now doing homework," Kai responded, placing her Michael Kors bag on the kitchen table and heading over to the stove where Mz. C was stirring her sauce. “Morris is watching them.”

The smell of garlic blended perfectly with the fresh basil and rosemary that Kai’s mother was known for chopping up and placing in her sauce. Kai reached for a dish towel and opened the oven to pull out the loaf of garlic bread that was perfectly golden and ready to be eaten. She placed the pan on the stove next to the pot of noodles and smiled over at her mother. “You did this on purpose didn’t you Missy?”

Mz. C waved her off. “Girl, I don’t know what you’re talking about.” She retrieved the strainer so that she could drain her noodles.

“You cooked all this food to entice me to stay here longer than I need to so I can get the itis and have to fall out on your sofa.” Kai laughed at the conspiracy that she’d concocted in her own mind.

“Nobody’s trying to entice you to do anything,” Mz. C stated. “But if you want to stay you know you’re more than welcomed.”

Kai picked at a stray noodle as her mother transferred noodles over into the saucepan with the simmering spaghetti sauce. “Un-uh, I needa get back home to my computer where I can concentrate in silent because I have an interview online at 6:30 so where’s Khy?”

“Upstairs somewhere on the phone, honey.”

“Didn’t he just get out of school?” Kai asked.

Mz. C didn’t respond as she continued to add noodles to the sauce.

“Why’s he caking on the phone when he just got home from school?” Kai inquired. “Like, didn’t he talk to her enough in school to take a break for a couple of hours and get his homework done? Does he have homework?"

"I don't know," her mother responded.

Kai didn't bother to pose another question. She turned from the kitchen and made the trek to her brother's room. She found him in his favorite position—laid out in the middle of the bed with his cell phone plastered to his ear and his eyes fixated on the ceiling as if it held the script for whatever game he was running.

"This how we do homework now?" Kai asked from the door way.

Khy looked over at his sister, surprised to see her standing there. He flashed her a gorgeous smile that immediately placed her in the mind of a young T.I. Her brother was adorable and she knew that the girls were clamoring over themselves to get into his good graces. But, Khy was a good guy. He had one girl that he'd been dating for quite some time and it was amazing to Kai how enamored Jenay was with her brother.

"Aye what's up?" Khy greeted his sister, moving the phone away from his mouth, but keeping it at his ear.

"Nothing," Kai responded nonchalantly, crossing her arms to indicate that she wasn't going to move from that spot.

"What you doin' here? You bought the boys or something?"

Kai shook her head. "I can't just come by?"

"Naw, I'm saying usually when you come by it's for a reason or something." Khy's attention was obviously averted back to his phone and his eyes looked away from

Kai's. "Naw, that's Kai." After a second he looked back at his sister. "Jenay said hey."

"What's up boo?" Kai said loudly enough for Jenay to hear. "When you coming back over to the house? We need to do a girls' day."

Khy listened for a second and then relayed the message. "She said she gon' call you."

Kai crossed the floor and took a seat at the foot of her brother's bed. He caught the hint that she wasn't about to leave any time soon. As if her piercing eyes didn't help drive that point home, Kai snapped her fingers and pointed at the phone.

"Aight, I'ma call you back later," Khy told Jenay. "Love you too," he said quickly, unable to look in Kai's direction out of embarrassment for his mushiness. He placed his phone down on the bed and sat up against his pillows. "What's up?"

"You tell me."

"Ain't nothing. You came in here like you had something you want to say? What? You feeling neglected and need some brotherly love or something?"

Kai raised an eyebrow. "Are you kidding me right now? Trust me, I got enough stuff on my plate that I am not at all feeling neglected by anyone."

He gave her a concerned look as frightening scenarios ran through his head. "Everything alright?"

She could see in his eyes that he was worried about her. Given her history of medical issues, he was afraid that she'd come to break some bad news to him. "Relax," she told him. "Everything's fine. I'm just checking on you."

There was a noticeable sigh of relief that escaped his mouth as his body relaxed from the tense position he'd fallen into. "Checking up on me for what?" He inquired.

"How's school?" Kai asked.

Khy shrugged. "I mean it's cool. Same ole' boring ish."

"Boring or not, you better be on point and stay on point. You don't have much longer."

"Oh, you came all the way over here to give me a lecture? You could have done that by phone."

Kai pointed a perfectly manicured finger at her little brother's mouth. "That right there. That's what I came all this way for. Ya' mouth."

He sucked his teeth, placed his hands behind his head, crossed his feet at the ankles, and leaned further back against his pillows with a smirk. "Man, whatcha talkin' 'bout?"

"Do I look like a man to you?" Kai snapped. "I heard that you been getting real fly at the mouth lately, so I was wondering if you needed somebody to come wash it with soap for you real quick."

"Ain't nobody washing my mouth with no soap. I'm good on all that."

"Humph. I heard you got kicked outta class because you don't know how to keep ya' mouth shut."

Khy shrugged.

"Oh, you don't have anything to say now?"

"What you want me to say Kai? The teacher got smart, I got smart back."

"Okay, while I'm all for not letting anybody disrespect you, I also know you weren't raised to be popping off at adults and acting like Billy Bad Ass at school. You're this close to being done with school so why would you wanna mess around and get disciplinary actions against you and stuff? Don't you know colleges look at mess like that? Your grades can be stellar, but if you pose as a disciplinary problem no college is going to welcome you onto their campus."

"Who said I was going to college?" Khy mumbled under his breath.

"What you say?" Kai was stunned. The thought of her charismatic, intelligent brother who held such a promising future not going to college baffled her. "Excuse you?"

Khy looked her dead in the eyes. "Who said I was going to college?" He repeated without a crack in his voice.

Oh, this dude is serious, Kai thought. "Then what you gon' do? You can't live up in here with ya' mama forever and you shoul' not moving into my house with any of that foolishness."

Khy shrugged, not really feeling like getting into a long discussion about his plans for the future. He knew how big Kai was on academic excellence, not that his grades were subpar, but he wasn't sure if she'd support the ideas he had in mind.

Kai looked at her brother quizzically. "What's that?" She asked in reference to the way he'd attempted to shrug off her question. "Obviously you have something in mind for yourself so share it."

"College ain't for everybody," he stated.

Kai nodded. "True. But the question was, what are you going to do?"

"I want to go into the Marines."

The statement hit Kai like a swift wind blows a light twig around. She was caught off guard and her head whirled from the thoughts and emotions that his revelation evoked. The idea of her brother, her baby, going away and joining the military had never occurred to her. While she commended him for thinking of his future, she wondered where the decision had come from.

"What brought that on?" Kai asked, softening her tone.

"I just wanna do something productive man. I don't wanna be getting up every morning going to some job hate making peanuts. I don't wanna live paycheck to paycheck. And I'm not sure I want to go to college. If I decide to go the military will pay for it, so I won't go in debt trying to pursue higher education."

It all made perfect sense to Kai and she looked at her brother with a newfound respect. Gone was the baby boy that she'd helped raise. Sitting before her was a young man who had a bright future ahead of him. "That's what's up," she told him. "But, in the meantime you still have to focus on graduating and staying out of trouble."

Khy cleared his throat and Kai's eyes grew wide. She could tell that there was something else he wanted to say.

"You might as well get it all out now," Kai said.

"I wanna go to YCA," he said blankly.

YCA— Youth Challenge Academy was a military based school in Augusta. Kai was very familiar with it due to the fact that her other brother, Morris, had been court ordered to attend the institution in 2008. Kai had never heard of someone volunteering to enroll in the rigorous program. She wondered if there was more to this than he was telling her.

"Why's that?" She asked, probing for more information.

"Because man…I'm bored going to regular school every day and not feeling like I'm really being prepared for anything. At least if I go to YCA I can get my diploma and get prepared for the Marines. It's a win-win."

Kai considered it. "Yeah, it would also help you get your attitude in check before you get out there with those grown men trying to get buck and getting your chest caved in."

Khy shrugged yet again. "I guess."

"You told mama?"

He shook his head. "She's just gon' feel some kinda way about me leaving and stuff. But I wanna do it, Kai. I think it's for the best."

Kai nodded. She understood his dilemma. Khy was Mz. C's last child to leave the nest. In some ways, Khy felt obligated to stick around for his mother's sake, but Kai knew that her brother was going to have to branch out and live for himself, not for their mother. She had plenty of grandkids to love on. She would be fine whenever Khy did move out and move on. "Focus on watching your mouth and keeping your grades up. I'll talk to mama and we'll see if we can get you enrolled for next year. We'll start getting whatever paperwork together so that you can have everything you need. It'll be okay," she assured him.

Khy put his arms down and moved forward as if he wanted to put his arms around his sister. After an awkward hesitation, he went ahead and gave her a heartfelt embrace. "Thanks, sis."

"You know I got your back," Kai told him. "As long as you're doing something positive and staying out of trouble I've always got your back. You can believe that." Kai pushed him away playfully and rose from the bed. "Alright, do ya' homework before you go back to caking on the phone and I'ma talk to you later."

Khy chuckled. "A'ight then."

Kai glided through the house and into the living room where her mother was comfortably positioned in front of the television and sipping from a cup. Without saying a word to Mz. C, Kai returned to the kitchen, fixed herself a to-go plate of the Italian dinner her mother had prepared, retrieved her purse and headed back to the living room. "Aight, I'm gone, honey."

Mz. C. looked up at her daughter. "Everything okay?"

Kai threw her hand up. "That boy's fine. I talked to him, reinforced him getting his act together and we talked about the future. Everything's good." She'd promised Khy that she would talk to their mother about him going to YCA, but that conversation wouldn't be today. She wanted to get her own mind completely wrapped around it and have all of the information in front of her before approaching Mz. C. with the idea.

Mz. C looked at Kai cautiously, yet trusted her daughter's judgment. If she said everything was fine, then everything was fine. "Alright. Why you not taking plates for the babies?"

"I'm gonna make them some chicken tenders for dinner. They'll be alright. I'ma call you later." Kai approached the door and reached for the knob.

"Oh, and happy release day baby!" Her mother called out.

Kai smiled, glad that her mother had remembered, because for a very brief moment she herself had forgotten. "Thank you, thank you!"

"I see all your friends and people liking the link and sharing it on Facebook."

"Yes! My team rocks."

"You heard from DeWayne?"

The mention of his name made Kai want to spit nails. Her day had been going just fine. Why did her mother have to bring him up and ruin what would have been a perfectly peaceful day otherwise?

Kai shook her head. "Naw, and it doesn't matter," she said, opening the door.

Mz. C frowned. "He hasn't even texted you to say congratulations or nothing? What kind of mess is that?"

"I'm not even worried about it. I don't do this for his recognition or anybody else's anyway, so it doesn't matter to me one way or the other."

Mz. C. felt ill-at-ease. She could sense how much her daughter loved the man she'd married, but as time grew on she feared that Kai's heart was growing cold as a result of the disconnect between herself and DeWayne. It pained her to see her daughter not having the love she so deserved and a part of her wished that she could reach out to DeWayne and slap some sense into his head. Marriage was supposed to be forever. She knew that Kai didn't really want to admit defeat and go forward with the divorce, but with the way things were steadily falling apart, it was apparent that the Davis' marriage was headed toward the end of the road.

"Hmmm," Mz. C. mumbled. "Well, call me later."

"Will do." Kai let herself out and hurried to her truck. During the ride home she couldn't help but think about her husband. Lately their conversations were refined to 'Hello, hold on' on her part as she promptly handed the phone over to Landon to speak to his father. She then allowed Landon to disconnect the call whenever he was done talking, which seemed to be only moments after he'd begun. DeWayne would text and ask why it was that Landon didn't want to speak to him. At times she would ignore the message and other times she would send a short reply back explaining that the child had very little to say.

It didn't surprise Kai at all that Landon was also becoming detached from DeWayne. For most of the child's very short life he'd mostly been around Kai. DeWayne was frequently absent from his son's life. Kai understood that this was all because of work and the distance between them, but as a child all Landon knew was that his dad wasn't there. Kai knew that despite the differences that stood between herself and DeWayne, if he was to return home he would make an effort to be active in Landon's life. But it was difficult to persuade a young child as such. At Landon's age he could pretty much only grasp what he could see and what he saw was that it was mommy who was consistently around and there for him. For that reason, Kai felt herself going the extra mile to try to compensate for the fact that her son was short a parent. Additionally, she was eternally grateful to Bill for the role that he played in Landon's life. Although he wasn't the child's biological father, he never once made Landon feel left out. Whenever Bill took Billy he asked for Landon as well. Whenever Bill shopped for Billy, he shopped for Landon as well. Kai appreciated the support and was glad that despite DeWayne's absence, Landon still had a positive male role model in his life.

By the time she got home, Kai was exhausted. It didn't take much for her to feel over-extended and she knew that she needed to get somewhere and sit down in order to catch her breath. With less than thirty minutes before she needed to log in to Facebook for the interview she was scheduled for, Kai stopped in the kitchen to get herself a glass of water.

Landon came flying down the hall and into the kitchen upon hearing her moving around. "Hey mommy!"

"Hey Munchie! You did your homework?"

"Uh-huh, yes, ma'am! Come see the flowers mommy." He pulled on her hand as she used her free one to put the cup of ice cold water up to her lips.

Kai allowed herself to be dragged down the hall, but she pressed the brakes the moment she reached Billy's open bedroom door. "Hey, Pop!" She greeted her oldest.

He failed to look up at her due to his eyes being plastered to the screen of his Nintendo DS. "Hey mom."

"You did your homework?"

"Yes ma'am."

"Where's your uncle? Downstairs?"

"Yes ma'am."

"You got your stuff out for practice? Your dad's gonna be here in a minute."

"Yes ma'am."

"You put the peanut butter on your head?" She pulled her hand away from Landon and placed it on her hip as she stared at Billy.

"Yes ma'am…wait…what?" Billy looked up at his mother as if she'd grown an ear on her forehead. "Peanut butter on my head?"

"Oh, I was just seeing if you were really listening, because you kept giving me robot-type automated answers."

Billy laughed. "Something's wrong with you mom."

"Nothing's wrong with me. Something's wrong with you. You didn't have anything more to say to me other than yes ma'am. No, how you doing…how's your day…"

Billy jumped up from the bed and ran over to give his mother a tight bear hug. "How was your day?"

"Uh-huh. Now you're interested, huh?" Kai joked with her son. "It was cool. Be sure you have everything ready to go when your dad gets here. I'm about to be working on my computer for an hour. I have an interview."

"Okay, I'm ready to go! You work hard mom," Billy said returning to his bed and his game. "You're always doing something."

"Make sure you find a woman like ya' mama," Kai said as Landon took her hand once more.

"Come see the flowers mommy," Landon urged.

"You're still my Chocolate-something-amazing," Billy said softly.

"What flowers?" Kai finally asked almost simultaneous to Billy's statement.

"Oh, somebody sent you flowers mama," Billy replied.

Landon took this opportunity to yank his mother on down the hall and she willingly allowed herself to be led, interested in seeing the surprise flowers from the secret sender. As she entered her room the vase was sitting on the table. She guesstimated that there were two dozen of the long-stem red roses resting in the vase. Leaning over the bouquet she sniffed a random rose and reveled in the heavenly fragrance. To the left she noticed a gift card situated on a clear stick. Her fingers gently pulled out the stick as her nose took a final sniff of the flowers. Glancing down at the card she quickly read over the short message.

Congrats on your release beautiful. Wishing you much success. –Jayson

Her heart skipped a beat as she stared at his name emblazoned in black ink on the card. Everything she'd ever wanted in a man was manifesting in this one guy and she could hardly believe it. The circumstances surrounding their budding relationship forced her to keep her feelings at bay. After all, she was still dealing with getting a divorce. But, she couldn't overlook Jayson's genuineness, his concern, sincerity, thoughtfulness, and affection. If she was being honest with herself, she had to admit that she also couldn't ignore his take-charge demeanor and his sex appeal. Outside of Billy and DeWayne, Kai had never felt this drawn to a man. Many had tried to woe—flowers here, money every now and again, promises of how they wanted to take care of her— but when these things came from Jayson it didn't sound like the typical load of crap that she chalked it up to being when it came from other dudes. It all was very sweet and very sincere coming from him.

Taking a seat at her computer and pulling up her internet, Kai quickly pulled her cell phone from its secured place in the cup of her bra. Quickly she shot him a text in acknowledgement of the roses.

Thanks so much for the beautiful flowers. You're the best.

She felt special and was certain that Jayson was moving in the direction of wanting a solid commitment from her. She wasn't sure how she would respond whenever the words made their way out of his mouth, but in the meantime she was enjoying the attention and affection that he showered her with. There was very little that could deter her from committing to this wonderful man. With as great as he was to her, he had one flaw that wasn't his fault and he'd never be able to fix it or overcome it— he wasn't DeWayne. Kai wasn't certain why the thought of her husband seeped into her mind in relation to this thoughtful thing that Jayson had done for her. She never wanted to purposely compare them for fear that it would negatively impact the progression of her relationship with Jayson. But, she couldn't help but realize that if DeWayne was a tenth of as affectionate and attentive as Jayson was then perhaps the roses she was gazing at would have been from him and they wouldn't be facing a divorce.

Kai shook her head. It was pointless to rack her brain with all of *the shoulda coulda wouldas and what ifs*. The only thing that could change DeWayne was DeWayne and it was clear to her that he wasn't wavering in his current lack of caring. She had to move on, mentally and emotionally, if she was ever going to have a healthy relationship with another man whether it was Jayson or not.

Holding on to how DeWayne used to make her feel and how she wished he'd behave wasn't doing any of them any good. Kai sighed and focused her attention on the screen ahead of her. It was time to work on promoting her new release and time to work on keeping DeWayne out of her thoughts.

~ CHAPTER 11 ~

"What's up Fat Girl?"

Kai rolled her eyes as she headed into the post office. She chastised herself silently for not allowing the phone to go to voice mail. "What's going on?" She asked nonchalantly.

"What you doing?"

"I'm working," she snapped. "About to mail out these book orders and get back to the house to work on my notes for Flatlined."

"What's that?"

It grated Kai's nerves that he was so outside of the loop with what was going on in her life. Sure they didn't communicate much on a personal level, but every contact on any of her social media pages knew that she was preparing to release her first novel in May on the anniversary of her Lupus diagnosis. The fact that he didn't know it made her livid.

"My next book," she stated blankly as she sat her packages down on the counter to check that they were addressed properly before approaching the counter to ship them.

"Oh yeah, that's right. I saw that. You just keep putting them out don't you? I'm proud of you."

She was in no mood for him to stroke her ego. It was almost Jayson's lunch hour and she knew that he would be calling soon. Not that she was doing anything wrong or owed it to him to not be speaking to another man, but when

Jayson phoned she didn't want to be stuck on the line with DeWayne. "What's up?" She asked to encourage him to speak his peace and then get off of her phone.

"Just letting you know I'll be home in May," he said.

"At whose home?" She questioned.

"Just saying I'll be back there…in Atlanta."

Kai sighed heavily. This wasn't the most opportune time to finally discuss the fate of their marriage. "Okay so…then what? Where are you going to stay?" It was her subtle way of telling him that he wasn't allowed to stay in her home. It just wasn't going to work out.

"I'm going to get an apartment after I get there, but in the meantime I'm going to stay with my sister I guess."

Kai nodded as if he could see her. "That's a good idea. And then when you're here we can finally go over all of these papers so I can get them turned in and we can be done with this."

"Yeah, that'll work. What about Landon?"

"What about him?" Kai dared DeWayne to say something foolish like he wanted to assume custody of their young child that barely knew him from the next man seeing as though he'd been away for the greater part of the child's life span.

"How will we do visitation until the court documents get filed and stuff?"

"I mean, you wanna get him on the weekends you just let me know. I'm not one to keep you from your son, you know that. Whatever apartment you get you need to have sufficient space for a child. You can't coop Munchie up in no one bedroom or studio type place. He needs his space."

"Mmmhmm. Okay. Gotcha."

Kay thought about the return of her husband and a thought hit her. "So you're done for real?"

"Yeah, man. I think it's time for me to come home, you know? Get settled and do something else with my life. Tired of being away from everybody…you know? Away from my family, my son…"

"Yeah, I guess that does get tiring and lonesome after a while. You know I know."

"Yeah."

They were both silent. Soon Kai realized the time and knew that she had to move on.

"Okay, well…let me know what your plans are. I'm sure Munchie will be glad to have his dad back."

"Alright. I'll call y'all later."

Kai sensed that there was something else he wanted to say but she wasn't down to stick around on the line to find out. "Okay. Bye."

As she gathered her packages and headed to the counter to be serviced she wondered how the transition would flow once DeWayne returned home. Now that they could finally get the divorce over and done with barring no excuses, she'd be able to fully give her all to someone that was ready to fully give their all to her. As the thoughts played out in her mind, her cell phone began to chime. It was Jayson calling. *Speak of the devil*, she thought, though in her eyes Jayson was nothing short of an angel.

***

It was Valentine's Day and Kai was in pain. She'd stayed up into the late hours of the night working diligently on her book, but the pain wouldn't allow her to keep going. Forced to listen to her body, Kai retired to her bed. The discomfort was more excruciating than it had been in a long time. She remembered a time when she'd hit up Blacc or Jermaine to help soothe her but now all she wanted was Jayson.

Kai: *In pain*

Jayson: *Is it bad?*

Kai: *Very*

Jayson: *Want me to kiss it and make it all better?*

Kai: *LOL, you just want to kiss me anyway. Don't use the pain as an excuse*

Jayson: *You think you know me now?*

Kai: *I know enough and I know more than you think I do*

Jayson: *Tell me what you know*

Kai: *If I tell you then I'd have to kill you. LOL*

Jayson: *Ain't nobody scared of you. You know I can handle your petite self*

Kai: *Right. I bet you can.*

Their text conversation went on for hours and Kai was thankful for the distraction. By 2:00 AM. Jayson asked the magic question.

Jayson: *You want company?*

Kai: *Sure*

It took him about an hour to get to her coming from his home in Buford, Georgia, but once he was there everything seemed alright. He laid next to her on the bed and held her hand as they talked about a plethora of topics. Before she knew it, Jayson turned the conversation into a monumental one, changing the course of their relationship.

"You know I care about you, right?" He asked her.

"I can tell. Not too many are going to get out of their bed in the middle of the night to just come and sit and talk just to help me feel better," Kai stated.

"I'd do anything for you. Do you know that?"

"Is that right?"

Jayson repositioned himself and gently turned her face toward his so that she couldn't miss the emotion in his eyes and the sincerity of his words. "I want to be more to you than just your friend Kai. I've respected your boundaries and your situation with regards to divorcing your husband, but you can't deny that there's a special chemistry between the two of us."

"I won't deny that," Kai responded softly. She knew where he was going with this and she'd known for a while that it was coming. Now that the moment was upon her, she wasn't sure how she could deny him the request he was about to give voice to.

"Are you sure that you're done with it?" He asked her. "Are you sure that you're done with the marriage and that there's no chance of reconciliation there."

"It's over and done," she assured him. "Just as soon as we can get this paperwork done."

He looked at her long and hard. "And you're sure that you're not in love with him anymore."

Kai slowly nodded her head.

"I need to hear you say it." His voice cracked as he spoke the words.

"I'm not in love with him anymore, but we share history and a child, so I do love him. But no, we're not in love anymore."

Jayson swallowed hard. "I couldn't handle even the idea that you would wake up one morning and realize that you'd rather give dude another shot…give your marriage another chance. I understand that that's something you can't just easily walk away from, so it's important for me to know that there's not a chance that that could happen. Because with the way that I love you, Kai I just want it to be you and me…I just want it to be us…and that can't happen if there's still a possibility of you and him…" His words trailed off and he had to work hard to get his emotions in check.

It was the most heartfelt moment they'd ever experienced together. The passion in his voice was so moving that Kai beared through the pain as she lifted her hand to gently touch his face. She was afraid of moving forward yet afraid of being still for fear that she'd lose out on the opportunity to have a real, lasting love with a man that wanted her and cared for her so intensely.

"I'm done with it," she told him once more.

He grabbed her hand with both of his and placed it at his lips. His kisses covered the delicate skin on the back of her hand and Kai felt tears well up in the corners of her eyes.

"So it's you and me," he said, solidifying the fact that they were now a couple.

"You and me," she reassured him.

Jayson pulled her into his arms and despite the discomfort she allowed him to cuddle her. The moment was so serene and perfectly romantic that for a second she pushed aside the wavering doubt that lingered in the back of her mind. She wanted something more than the broken fragments of a shattered marriage which she'd been holding on to for far too long. Jayson was her second chance at the happily ever after she knew she deserved.

~ Chapter 12 ~

Things were progressing. Kai and Jayson's relationship was shaping up into something beautiful and people were becoming accustomed to seeing Kai with her new beau. The co-parenting relationship with DeWayne and Kai was becoming a little less stifled although they often hit a few bumps in the road. It had been difficult to transition from being with DeWayne and being his loving wife, to being separated from him physically and legally, and then to being separated relationship wise yet having to see him on a regular basis now that he'd returned home. Just when it seemed like a routine was settling in and everything was falling into place, the wind shifted and Kai's world was once again rocked.

Kai was in the kitchen pouring herself a cup of juice. She was fully dressed and was waiting for Jayson to pick her up for their usual Friday night date. The front door opened and Kai walked to the threshold of the kitchen door to see who had entered. It was DeWayne coming to retrieve Landon for the weekend.

"Hey," he greeted her.

"Hey you," she said back.

"The boy ready?"

"Not quite. He's in there trying to put his things in his little Ninja Turtle book bag." Kai turned and headed back to the refrigerator to get ice for her drink from the freezer.

DeWayne noticed a bandage sticking from under Kai's arm. "What happened to you?" he asked.

"What?" She looked over her shoulder in the direction that his eyes were fixated upon. "Oh, I had these like boil type things under my arm they were bothering me like crazy. I went to the doctor this morning and they biopsied them to see what was causing them to rise up on my skin like that."

DeWayne failed to respond and Kai just assumed that he was disinterested as usual. He sat his keys and cell phone down on the kitchen table and watched his wife. For months he'd been home and hadn't had an opportunity to really talk to her the way he wanted to. "You got plans tonight?" He asked, taking in her appearance in her high-waist jeans and halter top.

"Yep. Got a date with Jayson."

It was no secret now that she was dating someone. They were each very clear on their positions in one another's life and it was mutually agreed that their marriage was done. They'd taken the mandated parenting class and now they were still trying to work out the terms of their settlement agreement without having to involve the courts any more than they had to. They were both moving on.

DeWayne nodded his head and bit the inside of his jaw. Anything that he'd planned to say was now stifled by the fact that Kai was waiting for another man to whisk her off. "I'ma go help him finish getting ready," he said before quickly exiting the room.

Kai was unfazed. A chirping sound occurred from the table and her eyes rested on her phone. Walking over to the table she quickly picked up the phone to view the text message that had just come in.

Baby, call me when you get a chance. Wanted to see if you wanted me to come through tonight. Missing you...

Kai was confused. Her eyes drifted up to the name on top of the text. "Who the hell is Ashleigh?" She asked herself in a whisper. She read the message again and it was clear to her what was going on. She'd obviously picked up DeWayne's phone instead of her own, but she was floored because as honest as she was about the fact that she was seeing someone, he'd been keeping his liaisons a secret. Kai was livid. It was irrational and uncalled for, but her anger had her blood boiling and the sight of the woman's name on his screen made her see nothing but red.

Kai returned DeWayne's phone to the table and placed hers inside of her purse in an attempt to not make the mistake again. For a moment she tried to regain some composure and shake off the emotions that were rapidly beginning to cloud her judgment. As much as she tried, she simply couldn't let it go. She walked down the hall to Landon's room and peeped her head in. The child had apparently fallen asleep when he was supposed to be packing. DeWayne was now trying to appropriately dress his son in his sleep.

"Can you come outside with me for a minute?" Kai asked DeWayne.

There was urgency in her tone that made him stop in his tracks. He didn't even bother with a verbal response, electing instead to give her a head nod followed by trailing behind her up the hall, down the stairs, and out of the front door.

"Close the door," she ordered.

DeWayne promptly pulled the door closed and gave her a questioning look. "Everything alright?"

"Are you dating anyone?" She didn't waste time beating around the bush. She wanted to give him a final opportunity to be honest about his personal affairs.

"No," he said nonchalantly.

Kai rubbed her chin and then crossed her arms. "Okay, well are you sleeping with anyone?" It took everything within her not to claw his eyes out at that very moment. How dare he bring her to this point where she was practically threatening him to be honest?

"No," he stated once again. "You brought me out here just to ask me that?"

"I'm not one to turn up in the house where my child is."

DeWayne was confused. "Turn up for what."

"I'ma ask you one more time. Are you messing around with someone?"

"No! I—"

"So you just gon' sit here and lie in my face?" she asked, cutting him off. With every no he gave her, Kai's temperature rose higher and higher. She was on the brink of exploding.

"Kai, man, what are you talking about?"

She stared him dead in the eyes and spoke through gritted teeth. "You know I'm dating someone. I don't lie to you about it and I don't hide it, so why are you lying? Who is Ashleigh?"

A temporary deer-in-the-headlights look occurred in his eyes before he threw up his hands and feigned his innocence. "I don't know an Ashleigh."

Kai hated being lied to. It was demeaning and insulting. It insinuated that he didn't think she was intelligent enough to know when he was lying even though she'd been married to him for several years. Looking at him struck something within her and before she could gain any control over her thoughts or actions, her fist connected with his nose in one swift, fluid movement. At that point, the flood gates were open and the match was struck. Kai was out for blood. Despite him throwing his hands up to defend his face, she continued swinging wildly. She didn't feel the pressure of her blows as she pounded him, nor did she feel the pain of the cuts under her right arm from the procedure she'd had done earlier in the day. None of it mattered. All that she was concerned about was beating the daylights out of the man that had caused her so much anguish and pain over the years. All she could see was his face being repeatedly assaulted by her hands, which she hadn't realized were so powerful until that very moment. Every tear she'd ever shed, every misgiving she'd ever experienced, every crack that had been etched in her heart because of him had manifested into this physical altercation. It was all due to the sight of another woman staking a claim on the man who was supposed to love her forever.

DeWayne grabbed Kai by her arms in an attempt to cease her frantic flailing. The feel of his hand against her skin only ignited her fire more.

"Don't you touch me!" She screamed as she struggled to break free of his embrace and commenced to once again attacking him. "Don't you ever put your freaking hands on me! I will kill you. I will kill your ass if you even think about laying a finger on me!" She screamed between blows.

By this point, their altercation had relocated from the porch to the driveway in DeWayne's attempt to get away from his wife. Kai was not letting up. She was now swinging blindly through her tears and attempting to beat DeWayne as if she'd forgotten that he was a man and she was woman. Gender was of no consequence. As far as she was concerned, he was merely her target and today she was about to assassinate him. As she drew back to land yet another punch a hand grabbed her wrist in mid-air. Before she knew it she was lifted off of the ground and spun around, away from DeWayne.

"Kai, are you crazy!" Morris shouted. He looked into her glazed over eyes and shook her feeling that his sister was surely possessed at that moment. "What's wrong with you, woman? Out here beating on this man?"

"You better get yo' sister man," DeWayne had the nerve to say.

Kai turned on her heels quickly and stepped off to approach him, but Morris grabbed her by the waist yet again and held her firmly. "Stop it man! Stop it!"

DeWayne was already hurrying down the drive way to jump into his burnt orange car that he'd purchased months prior. Watching him as he sped away Kai fought the urge to run after the car and throw a brick at it. Her makeup was smeared and her hair was a mess. Her chest heaved painfully as she stood in her driveway fuming.

"What happened man?" Morris asked. "Why you out here wildin' like that? What he do?"

What did he do? All Kai could remember was the name Ashleigh. Why had she reacted so violently following the revelation that he was seeing someone? She was over him wasn't she? It further infuriated her that he had stood in her face and lied about something so simple. Didn't he realize that she already knew the answer to her questions before she'd even asked them? She was pissed with him for causing her to be filled with so much anger and rage. They'd been married for nearly seven years and this was the thanks that she'd gotten. Being mistreated and unsupported for the last four years only to be lied to in the end. She was done taking his crap. She was done taking crap from anyone. But most importantly, she wanted to be done feeling any type of emotions for this man. After all she had a boyfriend now— a loving, supportive, and caring boyfriend who wouldn't cause her this much frustration.

Jayson, she thought. Taking stock of her appearance she knew that there was no way she would be able to follow through with their date. She hurried into the house with a confused Morris following behind her. Quickly she pulled out her phone and shot Jayson a quick text with two words— Rain check. She couldn't think of anything else to say because the truth would have been damning. To tell him that she'd just punched her husband because he'd gotten a text from another woman would have been to admit something that she wasn't ready to believe herself and she just couldn't do that to the man that had been so patient and loving over the last few months.

"Ummmm…Kai," Morris called from the living room. "You got a problem."

Kai sat her phone on the table and walked into the living room where Morris was standing at the window. "What?" she asked breathlessly. She walked over to the window and stood beside him. "What the heck?"

A black DeKalb County Police car was sitting in front of her neighbor's house directly across the street and DeWayne's car had returned to her driveway. The wheels in Kai's head spun quickly. She tore away from the window and ran back to the kitchen to get her phone. Frantically she called her grandfather.

"Baby girl," he answered in a jovial tone.

"I'm going to need your help," she said quickly. "I just got into a fight with DeWayne and now the police are outside. My nosy ass neighbor called the police, so I'm really not sure what's about to go down. So, I may need your help in case they take me in or something."

"He hit you?" The fury in his voice was evident.

"No, he didn't. I hit him. So, just be prepared in case I need you please."

"I'm here," he assured her.

Kai didn't bother to say goodbye as she disconnected the call and hurriedly dialed her mother's number.

"They're walking over here!" Morris called out giving her the play-by-play from the window.

"Hello," Mz. C. answered the phone.

"Ma, the police are at my house and I might go to jail…I don't know. I punched DeWayne two, or three times and the neighbors called the police. I need you to get ready now to come down. They'll most likely take me to the jail on Memorial."

There was a heavy knock at the door. Kai stood in the doorway of the kitchen and locked eyes with Morris. She nodded at him and held her hand up, letting him know that she had it.

"I gotta go now ma." Kai handed Morris her phone and headed to the door. Her heart thudded in her chest and she struggled through the difficulty in breathing that she was experiencing. She took a painful, deep breath and opened the door.

"Are you Kai Davis?" The officer asked with no salutation.

"Yes," Kai responded.

The next words out of his mouth nearly caused her to pass out. "Kai Davis you are under arrest for the assault of DeWayne Davis. You have the right to remain silent—" The remainder of the Miranda Rights that he recited to her were lost upon her ears as she was turned around and placed in handcuffs.

Kai was grateful that her kids were not around to witness the embarrassing, life changing moment. As the officer led her out of the house, down the stairs, and toward the squad car, Kai's eyes landed upon DeWayne. She wanted to snatch free of the hand cuffs and scratch his eyes out for placing her in such a compromising position. It was just one more thing to add to the list of reasons why she couldn't stand him.

"Sir, is this necessary?" DeWayne asked the officer. "I don't want to press charges."

Kai's eyes filled with hope at his statement and she turned to look in the officer's face.

"I'm sorry sir," the officer stated. "We have enough witness accounts that it doesn't matter whether you wish to press charges or not. It's still a public disturbance and the physical assault was a public siting so…"

DeWayne had a woeful look on his face as his eyes took in the defeated look on Kai's. Seeing her in handcuffs ripped at his heart and he knew that there was no way they could ever come back from this moment. Things would never be the same.

The officer opened the back door of his squad car and looked at Kai.

Kai spoke softly. "I have Lupus and I'm going to need my medication in thirty minutes," she informed him.

He nodded and there was sympathy in his eyes. "I'm sorry for this. I'll make sure the officers in intake know about your medical condition and that they're prepared to care for you once you get there." He motioned for her to watch her head and then assisted her into the back seat.

The moment the door closed Kai felt overwhelmed by the closed in space of the backseat of the squad car. How had things come to this? With her home being located off of South Harriston Road in Decatur, she was only a twenty minute drive from the county jail located on Memorial Drive. But, that ride from her house to the jail felt like longest commute of her life. The entire way there she'd been forced to replay the manic scene from earlier. All she could truly recall was her fists repeatedly flying towards DeWayne's face. Releasing her frustrations had awarded her this trip to a place she'd never wanted to visit.

As soon as she was escorted to the booking area an officer whose badge read Kelley took one look at Kai's facial expression and body language and huffed. "Oh, we got one with attitude." She looked at the papers that had been handed to her and then back up at Kai. "Oh, you'll be here for a while."

Kai wasn't intimidated by the bad bodied woman with the horrible skin. She rolled her eyes and refused to let the woman get to her. "I doubt it." She'd done the smart thing by calling Big Tony and her mother before being officially arrested. She knew that Mz. C. was already in route to rescue her and that Big Tony was standing by in case they needed money or some calls to be placed. She wasn't going to sit in that jail a minute longer than she had to.

~ CHAPTER 13 ~

Kai was officially booked into the DeKalb County Jail and was placed in a holding cell with two other women. One was an older woman who sat quietly on a bench with her head down, never once making eye contact with anyone else. The other woman was about Kai's age. She sat on yet another bench and was sobbing uncontrollably. Kai wanted to tell the girl to woman up, but she felt it wasn't her position to say anything to anyone. If things went accordingly she wouldn't even be there long enough to care. When given the opportunity Kai placed a call to a number she knew very well.

"Big Tony, it's me," she said into the tattered receiver of the phone that was for inmate usage.

"You okay, Baby Girl?" he asked her.

"I'm ready to get the hell outta here."

"Sit tight. Your mom's on her way down there. You know we got you. Shouldn't take too long, okay?"

She knew that she could always count on her grandfather to come through for her. After the call Kai took a seat at the far end of the bench that the older woman was on. She figured that she'd be released within an hour. As long as it stayed quiet with just the three of them in the holding cell, she assumed that it would be a smooth wait. That was until they were joined by two other women.

Stacy was at least 5'11 and her companion, Amaya was no more than 5'0 even. It was quiet for all of five minutes following their entrance. Even the young girl had stopped crying. For a minute Stacy and Amaya stood huddled together whispering secretly before Stacy moved over to the door and Amaya went over to the stall which housed a steel toilet and no door. It was clear that Stacey was playing lookout as Amaya did something that was completely wrong and risky.

Kai slid closer to the end of the bench to make it clear that she had no association with these women and their shenanigans. She didn't even want to give the impression that she was knowledgeable about what was going on. Within seconds Amaya resurfaced with a small, plastic baggie of marijuana, an already half smoked blunt, and a lighter. The older woman gave Amaya a look of astonishment.

Amaya laughed. "Shoooott…they missed it when they booked me and I dang sure ain't about to let it go to waste," she said as she boldly lit the blunt.

Kai tried to avoid a contact high as the girl puffed gaily on her weed. A few seconds passed before Stacey and Amaya switched places so that Stacy could take her turn with the joint. Kai was impressed by their gall, but dismayed by their stupidity. The scent of weed lingered in the cell and she knew it wouldn't be long before an officer came down to inquire about it.

Satisfied with the high that they were able to achieve, the women flushed the remaining weed down the toilet and took a seat on the bench near the younger girl as if nothing had happened. It didn't take long for Officer Kelley to surface. She opened the cell and took a stern look around at all of us. "Kensington!" She called out to another officer.

Officer Kensington approached and immediately locked eyes with Officer Kelly. After sharing a knowing look, Kelley motioned for the women in the cell to get up.

"Get out here and form a line!" Kelley ordered.

The women followed instructions and stood side by side in a line as the officers grilled them about the weed.

"Which one of you was smoking?" Officer Kensington asked as if someone was really going to voluntarily confess.

Once they saw that no one was going to take responsibility for the dirty deed, they began to ask each woman individually. When it was Kai's turn to be questioned she drew back upon what she knew of the code of the streets from growing up in Yonkers, New York. Where she was from you didn't snitch no matter what. Kai respected the code and despite whatever the officers thought of her, she wasn't about to defy it for them under any circumstances.

"Tell me who was in there smoking," Officer Kelley demanded rather than asked.

Kai was turned off by her attitude. Even if she was a snitch she wouldn't have told the woman a thing for the simple fact that her attitude was unbecoming. "I don't know anything about that," Kai said flatly. "And I don't smoke so…"

The look on Officer Kelley's face spoke volumes. She was completely livid by the way Kai had no regards for her authority. "Didn't you tell us that you have Lupus?"

"Mmmhmm," Kai said, holding up her medical ID bracelet as proof of her claim.

"And don't you need to see the nurse for your medication?"

Kai eyed the woman suspiciously, not liking her tone and where she assumed the officer was going with her line of questioning. "Yes, ma'am," she answered slowly.

"So, let me ask you this one more time." Officer Kelley paused for dramatic effect and gave Kai a hard, cold stare. "Who was in there smoking?"

Kai smiled curtly. *If this chick thinks she's going to rattle me she has another thing coming to her*, she thought. "I...don't...know..." Kai's answer was drawn out yet unchanging.

She dared this woman to compromise her own job and livelihood by denying her proper medical attention. Kai wasn't about to break under the pressures of the woman's illegal punishment. Her tolerance for pain was high and she'd already endured two experiences when she FLATLINED in her life. Surely she could make it through this heifer's torture. It was clear that the woman didn't know who she was dealing with and what Kai was capable of. Kai had every intention of penning a letter to the county commissioner to let him know exactly how his officers treated the inmates. Heads would surely roll starting with Officer Kelley's.

After getting no answer out of any of the four women, Officer Kensington decided to step things up a notch. "Fine! Let's strip search them."

Kai found this tactic laughable for several reasons. It was idiotic of them to believe that a strip search would yield any evidence as to who had been smoking considering that the evidence was long gone. Secondly, she was pretty certain that the strip search was more of a means to humiliate the women into tattling than anything else. With her they would still fail miserably because Kai had grown extremely comfortable with her body by this point. Sure she'd gained a few more pounds than she was used to having, but she knew that she was thick and luscious and if anything the women would feel embarrassed to have to witness how great her body looked in comparison to their own.

One by women the women were ushered into the restroom so that Officer Kelley could perform a rather routine strip search with some level of privacy. When it was Kai's turn, she was instructed to undress, bend over, and cough. She endured the invasion of her privacy without protest and after it was over she couldn't help but notice the grimace on Officer Kelley's face. Not only had she not found what she'd been looking for, she also knew exactly how well kept up Kai was.

Once more the inmates were lined up side by side. The officers were now at their wits ends and were feeling infuriated by the lack of cooperation they were getting by way of a confession.

"Since no one wants to step forward we have no choice but to charge all of you with possession of illegal contraband," Officer Kensington informed the group."

Kai had to chuckle at the irony. She'd had to come to jail of all places in order to catch a drug charge. Her patience was wearing thin. The hour that she thought she'd had to spend in jail had become three hours and she was starting to develop an uneasy feeling. Surely her mother should have been there by now. Once more she placed a call to Big Tony. She needed an update on when she could expect to get away from this place and these people.

"Baby Girl, we've run into a few problems," he told her once their connection had been established.

Kai's left eyebrow rose and she felt her head begin to pound. She knew that whatever was about to come out of his mouth wasn't good.

"Your bond was set at $500," Big Tony stated. "I sent that money and your mom took care of it, but when she did the county told her there's an outstanding warrant for you in Rockdale County."

"What?" She couldn't believe her ears. This was news to her.

"Yeah, for failure to appear six years ago."

Six years ago? Were they serious? Kai was fuming. She stared long and hard at the wall ahead of her as she bit her lip in an effort to not scream. She couldn't even remember getting a ticket six years ago and wondered why on earth Rockdale County would go so long without acting on it. The whole situation was becoming more and more of an outrage and all Kai could do was link the whole series of unfortunate events back to the fact that her husband had more or less screwed her over.

"Hello?" Big Tony's voice resounded in Kai's ear. "You still there?"

"Mmmhmm," Kai managed to get out. "I'm here. So….so what now? What do we do?"

"Well, we took care of the fine for Rockdale, which was $485."

Kai felt a little beckon of hope. "Okay, that's good then, right? So why am I still here?"

"Your mom is still down there where you are pitching a fit, but they're telling her that you have to be transported to the Rockdale County Jail in order to be released and processed out of their system. DeWayne and Terry are down there too. Everyone's trying to talk to the folk and see how to get you outta there without having to go to Rockdale."

Kai slapped the wall out of frustration. "This doesn't make any sense. I'll call you back." She didn't wait for her grandfather to respond. She racked her brain to remember her mother's cell number and then quickly placed the call.

"Hello?" Mz. C answered.

"Ma, what is going on?" Kai asked as if Big Tony hadn't just given her the run down.

A blend of voices could be heard in the background as her mother replied. "I'm working on getting you out Kai. It's…it's complicated."

"This is a bunch of mess. In just a matter of hours I've racked up three ridiculous charges."

"Three?" Mz. C asked in astonishment.

"Simple battery, possession of illegal contraband, and failure to appear," Kai rattled off the list.

"Possession?" Her mother questioned.

"I went from being a stand-up citizen to having a freakin' rap sheet. This isn't cool and I been in here too long and without my medication. I can't do—"

"I am trying to get you out, Kai!" Mz. C snapped. "I need you to hold on and be a little more patient with me. You have got to learn to control your temper. Not only has it landed you in jail, but aside from that you're never going to feel well carrying around all of that anger and hostility.

Pray about whatever is bothering you Kai and stop lashing out."

Kai remained silent. It took a lot for Mz. C. to step out of character and put you in your place, but once she did it you had no recourse but to sit and listen.

"Got folks worried about you," her mother went on. "I just got off the phone with Racquel. She called me checking on you because she said she hadn't heard from you all day. I went ahead and told her what happened…I didn't think you'd mine me telling her. But, she told me to tell you that she's staying by her phone until you're released and for you to call her."

The stress was raising Kai's body temperature. She could feel the sweat rolling down her back inside of her shirt and beading up along the curve of her forehead. She reached her hand up to wipe away the moisture and felt the heat radiating from her face. "Mom, get me the hell out of here!" She yelled. "I'm already getting a fever and I'm feeling a flare up. This sloppy, ignorant officer won't give me my medicine, or let me see the nurse because of some mess that didn't have anything to do with me."

"What mess?" Mz. C asked.

Kai ignored the question, too caught up in her own rage and dismay. "I've been in here too long. This is ridiculous! Wait 'til I see DeWayne. I'm gonna punch his lying ass dead in the mouth. Bet he won't tell another lie ever. This whole thing is his fault!"

"You need to calm down," Mz. C. said sternly. "Making yourself upset like that is only going to make you sicker. The truth of the matter is that no matter what DeWayne did or didn't do, you have to learn to control *your* temper. You can't control other people, you can only control yourself. DeWayne doesn't have Lupus. *You* do. So when you get all pissed off and mad you're only hurting yourself. You're only making yourself stressed out and sick. And now you got ya' self stressed out, sick, and in jail. Jermaine called. He said that jail is not the place for you Kai. You better get it together until we get this thing worked out."

Kai was quiet as she felt her strength weakening. She felt that she would slide to the floor and pass out at any moment. It didn't help that the ornery officers and trifling women she was currently sharing a cell with would be her only source of help.

"Have you even thought about what you're going to tell Jayson?" Her mother asked.

The mention of Jayson shook her. Kai knew that he had to have been blowing up her phone by that point. They spoke religiously at set times every day. She knew that he would especially be trying to get at her following the text she'd sent canceling their date. How she was going to explain everything to him had become the very least of her worries, but she knew that ultimately she was going to have to face him. In the meantime, her mother was right. She was getting worse by the minute and she needed to get her anger in check in order to focus on remaining strong enough to make it out of that jail.

"Let me get back to seeing what I can do," Mz. C. said following no response from her daughter.

"Please hurry," Kai said weakly before hanging up the phone.

But, her plea was of no consequence. Within the next half hour Kai was issued an orange jumpsuit with standard white county underwear and the inmate number 12041984. Stripped of her identity and being placed among a sea of women who'd done Lord knows what, Kai was ill at ease. It bothered her to be wearing undergarments that weren't her own. It bothered her to be suffering the way she was in a place where no one cared anything at all about her health. After changing into her new attire, Kai was handcuffed to yet another woman that had been booked and they were both ushered upstairs where they would share a cell. Kai noticed that the woman's scrub like uniform was a different color from hers. After inquiring, Kai learned that the woman was a fugitive from Alabama who had been on the run for over ten years for check fraud.

The moment they were inside of the matchbox cell and the gates clanked shut and the locks resounded, Kai felt herself become overwhelmed with emotion. Lying on the uncomfortable bed that was now hers she turned to face the wall and cried silently, yet uncontrollably. She was certain that her fever had spiked to over 102 because of the way her body felt. She was used to it, but she was also used to getting the medical attention that she needed when she needed it. The cell they'd stuffed her in was about the size of her master bathroom. It wasn't sufficient living space for two human beings and already Kai was beginning to feel claustrophobic.

Nothing was working out and her greatest fear was dying right there in that stale cell on the uncomfortable cot in the presence of a white collar criminal. All she wanted was to go home. Her tears sealed her eyes shut as she tried to block out the nearly unbearable pain that her anger had initiated. In the midst of her quiet breakdown Kai did the only thing that was left for her to do. Following her mother's advice, she prayed.

***

She must have fallen asleep because the sound of her name being called out rocked her. Her eyes popped open and the memory of the pain resurfaced as her body screamed out in agony. She glanced around trying to place her surroundings and quickly the entire turn of events dawned upon her. She remembered. She was in jail.

"Kai A'Marie Davis." The voice sounded faint and far away.

Kai remembered that she'd been praying. Was God finally answering her? Was this the moment that she needed to be completely still to listen to him impart the wisdom that she needed to get out of this horrid situation? The locks of on her cell door clicked and the clanking of the door opening caused Kai to turn around.

"Kai Davis," the voice repeated itself. "You're being released."

Indeed God had answered her prayers. Despite the pain in her body, Kai moved as swiftly as she could off of the bunk and eagerly followed the officer down a flight of stairs where she was then handed off to another officer in order to be escorted back to the area where she could retrieve her own clothing. She changed with a sense of urgency as tears stung her eyes. Once she was processed out, Kai was met by her weary-looking mother and an apologetic DeWayne. Kai had never been so happy to see either of them in her whole life, despite her disdain for

DeWayne. She was free and at that point that was all that mattered.

~ Chapter 14 ~

Once Kai was home safe and sound she showered and had her medication in her system. She knew that she had one more problem to attend to— Jayson. She'd gone through her phone to see the multitude of missed calls from him and the many text messages. She knew that he was feeling a mixture of worry and anger and could only pray that he'd be understanding once she gave him the rundown of all that had happened. She got herself situated in bed and took a deep breath before dialing his number.

"Hello?" He asked before the phone could ring all the way through one good time.

"Hey, it's me," Kai said as if he hadn't seen her name appear on his CALLER ID.

"What's up?" The tone of his voice made it clear that he was very guarded about whatever it was that was about to come out of her mouth.

"I just wanted to give you a call and let you know what happened today. You know it's not like me to cancel a date, or to just not answer your calls."

"I was worried about you. Are you okay? Were you sick?"

"I got into an altercation with DeWayne when he came over to get Landon," she began explaining. "Like, an actual physical altercation. And then my neighbors called the police and I ended up getting arrested for assault against De. Then I get to the jail and this hateful officer kept giving me crap for every single thing, like she just had some kinda vendetta against me from the moment I walked in the door. Some chicks were in there smoking a blunt or whatever and when I wouldn't tell her who was doing it the officer threatened not to get me the medical care I needed. I was already having trouble breathing and I was so pissed off that I had pushed myself over the edge and was flaring up. But this chick just flat out refused to let me see the nurse and I didn't get my medication the whole time I was in there.

"Oh, and because no one would tell who was smoking they charged all five of us that were in the holding cell with possession. What kinda mess is that? All that time I was waiting for my mom to get me out and my grandfather had made sure the money was available for my bond and what not. So I called him to see what was taking so long with my release and he tells me that I had a warrant out in Rockdale County. So there was some mess with that but before my mom and De could get it all straightened out they'd already placed me in the general population in a damn orange suit and everything. I was flaring, fever off the meters, and all kinds of pissed. But, somehow they worked it out and before long I was released."

Kai finally took a breath following her long recap of the day's activities. She realized that Jayson hadn't uttered a word. Concerned about what he was feeling and thinking, Kai called out to him sweetly. "Jayson?"

"Yeah, I'm here," he replied. "I'm glad to know that you're okay. You should get some rest. We'll talk tomorrow."

"Oh, okay." Kai felt deflated.

"I love you."

"I love you too."

She placed the phone down and snuggled down into her covers. She knew that Jayson was beyond angry and she couldn't blame him. She wasn't sure what she could do to fix it and she wondered if perhaps their relationship was now too impaired to be repaired. It was clear that they each had trust issues going in. He was often concerned about her still being legally married and she was secretly worried about the situation he had with his baby's mother as well as her misgivings about being able to trust a man after everything she'd been through. Now her recent actions had done nothing but heighten his insecurities. Jayson was a good guy and she didn't want to lose him, but she had no clue as to how to erase the hurt that she was sure he was now feeling.

***

The next day Kai busied herself with attending to some other issues that she'd been made privy to following her release. Apparently she had two unpaid traffic tickets in Rockdale County which resulted in her license being suspended, both of which were news to her. She spent $200 total clearing up the fines in order to reinstate her license, but was informed that she would still have to appear in court. The thought did not appeal to her at all.

After dealing with her legal issues Kai was reminded of how much she disliked DeWayne at that time. She still contended that everything she'd endured in the past 24 hours was completely his fault. As much as she wanted to ride over to his apartment and give him the business once again, she remembered what her mother had told her. She needed to learn to control her temper despite how

DeWayne infuriated her. Since he still had Landon, Kai decided that the best way to take her mind off of the recent events and her frustration with DeWayne was to work on salvaging her relationship with Jayson.

She shot him a text asking if he wanted her to come over. Once he confirmed, she packed her bags for her typical overnight stay and made the trek out to his home in Buford, Georgia. His reception wasn't as inviting as usual as he gave her a halfhearted hug and no kiss, but Kai didn't complain. She understood his position. They sat on the sofa and Jayson muted his large screen plasma television so that they could have the conversation that they both dreaded.

"How you feeling?" He asked cautiously.

"Much better than I did yesterday," she answered. "How are you feeling?"

"Pissed," he said honestly. "You told me everything that happened yesterday and while it was all very unfortunate for you and messed up, I'm still unclear on something."

"Uh-huh?"

"What were you and DeWayne fighting about?"

Kai wasn't sure how to answer the question. She didn't want to say anything that was going to be disparaging and potentially fatal to their relationship, but she also didn't want to lie to him. "We weren't fighting," she said. "It was just me constantly swinging on him. The most he did was try to hold my hands still. But, I think I just got so fed up in general that it was just a combination of everything he's ever done or said that just made me… I don't know…snap. I just lost it and wanted to take him out for all the heartache he's caused me." It wasn't a lie, but it wasn't the complete truth either. She gave him just enough to understand what had happened with crushing him with the exact logistics.

"So this lashing out at him…if you're over it and you're over him why the need to go all Rambo on him?"

Kai shrugged. "I mean…I'm human. What can I say? Anything can trigger a person's emotions and cause them to snap. And that's what happened to me. It doesn't mean that I'm not over it. It just means that I had some pent up hostility and aggression which I promptly took out on the person that instilled it in me."

Jayson looked at her as if searching her eyes for the truth. "So you're not still in love with him Kai?"

"No." She decided to give the simplest most direct answer without trying to oversell it.

He leaned back and sighed deeply. "That's some real messed up ish Kai."

She nodded. "I know. I know. And I know I need to work on my temper. I promise you that nothing like this will ever happen again. I'm so sorry."

Jayson hesitated for a moment and then pulled her close, kissing her gently on the forehead. To Kai's understanding, the air was clear and the crisis had been averted. All was well until she used his bathroom to prepare for bed. She changed into her night clothes and brushed her teeth, but on the way out of the bathroom something on the floor caught her eye. She picked it up and stared hard at the small square packaging that she knew all too well. She exited the bathroom and stood at the foot of his bed holding up what she'd found.

"Where'd this come from?" She asked, her voice filled with attitude.

Jayson looked at the condom she was holding and shrugged his shoulders. "I don't know. Where you find it at?"

"In your bathroom on the counter. How did it get there?"

"I don't know, Kai," he said once more in a testy manner. "Anybody that visited could have dropped it for all I know." He caught her facial expression and frowned. "What? You accusing me of stuff now? You should know me better than that man."

Kai was fuming, but in light of the fact that they'd just made up she didn't want to create a big scene. She discarded the condom and they silently went to bed without the intimacy they had become accustomed to sharing.

During the ride home the next morning, Kai's emotions ran rampant. She wasn't a dumb girl. Common sense told her what her heart didn't want to accept. *Did my boyfriend really cheat on me*, she asked herself. *Is this the thanks I get for getting all riled up over the love-life of my soon to be ex-husband?* The way she figured it either he'd done the deed and actually slept with another woman, or he'd intended to. Either way, she felt a violation of their relationship had occurred and the fact that he'd lied in her face verses owning up to his mistake crushed her. She'd just popped off at DeWayne for lying about a woman and now here Jayson was doing the exact same thing. Kai's faith in love plummeted at that moment. Perhaps it was impossible for a man to be everything she needed. Perhaps romantic love simply didn't exist for her.

***

"Nikkiiiii!" Kai whined.

"What's up boo?"

Kai tilted her head to the side as she signed the two copies of her latest release to be mailed out to two customers who had purchased them online. "I am completely and utterly at a loss right now."

"Why, boo?" Nikki Love's chipper tone filled Kai's ear.

"Girl, once I tell you all of the mess and drama I've been through over the last few days you're not even going to believe me."

Nikki giggled. "What happened girl? Don't tell me you had to turn up on somebody."

Kai paused and nearly dropped her phone. It was amazing how well her best friend knew her. "Girl, did I! De made me have to show out on his behind honey. I'm talking about, I was whacking the crap out of him out there in the front yard."

"Are you serious? Why?! What happened? What he say to set you off like that?"

"Being his ole' trifling self. Lying about his shenanigans."

"What he lie about though?"

Kai wasn't sure if she wanted to give Nikki full disclosure, but then she realized this was her best friend, her baby's mama, that she was talking to. They had a nonjudgmental relationship. If anything, Nikki would be on Kai's side whether she was wrong or right. "I saw a text in his phone from some chick and he lied to me talking about he's not dating nobody or sleeping with nobody. Pretty much argued me down saying he didn't even know the chick. Which, clearly that was a big lie because the girl's name and number were programed in his phone."

"Wow! Nobody ain't never told him that he ain't gotta lie to kick it?"

Kai laughed at Nikki's remark. "Somebody shoulda told him at least not to lie to me. At least! Girl, the moment he lied to me for like the third time I just starting tagging him. There was like no end in sight. I was justa swinging."

"He didn't hit you back did he?" The concern in her voice was apparent.

"Naw," Kai answered. "He might be a liar, a cheat from time to time, and an insensitive bastard, but he's not a stupid brother. He knew better than to place one blow in my direction or I'd still be in jail for killing him, honey."

"Wait, hold up! You went to jail?"

"Oh yeah, I was gon' tell you that part." Kai shook her head at the memory. Each time she told the story she still couldn't believe that she'd personally endured it. "Girl, the neighbors called the police and they arrested me."

"He pressed charges against you? Oh see, he's gon' make me come over there and have to mess him up." Nikki was feisty and at the thought of DeWayne getting out of line she was ready to go to war.

"No, he told them he didn't want to press charges but the officer said they had to take me anyway because of the witness testimonies and public disturbance. It was a mess. I was in there dealing with foolishness…flaring…just horrible." Kai went on to relive the entire experience with her bestie and by the time she got to the end she herself was flabbergasted.

"I'm so sorry you had to go through all of that," Nikki stated. "That really sucks."

"Oh, but it gets worse," Kai advised as she placed the books into their respective packages. "How about the next day I go over to Jayson's to hash it out with him right and I found a condom in his bathroom."

"What the hell? Like, a used one?"

Kai's nosed turned up. "Ewww, no girl. It was still in the wrapper. But the thing was, why you got condoms out when I wasn't even there? Who'd you have up in your house that you were boning, or planning to bone while I was going through some things? That's all kinds of shady."

"These men! They on some other type stuff today. I was rooting for Jayson too, but that's some trifling mess."

"Yeah, so I am in desperate need of an escape from De, from Jayson, from work. Everything. I feel like I might snap or something."

"Whoa! We don't want you to do that. The last time you did that your butt ended up in jail." Nikki laughed at her own joke.

Kai could chuckle about it now, but there had been nothing funny about the situation while she was actually living it.

"So what you wanna do?" Nikki asked. "You wanna go away for the weekend and take a breather? Just to get away from everything? I'm free, we can do it girl."

"But where?" Kai asked, really giving her friend's suggestion some serious thought.

"It's gotta be somewhere that's not too far so we can ride out and ride back, you know?"

"Hmmm."

"Think about it and I'll be over after work."

"Cool."

True to her word, Nikki arrived at the house after work and a game plan was put in action. They settled upon Chattanooga, Tennessee because of its proximity and the myriads of things to do in the city. Without hesitation, the duo packed up the kids and headed out of town with the intent to do nothing but relax and enjoy their sporadic mini-vacation.

Kai was depressed. She tried not to voice it, but even if she didn't say a word it was obvious in her facial expression, tone, and body language. It felt as if everything was spiraling out of control. Just when she felt that she was getting some kind of a handle on her health issues, her personal life began to fall apart at the seams. She was used to DeWayne causing her to feel so broken and hurt over the years, but she'd expected more from Jayson. It had taken a while for her to let her guard down and decide to move on with someone new. Given his trust issues and how he'd appeared to be so sincere about wanting them to have a good, healthy relationship, she would have never guessed in a million years that she'd be reliving the battle of infidelity and insensitivity via Jayson.

Thoughts of him made Kai pull out her cell phone. She hadn't told anyone at all about her spur of the moment getaway. Quickly, she sent Jayson a text letting him know where she was going and when she'd be back. Although she was pissed with him and was certain that their relationship had reached the point of no return, she still felt obligated to check in. She wanted it to be clear to him that she was with the boys and Nikki because she didn't want him thinking that she'd ever stoop to his level of sneaking around and creeping. It simply wasn't her style. She considered sending DeWayne an update and then decided against it. If he called looking for her he'd just have to be on pins and needles until she got back. They needed a little space and distance between the two of them anyway.

The trip to Tennessee was worth every hour of the drive. Not only did it afford Kai a change of scenery, but it also took her mind off of her man problems and gave the children a fun adventure to enjoy. Kai especially enjoyed the Captain's boat ride that they took allowing them to enjoy dinner, a bottle of Moet for herself and Nikki, as well as the terrific waterside view. It was relaxing and fun at the same time. The peacefulness engulfed her and Kai couldn't help but to exhale, releasing all of her frustrations and anxiety into the calmness of the crisp, evening air.

Following dinner they decided to do something that the children would truly enjoy. With Landon being a big Ninja Turtles buff, Nikki figured it would be cool to see the movie at the IMAX Theatre close to their hotel. The thought of seeing the Ninja Turtles in 3D excited the children. The clan dressed up in their Ninja Turtle gear, which was basically character t-shirts and pajama bottoms, and hit the theater. It felt good to be in a position to whisk the kids away for the weekend with no qualms, regrets, or hindrances. In that aspect, Kai felt blessed that her life was in a place that afforded her the opportunity to do that. Seeing the smiles on the boys' faces and hearing the laughter that spread between the four of them did wonders to lift Kai's mood. That was until her phone rang.

Kai took the call outside of the theater seeing that it was her general practitioner's office calling. She was surprised to be receiving a call at that time of day on the weekend and figured that whatever it was, it was an urgent matter. "Hello?" She answered the phone with a shaky voice.

"Kai? It's Dr. Anderson. You have a minute."

"Considering you're calling at an odd time indicating something's not right…sure!"

"We got the biopsy report back from the legions under your arm…I really need you to come back into the office in the morning. You tested positive for Staph Infection. We needa get you on antibiotics immediately."

Kai's heart plummeted. If it wasn't one thing it was another. She was sick of it all. Not only were the men in her life failing her time and time again, but her body was constantly failing her as well. She'd attempted to get away from everything, to relax for a moment, only to have something else dumped in her lap and be forced to return back to her reality prematurely in order to deal with it all.

After assuring the doctor that she'd be there the following morning, she linked back up with Nikki and the boys and regretted having to tell them that their impromptu trip was being cut short. She fought back the tears of defeat and the drive home was bittersweet. Lost in her thoughts as she drove along the highway, Kai felt Nikki nudge her.

"Your phone's ringing," Nikki advised.

Kai was so caught up in the turmoil that mentally plagued her that she hadn't even heard the phone. Quickly she placed her ear buds in and pressed TALK on her cell. "Hello?"

"Hey baby girl. What's good?" It was Sissy. Kai could hear the smile in her sister-in-law's voice.

"Hey girl. Nothing much. I'm in the car driving back home."

"Coming from where?"

"Nikki and I took the kids for a little getaway but we're coming back a little earlier than expected...something came up."

"Oh…well at least you got to go have fun for a bit."

Kai sighed. "Yeah, it was fun. What's up with you?" She wondered if maybe DeWayne had called Sissy inquiring about her whereabouts, although she hadn't discovered any missed calls from him.

"Nothing, boo. I heard about the drama and stuff with De and I wanted to reach out to you. I sensed that you need a little girl time so we need to schedule that in, Ms. Busy Author."

Kai smiled. "Yes, we do." It warmed Kai's heart to know that despite whatever happened between her and DeWayne she still had a sister in Sissy. "Let's work on that."

"Okay, hun. Give me a call back after you get home and settled."

"I will."

"Kiss the boys for me."

Kai smiled again. "Okay, boo. Love you."

"I love you too."

The rest of the ride filled Kai with trepidation. She couldn't fathom what else in her life could possibly go wrong. There had to be a turning point around the corner where things would start to balance themselves out. She wanted to believe the saying that ‘trouble don’t last always’, but it was starting to feel as if that was the only thing she ever had to look forward to—hardships and trouble. She was depressed. There was no way around it and none of the things happening in her life were helping matters. She needed a way to pull herself out of the funk, but wasn’t even sure where to begin.

~ CHAPTER 15 ~

A month later Kai appeared in court to deal with the assault charge that the county had placed against her. In what he defined as moral support, DeWayne sat in the back of the court room silently. She hadn't asked him to come, but she also hadn't demanded that he not show up. The sight of him grated her nerves and she was once again reminded that he was the very reason that she was even there in the first place.

The judge presiding over her case appeared to be uptight and insensitive. Kai could tell instantly from the way he held his lips in a thin line of indifference that he wasn't about to say anything that would be pleasing to her ears. She laced her fingers together and tried to remember what her mother said about keeping her temper in check. It wasn't an easy feat, but the last thing she wanted to do was show her behind in the courtroom and be thrown back in jail. She'd had about as much of jail life as she could take and didn't desire to ever relive the experience.

"Mrs. Davis," Judge Abraham called her name. "You've been changed with one count of aggravated assaulted and one count of possession of illegal contraband. The possession charge has been dismissed, but in the matter of the assault charge you are sentenced to twelve months probation."

"Twelve months," Kai mumbled in disbelief. A whole year of checking in with a probation officer simply because her husband had pushed her over the edge.

Judge Abraham gave her stern look before continuing on. "In addition to which, you're subjected to the fine of $1000."

Kai felt her jaw muscles tighten as she clenched her mouth shut tightly to refrain from cursing out loud. She was being punished repeatedly it appeared. Was there no mercy? Her body temperature quickly escalated and she prayed that the man would stop talking so that she could seek refuge outside in the cool air. Red flashed before her eyes, just as it had the day that she'd unleashed her frustrations upon DeWayne. Gripping the table with both hands, Kai tried her best to remain composed when all she really wanted to do was turn around and kick his butt again. She wondered if he was getting any kind of perverse pleasure out of witnessing her defeats and humiliation over and over again. It was sickening to her and Kai longed to be far away from the court room and the man that was making her life a living hell.

"I'm also ordering you to attend anger management. Failure to complete the course by the completion of your probation sentence will result in the subsequent jail time of twelve months. That's my ruling and it is so ordered." He banged his gavel to signify that the matter was over and done with.

Kai's feet had never moved so quickly as she bolted from her position at the table and past the mainly empty seats within the courtroom. Her eyes locked with DeWayne's for a moment and she could see his lips moving, but she couldn't process a word that he was saying. All she could make out was the fire blazing around him from the heated thoughts that were running through her mind. She knew it was in her best interest to get away from him before she found herself getting hit with yet another charge.

She tore through the doors of the courtroom and down the hall, leaving him to watch her retreating figure. As she made her way toward the exit her eyes fell upon the family law documents resting on a stand. Quickly she grabbed a divorce packet with the intent to get it completed immediately. They'd been dragging their feet on completing the process, but this was the last and final straw. She'd lost respect and now she'd lost her good name by way of receiving a criminal record because of him. Enough was enough. Time and time again, either he'd completed the papers or she hadn't signed or vice versa. This time it was going to be done whether she had to force his hand to sign the paper or hold him at gunpoint to get it done.

Kai was ready to start over. This life she was living now wasn't fit for her. The hatred and contempt that she was filled with wasn't doing her any good. Here she was not even thirty yet and going through all of this drama and heartache. At least, she was young enough to remarry and start a new life. The thing was finding someone worthy of rebuilding with. She wanted that someone to be Jayson, but with the way that things were going she wasn't even sure about that. Something had to give. Grandma Lucy had always told her to never allow anyone to make her unhappy because years down the line she would wish that she'd had the good sense to walk away. Kai appreciated the fact that Grandma Lucy always gave it to her straight. They were so much alike that it stunned even Kai. They shared that bluntness and sassiness that others came to expect from them.

As she waltzed through the doors of the courthouse she pulled out her cell phone and called Sissy to let her know how she was putting the nails in her brother's coffin.

"Hey girl!" Sissy answered the phone sounding as if she was beaming from ear to ear.

"Honey, I am 38 hot right about now," Kai huffed as she made her way down the stairs and in the direction of the parking deck.

"Where are you? Sounds like you're running or something."

"I am girl. Running away from that courtroom before I kill your brother."

"What?! What happened?"

"You know I had my hearing today, right? So how about I got hit with a $1000 fine, twelve months of probation, and then the judge ordered me to take anger management. I am beyond livid."

Sissy sucked in her breath. "Whew....that is a bit much. I'm sorry baby girl. But you've got to believe that your time is coming."

"Time for what?" Kai hesitated as she waited for a response.

"I just...I don't think that you two are really over. DeWayne is readjusting to being back home. The fact that he didn't relist and chose to come back to the states and be near his family is a big indication that his priorities have shifted. You've got to see that."

Was she serious? Kai bit her lip and had to remember that she loved Sissy and that deep down what she was saying was coming from a loving place. But, no matter how loving and intuitive she was attempting to be, Kai wasn't going for it. "That's some bull!" She screamed through the phone as she continued walking and approached her vehicle. "We are so done I'm already looking forward to meeting and marrying my next husband. Ain't nobody trying to keep putting up with this nonsense. Too much has happened to just sweep it under the rug and then skip off into the sunset. No! We're through. I'm over this mess."

Sissy remained silent. She knew that Kai was in her feelings and there was nothing that she could say to her in that moment to calm her down and get the girl to see her point-of-view. Sissy could admit that DeWayne and Kai's history had a lot of sordid moments, but she firmly believed that in their case you had to look through the blemishes in order to see the beauty of what it was that they shared.

Kai took a deep breath. She realized that she'd just blown up at one of the people she truly trusted and respected. Although she was pissed with DeWayne she knew that she didn't have to let it affect how she communicated with others, even though she was convicted in what she'd been saying. "My bad, girl. I'm just so frustrated right now that I can't even believe it's come to this." She cranked up the Explorer and put it in reverse to back out of her parking spot. "I can't even talk about this anymore. What's going on with you?"

"Oh there's nothing to report here. Believe me. My divorce is final and I'm just living life. Glad to be finally happy."

"When are you going to start dating again?"

Sissy laughed as if the notion was whimsical. "Are you kidding me? I'm done with that. I'm not trying to deal with anyone else and their craziness. Some people were designed to be in relationships while some of us were meant to do the single thing."

"I don't believe that," Kai said as she paid for her parking ticket. "I don't believe that at all."

"Believe what you want. I'm concentrating on me honey."

Kai pulled into traffic and began her commute towards home. "I hear that. Nothing's wrong with that. I just figured since you keep trying to play cupid with me that you should work some of that magic in your own life. But, you know…I'm glad you're happy. I'm glad you got yourself out of an unhappy situation and was bold and brave enough to go ahead and get that divorce. I can't even do that part because I don't have a participant who's willing to just get the damn process over with."

"That's because you and my brother were meant to be together." Sissy couldn't help but reiterate her belief. Her spirit was telling her that something kismet was going on between the two and she only wanted Kai to open up her heart to the possibility of her being correct. "I couldn't have picked a better woman for that boy if I'd handpicked her myself. You gotta know it's true girl."

Kai rolled her eyes as she continued along her route. "Uh-huh. You know that and I may know that, but it doesn't mean a hill of beans if he doesn't realize it, which he doesn't. So…I'll tell you what honey. You get a man and I'll work on my marriage. That's the offer I'm putting on the table." Kai laughed at her own humor knowing full well how Sissy felt about placing herself in another relationship.

Sissy joined in on the laughter. "Girl, please. Love ain't for everybody and by everybody I mean me."

Kai shook her head as she turned into the parking lot of an eatery. "You're hell girl. I'm going to lunch. I'll talk to you later."

"Alright, boo."

Following the call Kai thought about Sissy's last words—love ain't for everybody. She was starting to think the same was true for her given all of the mess that she'd been dealing with between DeWayne and now Jayson. But, she'd written a whole poetry anthology about the universal emotion of love in all of its formats so how could she readily dismiss the notion of romantic love? Perhaps true love really did exist, but she was being forced to wade through all the negative aspects of a relationship in order to appreciate the beauty of a real, everlasting bond whenever God was ready to place it before her. Kai shrugged. Anything was possible, but she was having difficulty seeing the light at the end of the dark tunnel she'd been traveling through for so long.

~ CHAPTER 16 ~

Time drifted on and Kai coasted right along with it. DeWayne still wouldn't sign the papers, always deflecting by saying something needed to be adjusted, or he was going to have an attorney look over them. Whether he signed or not, in Kai's mind there was no turning back. She'd already inquired via free counsel at the Family Law Help Center at the DeKalb County Jail how the process would be to file for a contested divorce. Before the year was over DeWayne's ass was going to be history.

Jayson was still around despite the feelings of betrayal that lingered within Kai's spirit. He would never admit it and quite frankly she didn't feel the need to have to inquire again, but Kai was certain that he'd been up to something foul the day she'd found the condom in his bathroom. For her, a red flag was raised where their relationship was concerned and she treaded very lightly as she waded through to see just how their story would end up.

Khy had been accepted to the Youth Challenges Academy after Kai firmly convincing her mother that perhaps it was the best thing for her son. Everyone was proud of him for making such a sound decision that would greatly aid in securing a lucrative future. It wasn't easy knowing that he'd be a two hour drive away, but as Bill had told Kai one evening by phone, they had to allow him to become his own man.

With everyone's lives so busy and complex, Mz. C. had demanded that they all take a family trip together. No one could deny the queen bee her request, so Kai's family packed it in and made a beeline for Panama City, Florida. It was just Mz. C, her offspring, and their significant others. Morris had Sarah, Khy had Jenay, I had Nikki Love since Jayson was unable to make it, and then of course there was Terri. All of Mz. C's grandchildren had been left at home with other adults to give the siblings and their mother an opportunity to bond and have some adult fun.

Kai enjoyed being away. Unlike the trip she'd taken previously with Nikki Love, she hadn't had any mishaps causing her to have to return home. She was in a place of acceptance where her relationship with DeWayne was concerned so she wasn't even allowing depression over the situation to ruin her mood. She'd even thrown caution to the wind by ignoring the guidelines of her probation by leaving the state. She didn't care. For too long she'd allowed herself to be consumed by anguish over things that were related to DeWayne and all of the crap he'd pulled. No longer was she allowing herself to be emotionally held hostage by the hurt he'd inflicted.

As she relaxed against the plushness of her hotel room bed following a long and exhausting, yet fun trip to the beach, Kai heard the chiming of her cell phone. She said a quick prayer in hopes that no one was calling her with bad news or an urgent emergency. She saw that it was Sissy calling and immediately assumed that the woman was only checking in. "Hey, Sissy!" She greeted her upon accepting the call.

"Hey, girl! I have been seeing your pictures on Facebook. I know you're having a good time."

"Girl, am I?! But you know me. I've sold about three copies of Flatlined since I've been out here."

"You took books with you?" Sissy was amazed. "Nobody ever taught you how to go on vacation?"

"Vacation or not, I'm a BOSS first and foremost."

"I heard that. Look, I know you're busy, so I'm not gon' keep you long. But girl, guess what?"

Kai was stumped as to what it was that Sissy could possibly be bursting at the seams about. "What? Tell me. I'm all ears."

"So, I went to grab some lunch one day right. I was minding my own business and you won't believe the dude that I met. I'm talking about, this is the most wonderful, most perfect man I have *ever* known!"

Kai sat straight up. Surely she'd heard incorrectly. "Say what? You met who now?"

"Yes girl! I met a man!" Sissy laughed, tickled by the turn of events in her life. "His name is Chico and he is finer than wine honey."

"Chico," Kai repeated the name with a smile upon her lips. "Oooh, okay. He sounds Puerto Rican."

"No, he's mixed and honey did you hear me when I said this man is fine? Tall, handsome, beautiful smile, manly hands…ooh, and no kids!"

"Okay now. Go 'head Chico," Kai joked.

Sissy laughed. "Chico is his old childhood nickname. His given name is Eric Giovanni."

"Oohhhh," Kai squealed feeding off of Sissy's excitement. "Eric Giovanni! I love it! Sounds sexy and exotic."

"Oh yes, he is so very, very sexy. I can't get enough of just looking at him."

Kai was in awe. This woman whom she'd once viewed as a cold-hearted cupid was now gushing over some man that she never thought she'd come across. Her complete change of heart where relationships were concerned had Kai wondering just who this man was that had given Sissy her new perspective. "Tell me how this all happened honey. You know I need full disclosure."

"Okay, so he was working on a traffic light by the building I was heading toward right. He was sitting in the truck doing something and then when he saw me he blew his horn. You know me, I don't respond well to that kind of thing and I just rolled my eyes and had half the mind to dismiss him as I would anyone else at any other time." Sissy hesitated as if she was envisioning that moment just as it had occurred. "And then something told me to stop. I don't know what it was, but my spirit just took the life out of my feet and I stood there like...what now? His coworker got his attention and told him that I'd stopped because originally it had looked like I was going to ignore him, which you know...initially I was. Girl, Chico jumped out of that truck and ran over to me and I immediately couldn't shake the fact that he was like some sexy god or something. I'm telling you that he had me all caught up from the moment I saw him get out of that truck.

"We talked for about 30 minutes and then exchanged numbers. I'm not the type to get all caught up in these things, you know. Honestly, I didn't know what his intentions were, or how things would play out, but we started talking on the phone, Skyping, texting...and everything. Now I cannot get enough of this man!"

Kai was completely overjoyed. Not only was Sissy her sister-in-law, but she was also her friend and Kai cared a great deal about her happiness. She was thrilled to know that Sissy was apparently very much enthralled by her newfound love interest. Listening to the way she spoke about Chico made Kai blush. It was that pure, untainted sensation of bliss that made Kai's skin tingle with the hope of one day gushing about her own fairytale love story. Sissy deserved a happy ending and whoever this Chico guy was, it was clear that he'd made an impact on Sissy that was monumental.

"I'm so happy for you," Kai told her. "I really am. You deserve to be happy."

"Thanks, sis, but let me get to the real reason why I called."

Kai's eyebrow went up. She'd been under the impression that Sissy's intent was to share her love story. Now she wondered what other bomb the woman was about to drop on her.

"So, remember that day when you told me that if I got a guy you'd work on your marriage?" Sissy asked.

Kai shook her head. She remembered the conversation well and she knew exactly where her friend was going. "Uh, let me stop you now. As happy as I am for you Sissy, it doesn't change the fact that your brother and I are done. I have no intentions of ever speaking to him outside of convos pertaining to Landon. But, as for us working on our marriage, it's a no-go boo. Yes, we're still married, but what we're dealing with is nothing like a marriage. I don't even know what to call it, but there's no gluing the pieces back together. There's no happily ever after coming out of this mess."

"That's just it Kai. I was so wrong about love not being for me. And well…maybe as wrong as I was about myself…maybe I was wrong about y'all too. I want you to experience this level of happiness, no matter if it's with De or some other man. I love you and I want you to be happy period."

Kai was surprised. "Well…my, my, my. Haven't we done a complete about face?"

Sissy chuckled. "I just wanted to tell you that boo. You go on and enjoy the rest of your trip."

"Thank you boo. And don't you smother that man over there."

"Oh trust me, he loves it."

Kai giggled and disconnected the call. A shift had occurred. Sissy was their biggest supporter and even she now realized that the era of DeWayne and Kai was long gone. With her acceptance maybe now fate was turning around and DeWayne would soon stop being a pain and just get on with the process. Kai smiled at the thought of Sissy and her new boo. After divorcing and moving on she'd finally found someone who made her smile. Kai could only hope for the same.

PART 3:

RESUSCITATED

~ CHAPTER 17 ~

Kai's nails tapped against the remote that lay by her side. It was late night and she'd just gotten off of the phone with Jayson. Her thoughts were all over the place with regards to what she needed to do workwise the next day. With so many projects in full effect it was becoming more and more of a chore keeping up with her own busy schedule. The beep of her text message alert pulled Kai out of her current thoughts evoking her to consider new ones. Who in the world was messaging her at that time of the night? Looking down at the screen she noticed that the text was from DeWayne.

"What does he want?" She asked out loud as she reached for the phone and clicked on the message.

DeWayne: *Hey Fat Girl. What you doing?*

Without thinking about it, Kai smiled. She couldn't help it. He'd been calling her Fat Girl for years and it seemed like eons since she'd last heard him say it.

Kai: *Watching TV and getting my thoughts together. What has you texting me at this time of the night?*

She stared at the phone waiting for his reply, wondering what he would say and if he was on some mess at this ungodly hour. Her test tightened and she was unsure as to why. Lately he'd been hitting her up randomly more and more simply saying hi, or letting her know that he was checking on her. It was never anything out of the way considering that he knew she was dating Jayson. It was never anything disrespectful considering that he was still in the doghouse for all the hardships he'd put her through in just the past year alone.

DeWayne: *Just sitting here thinking and my thoughts led to you.*

Kai: *What exactly?*

DeWayne: *Just thinking about if you were okay over there.*

Kai thought about his recent considerateness and somehow his one statement forced a sea of emotions and thoughts to come crashing to the forefront. Her fingers were moving so quickly as she typed the long texts that she was almost moving faster than her thoughts.

Kai: *I'm okay...but I'm just now wondering how the hell we got to the place where we are. Sometimes I'm so consumed with anger that it's unbelievable and I've been working hard on overcoming that. I mean, thanks to you've I've had to go through anger management. But during those classes I've learned a lot about myself and my triggers and you are my trigger De. It doesn't matter how much I try to ignore it, deny it, or work past it, you are my trigger. Thoughts of you trigger all kinds of emotions and stuff that I can't even comprehend and at the end of the day it all comes out as anger. I am angry with you De. I am so freakin' angry with you just generally speaking and I don't want to be, but when I see you sometimes...most times...I see red and I just want to kill you.*

She reread her last line and realized that it was a little harsh. She could imagine his face upon reading it— him biting his jaw trying to figure out how to respond, blinking profusely as he tried to recover from the verbal slap she'd given him. Once more her fingers assaulted the keypad of her cell.

Kai: *Not that I plan to kill you because I refuse to go back to jail for anyone after all the mess I went through honey.*

DeWayne: *I never intended for that to happen. You know I told them that I didn't wanna press charges.*

Kai: *I know that but the fact of the matter was that you pushed me to the point where I completely snapped...I shouldn't have even given a damn about you and what or who you're messing with but it goes back to all that business about you being my trigger. With you it can be the slightest thing that can make me fall all the way in love or just all the way in hate. And it did NOT help matters that you felt the need to lie to me. I mean, above everything else that had gone on you should never feel the need to lie to me EVER. I can't respect that.*

DeWayne: *I never meant to lose your respect. Rather than tell you the truth...rather than hurt you, I felt it was the better way to go. I mean, I didn't feel comfortable telling my wife that I have a girlfriend or I'm dating someone.*

Kai: *Oh so she's your girlfriend?????*

DeWayne: *No, that's not what I meant...I'm just saying telling you about some woman isn't comfortable for me. But you're right...lying wasn't cool...lying isn't cool.*

Before Kai knew it 2:00 A.M. snuck up on her and she was just ending a long text conversation with the man that she thought she'd never be able to have another civilized discussion with for the rest of her life. Her face was wet as she turned over to finally call it a night. During their texting she'd divulged a lot of feelings and emotions that she'd never been able to constructively voice to him since they'd fallen into the slump which ultimately led to the demise of their marriage. She'd learned in anger management that it was best to express your emotions and tell others how their actions made you feel rather than simply blowing up all the time. Tonight she'd done just that and all it had taken was writing out her emotions and thoughts verses being vocal. Through her tears Kai chuckled at the irony. Through writing the author was able to effectively communicate with her soon to be ex-husband. Feeling some odd sense of closure and peace, Kai drifted off to sleep.

The next morning she awoke to two text messages. The first was from Jayson sending his usual good morning text.

Jayson: *Good morning, sleeping beauty. I called you this morning but got no answer. I guess you're still getting that un-needed beauty rest. Meet me today for lunch? I love you, baby. Have a great day.*

Kai sat up in bed and smiled. She loved the way that Jayson made her feel with the compliments that he frequently showered her with. She wasn't usually fazed by men professing their love for her and their appreciation of her beauty. But, when Jayson said it she felt that it was heartfelt which made her giggle with giddiness in return. With her smile still plastered to her face she quickly shot him back an I-Love-You text and a confirmation for lunch at a restaurant down the street from his job which they'd frequented during the duration of their relationship. Following that, she clicked to see who the next message was from.

As she rose from the bed with her eyes glued to the phone, Kai almost stumbled over her own feet. The second message was from DeWayne. The smile she'd been donning fell instantly and she felt her heart rate quicken. It was just like DeWayne to disrupt the peace between them by coming back with some bull. Kai could only imagine what tricks he had up his sleeve this time.

Dewayne: *Hey beautiful. Have a great day.*

That was it. Kai tried to force the screen to scroll up to see if there was more to his message. But that was truly it. Where's he going with this, she wondered. Why's he being so thoughtful now? She was waiting for the other shoe to drop because Kai knew DeWayne and his pattern all too well. As soon as everything seemed to be all good and he had her with her guards down, he'd turn around and force her right back to the end of the spectrum to the point of hating him with a passion. After thinking it over for a second she decided to respond just to see what he was going to come back with.

Kai: *Thank you. You too.*

It was a simple reply. Kai washed her face, brushed her teeth, and picked out her clothes for the day all with no response. That was it. Apparently, he'd only wanted to tell her to have a good day with no hidden agenda. The thought that maybe he was really just trying to be nice made the smile creep back upon her lips, then she caught herself and shook her head. Her thoughts were all over the place. She recalled the day she'd found the condom in Jayson's bathroom and how she'd been infuriated with the belief that he'd cheated on her. She still wasn't completely over that and her guard was still up where Jayson was concerned.

Now here she was staying up to the wee hours of the morning texting DeWayne and smiling at his simple yet thoughtful text messages. She felt like she was sneaking around and the idea of it sickened her. She wasn't that person and she had no respect for people who tended to creep. What was worse, and completely bizarre, about the situation was that she felt like she was cheating on her boyfriend with her husband.

Her head began to whirl as the thoughts crowded her mind. Something was off. Something about this situation wasn't right and as much as she thought she was at peace with what was going on in her life the truth was that she was probably more confused now than ever. She wished that someone could just show up and point out to her whatever it was that needed to be done in her life to restore some real level of order or normalcy, but she knew that only she could determine what needed to be done. But how?

Moving on with her morning, Kai dressed and hurried off to drop by Raquel's to drop off some copies of her books that Raquel would be taking with her to a book event she was attending the following weekend. The moment Kai walked through the door Raquel gave her a knowing look.

"What?" Kai asked after hugging her friend.

"You tell me what. You just look like something's heavy on your mind."

Kai shook her head and played it off. "Naw, just got a lot to do. Trying to finish up my errands so I can be on time to meet Jayson for lunch." She handed Racquel the signed books she'd brought over. "Here you go boo. Thank you again."

"You know it's no problem." Racquel took the books and smiled at Kai.

"What?" Kai asked again, this time laughing at how intently the other woman was eyeing her.

"You can sit up here and tell me it ain't nothing all day long, but I know you. I know that something's running through that mind of yours. You know you ain't gotta try to hold everything in all the time don't you? Even the strongest person in the world needs to unleash some stuff every once in a while."

Kai opened her mouth to speak, but was silenced by the first bars of Beyonce's 'Resentment'. Instantly she bit her lower lip and stared at the phone as if trying to decide whether or not she should answer. Perhaps this was the moment when he'd show his true ass and get to the heart of why he'd been playing the role of nice guy here lately. Kai wasn't sure that she was ready to take a seat on the roller coaster ride that she often found herself on when dealing with DeWayne. But, despite her misgivings, like a fish to water she was drawn to him and felt compelled to answer the phone.

"Hello," she greeted, trying to keep her tone even.

"Hey, what you doing?" He asked her.

"About to leave Racquel's."

"I need you to meet me."

Her guard was up. "When?"

"In about an hour."

"Where?"

"Benihanas."

It was one of her favorite eateries, but she wondered what his reason was for requiring her to meet him there.

"Why?"

"We need to talk about this divorce stuff…these papers."

She nodded and stared at Racquel, whose facial expression denoted confusion. "Um…I have plans. You shoulda asked me earlier and I—"

"Sorry for the last minute request, but it's important and I kinda want to get it over with while I still have the nerve to do it. It's time. You know? So I'll see you there in one hour, okay?" He hung up without waiting for a reply.

Kai was rooted to the spot. The feelings she'd experienced earlier that morning returned. Her head was spinning and she prayed for the room to be still so that she could collect her thoughts. Everything seemed to be moving at the speed of lightening now. She'd prayed for some kind of restoration of her life and perhaps the universe was giving her exactly what she'd asked for.

"Kai?" Racquel called out, concern etched in her tone. "Sis, you alright?"

"I…I don't know." She looked at her friend and shook her head.

Racquel led her to the couch. "Okay, you don't look too good. You need to sit for a minute. Your breathing's all irregular. You need some water?"

Kai shook her head. "I'll be alright. I'm just…a lil' bit overwhelmed."

"What's going on? You got me over here scared like I don't know if I should call your mama, your doctor….what?"

"I have two dates right now," Kai said.

"What?"

"I have two dates. Jayson's waiting for me to meet him for lunch and DeWayne just said he needed me to meet him."

"DeWayne?" The mention of him made Racquel's eyebrow rise. "Hmm. You over here about to fall out like something's the matter. Girl, some women don't get two dates in a year, but you got two in a day. So, what's the problem?" Racquel laughed.

"My spirit is telling me that something is going to happen…that something needs to happen. I just…I feel this insecurity with Jayson and I don't like it. I mean, we're getting along fine now, but in the back of my mind I keep thinking about the condom I found in his bathroom and the possibility of him cheating on me. Then DeWayne's been playing nice for a while. Texting, calling, and just being the attentive man he should've been a long time ago. Now he calls me talking about come meet him now to go over the divorce papers."

Racquel nodded. "Ohhhh. He's ready to sign now huh?"

Kai shrugged. "It sounds that way."

"Isn't that what you wanted?"

Kai had to be honest with herself in that moment. "I never really wanted to get divorced. I just wanted my husband to act right. I just wanted him to love me."

Racquel took a deep breath. "You sound like you don't know if you wanna stay in a relationship with Jayson and you don't know if you really wanna divorce DeWayne....either way, you got to face somebody today. So, what are you going to do?"

Kai looked into Racquel's eyes for some hint of a suggestion at what move she should make. "I don't know," she said. "I just don't know."

***

Kai sat in the parking lot and reviewed her decision. It was too late to turn back now because she was already there. The choice, though it was difficult to make, made plenty of sense to her. She only hoped that the other would understand. Time had been invested into their relationship and she owed it to herself to handle it with delicacy. She needed to say some things and she wondered what his responses would be. She wondered how things would be once lunch was over and they walked out of those doors going in separate directions.

Taking a deep breath, she got out of the car and headed inside to the table where he was patiently waiting for her. He'd thoughtfully gone ahead and ordered a drink for her which she was in desperate need of as she thought about the text message that she'd shot to the other guy in hopes that he wouldn't choose now to call and inquire about her inability to show up and her aloofness as to why.

"I thought you weren't coming for a minute," he said, rising to pull her chair out for her.

Very chivalrous of him, she thought as she took a seat and immediately took a sip of her drink. "It was hell to get all the way out here. Plus I had something else to attend to."

He nodded his understanding. "You look nice."

She was wearing jeans and a black tank top, nothing special, but it was still kind of him to think so. "Thank you," she said softly.

"Mmmhmm. I just have a lot on my mind and after you asked me to meet you this morning a lot of feelings came to me that I think it's best if we discuss."

"Well, I want to go first if you don't mind."

She waved her hand giving him the floor.

"Kai, baby, I know I messed up." He took her hand and turned her face to look dead into his. "I messed up bad. I see it in your eyes all the time. I hear it in your voice. Even your demeanor, your body language is different when I come around now. It's hard for me to miss all of that and I know that it's because of me."

Kai was stunned. Was he about to confess all his sins and then paint the picture that they could live happily ever after? She was sick of being played like a yo-yo. She was starting to believe that this was the only game men knew how to play. The lying, the saying whatever they thought she wanted to hear, and the lack of trust was all too much for her. The feelings that she thought she'd buried deep within her soul rested right on her sleeves for the world to see as anguish took over her face. Was he about to tell her that he wanted them to work it out? He'd sat in her house telling her this exact thing before leading her to promise him that they were in it together, yet where had it led them to?

"Have I lied? Yes. Have I cheated? Yes. Have I been less of the man than you deserve? Yes. But you have to believe that I want to fix it baby. I'm broken over how much you've been hurt in the past and I don't want to add to that anymore," he told her. "I want you to allow me the chance to regain your trust and while I know that it's easier said than done, I know that I can do it. I know that I can be the man that you need, Kai. I love you with everything that's inside of me and all I want is to see you happy."

She was stunned. A part of her wanted to kiss the tears that he kept sniffling and working hard to keep at bay. The other part of her wanted to slap his face. Didn't this man know how much she'd been through? Didn't he understand that the role he played in her confusion was far too outrageous now for her to buy into the speech he was giving to her? There was a time when all she wanted was to make things work with this man that she found beautiful and irresistible, but that whole notion that maybe love wasn't meant for her was starting to sink deeper into her soul.

She searched his eyes for sincerity and couldn't deny the twinkle that flashed back at her. While there was something noticeably different about the way he looked at her, there was nothing different about the words that were coming out of his mouth. She'd heard similar verbiage before and wasn't emotionally equipped to deal with the mounds of heartache that followed the broken promises later on down the line. She was so sure that he was running game on her that she shook her head and broke their stare.

Not yet willing to concede and sensing that he was losing her, he grabbed her face with both hands, lifted her chin, and kissed her lips more passionately than he ever had. Though his eyes were shut, his tears fell swiftly and he didn't bother to mask them as he continued to make love to her lips with his own. Her tears began to fall, mixing with his as their lip-lock continued. It felt like an eternity had passed before he finally pulled away and looked into her eyes as she blinked through the tears that blinded her.

Kai had to admit that it was different—the public display of affection, the way his embrace rocked her core, and the trembling of his hands as he held her face so that she couldn't escape his kiss. Perhaps he wasn't toying with her emotions. Perhaps the man sitting before her was different from what she'd known and experienced before. Perhaps this man really did want to secure forever with her and build a lasting relationship.

"I want to make you happy," he reiterated. "In any way that I can." He reached over to the seat beside him and pulled some papers out of a briefcase that she hadn't seen resting on the neighboring seat. He laid the thick packet down on the table in front of her and returned his eyes to meet hers. "Even if it means granting you the divorce that you asked for. I just want you to be happy."

Kai was speechless. Just when she thought that DeWayne was staking his claim and had transformed into the Prince Charming she always knew that he could be, there he was offering her the one thing that she'd been dying for over the last couple of years. Just like that she realized that he wasn't there to procure forever. He was there to solidify the end. Sadness over came her and that familiar depression she'd found herself in and out of over the last few years immediately seeped right back into her body. But hadn't she come there for closure? Why was she so distraught over seeing the signed papers before her when all she'd wanted was to expediently end this chapter of her life?

She fingered the pages with one hand and with her other she picked up her napkin to wipe her eyes. She nodded her head in understanding. "It only took forever," she said softly.

"That's what I want," he told her.

She shot him a confused look. "What?"

"I want forever."

Kai was close to tossing her drink in his face for sending her in a tail-spin of emotions at that moment. "You just gave me divorce papers and you're saying you want forever?"

"I'm giving you what makes you happy Kai, but let me tell you what would make me happy. The opportunity to reclaim my family, keep a smile on your face, and show you all the love in the world...the chance to wake up to you in the mornings and put you to sleep at night. I want the chance to stand before God and all of our family and rededicate ourselves to something that I know could be great. I messed up…I own that baby. And seeing all the hurt I've caused you, seeing how it's affected you and our family makes me want to be a better man. It makes me want to be a better man for you."

"You ready order now?" The Japanese waiter asked out of nowhere with his broken English.

DeWayne's head turned slowly in the man's direction before he gave him a stern look. "We're kinda in the middle of a moment," he snapped.

The waiter nodded several times before running off.

DeWayne returned his focus to Kai and hunched his shoulders in an effort to loosen up his body and get back into the moment. She couldn't help but turn up the corners of her lips. There was something so sexy about the way he took charge. She remembered that trait of his and the way that it would make her fall over in lust whenever he exercised it.

The table next to them was beginning their hibachi experience as the chef brought out all of his necessary utensils and ingredients.

"I want to show you that I can be everything you need Kai," DeWayne said, getting back to the matter at hand. "I signed those papers for you only if that's what you want, because it sure as hell isn't what I want. So tell me, baby....we can go as fast, or as slow as you need to, but let me know if you're open to giving me that chance...to letting me win back your trust, love, and affection."

Words wouldn't form upon her lips and sound was vacant from her voice box. All she could do was look at him in awe of the fact that he appeared to be so openly invested in making things right. She wanted to believe him, but then again she'd grown so accustomed to the thought of moving on without him. Was she really ready to try the wife thing again? Was she really ready to open herself up to the potential of being hurt again? She'd just recently finished paying her fines and completing her anger management classes, but the memory of all the strife DeWayne had caused was firmly planted in her mind. Was she capable of forgiving him and moving forward? Was she capable of loving him again, let alone trusting him to love her wholeheartedly?

Sensing her hesitation, DeWayne reached for the divorce papers. When she didn't stop him he grabbed the packet and rolled it up tight with both of his hands. The waiter at the table beside them turned on his gas stove and lit a fire onto the grill. Instantly, DeWayne hopped up and took two steps to approach the nearby table. To everyone's surprise, especially the chef's, he tossed the rolled up packet into the fire on the stove contaminating the cooking environment, delaying the customer's dinner, all while making a bold statement.

DeWayne looked over at Kai who was laughing at the chef who was vehemently going off in Japanese. "I want forever," DeWayne told Kai. "And I'll go to my grave trying to prove that to you."

As the chef removed the burning papers and cleaned his stove, the restaurant's manager approached the seemingly crazed DeWayne. He didn't care. His eyes never left his wife's. He needed her to know that he was serious. As sure as that fire blazed the divorce papers to a crisp, his love for her burned eternally. He wasn't giving up. They'd loss so much time, now he'd die proving to her that he loved her past the moon.

~ CHAPTER 18 ~

"You stood me up and you've been evasive," Jayson said. "You sent me some nonchalant text about needing space which I can respect…I don't like it, but I respect it. But now you're telling me that you're done?"

She'd given it a lot of thought and even before DeWayne's declaration of wanting to create forever with her, she'd been battling with the decision to end things with Jayson completely. She'd told him that she needed space and they should take a break in her abrupt text the day that they were supposed to meet for lunch. But, now she was telling him that there would be an indefinite hold on their relationship.

"So, what is it? You just felt like trying something new until your man got it right?" Jayson asked accusingly.

She'd gone over to his place out of courtesy and respect for what they had. She wouldn't have wanted to hear it by phone if someone was breaking up with her, so she didn't want to do that to him. Now she was regretting the decision because seeing the hurt in his eyes was tearing her apart. "It's not like that and you know it. I was done. You know that."

"That's what your mouth said. But now your mouth is telling me that you're reuniting with the same dude that caused you to end up in jail. That's messed up man. You think a brother ain't got no feelings?"

"I'm respecting your feelings by letting you know what's going on and not leading you on. And I never said we were reuniting…we're just getting to know each other again and taking it one day at a time. I need this time to give my life and feelings together. I'd hope that you would understand, but I completely understand you feelings."

"Do you? Do you know that I loved you?" Jayson's voice cracked as he said the words. "I *still* love you."

The thought of the condom she'd found in his bathroom resurfaced yet again. She shook it off, not wanting to bring it up at that moment, but wondering if he loved her when he'd been prepared to use the condom. Kai sighed. "It took a lot for me to agree to a relationship with you in the first place. As much as I was drawn to you I wanted this whole mess to be over and done with before—"

"Wait, I know you're not trying to say I pressured you into a relationship," his voice boomed in the quiet of his living room.

Kai looked up at him from her seat on the couch and bit her tongue for just a second. She understood that he was feeling emotional, but she wasn't the type of chick that would let a man pop off at her. "No, if you'll listen to me and stop being so quick to snap…I was saying I wanted this whole mess to be over and done with before getting involved with anyone and I was so certain that it was nearly done. I didn't expect a turn of events. But rather than waste your time, or make you feel like I'm playing with your emotions, I'd rather walk away now and give myself time to figure out what's going on."

Jayson shook his head. "This is messed up. This is real messed up. What am I supposed to do now?"

Kai grabbed her purse and stood up to face him. "Move on," she said simply. She leaned forward and kissed him gently on his cheek. "I'm sorry," she said sincerely.

Jayson didn't respond. There were no words that could capture his feelings any greater than the facial expression he was giving her. Kai turned away and let herself out of his home, failing to turn back. She knew what she would see if she did—the face of a man fighting hard to hold his emotions end knowing that he'd lost what could have potentially been the best woman he'd ever had.

***

"Quinn, you gotta let me know if I'm showing too much," Kai joked as she perched onto the railing overlooking the pond at the gazebo at Piedmont Park.

It was a beautiful day and Kai was feeling blessed and joyous. Over the last few months her life had changed drastically. She and DeWayne had gone from her wanting to kill him most days, to dating casually, to slipping back into a familial routine, all the way down to living together once again. He'd been more attentive than ever and even though she still wavered from time to time on whether he was truly all in and if the other shoe would soon drop, never once did he revert back to the DeWayne that caused her to see nothing but red and fury.

Business was going well as she prepared to release yet another novel while going to school and still maintaining her event planning agency. Although the Literary Ladies of the ATL had managed to tap a few episodes in order to pitch the show idea, they were still constantly coming up with more creative ways to extend the brand. Even their camerawomen, Kierra, had found her niche in the literary community evolving her from behind the scenes to becoming a full-fledged Literary Lady of the ATL. Kai's business was booming and her personal circle was small—it was the recipe for a happy, stress-free, fulfilling life.

Click, click. Quinn snapped away with his camera taking picture after picture of her in the beautiful light of day. Kai was preparing to put together a new line of promotional materials for her many projects and Quinn was the only photographer in the world who could photograph her to her liking. He'd been her photographer for years and she loved the working relationship that they had.

The wind blew a little moving her braids and Kai smiled into the camera. *Click, click.*

"Beautiful!" Quinn exclaimed. "You're making my camera happy."

Kai laughed and then her eyes were averted toward a figure moving in their direction. A man was carrying a vase of roses and he looked intent upon coming up to them.

"What in the world?" Kai asked as Quinn snapped a photo of her capturing the sincere look of wonderment.

The stranger approached her. "Kai Davis?" He asked.

She nodded.

"These are for you." He handed her the vase.

Kai took it and looked through the flowers for a card, but there wasn't one. She sniffed the roses as the stranger walked away and looked up at Quinn. "Did you have him bring these?"

Quinn flashed his beautiful, bright, toothy grin. "I would take credit for it, but I can't tell a lie."

Kai was stunned. "Who would just send flowers out to my photo shoot?" She sniffed the flowers again just as

Quinn snapped yet another photo. She sat the vase down and shook her head. "Whoever it was will probably call soon to see if I got it," she rationalized.

"Back to work Boss Lady," Quinn urged.

"Right," Kai agreed, standing up and getting back into her modeling frame of mind.

Quinn snapped a couple more shots before two young women rounded the corner and down the sidewalk in their direction, each carrying a vase of red roses.

Kai laughed out loud. "Wait a minute now. One, maybe, but three…something's going on here."

The women smiled, yet said nothing as they sat their vases down next to the first one and turned to walk off. Kai examined the flowers, but still there was no card in sight. She looked at Quinn whose bright complexion was starting to look flushed. She felt like he knew something.

"You want to tell me what's going on?" She asked.

He shrugged his shoulders. "I'm just here to take your picture. Your guess is as good as mine."

Just as he finished his statement the sound of music faintly filled their ears. They both turned to watch as a horse and carriage took its time descending the sidewalk. Kai squinted to see who was sitting in the carriage. This was different. She'd never seen a horse and carriage prancing through Piedmont Park in all the times that she'd been there. The sound of lyrics from Brian McKnight's '6,8,12' grew louder and more distinguishable. Kai stood still staring at the carriage and found herself caught up in the melody that was drawing the attention of others nearby. As Brain cooed about the difficulty in passing the time while unable to get his love interest off of his mind,

DeWayne's face came into clear view. Kai's knees grew weak and she had to reach out for the pillar to her left to sturdy herself.

Quinn snapped candids as Kai watched her husband get out of the carriage and approach her in a red and white plaid shirt and jeans that matched her red and white apparel perfectly. Her favorite song continued to blast from the top of the hill as DeWayne got closer, holding out one perfect long-stem red rose.

Click, click. Quinn didn't miss a moment of the surprise, or the expressions that flickered across Kai's face.

"What are you doing?" Kai asked on the verge of tears.

"I'm showing you my intent," DeWayne explained. "Things have been good…being around you, being back in a good place. But, I want things to be perfect." He lowered himself to one knee as the camera flashed and Kai sucked in a deep breath.

"Oh my God!" Kai exclaimed.

The moment was extremely surreal as those passing by stopped to witness the grand display of romance occurring before them. The onlookers were of no consequence to DeWayne. He only saw Kai. He was on a mission to solidify the rebirth of their love and the rededication to their marriage. From his pocket he pulled out a tiny black box and took his time opening it to expose the 4.35 princess cut, antique custom-designed diamond platinum engagement ring with emeralds on the sides and crushed diamonds encased in the band, which lied nestled inside of the velvet cushion.

"I love you more than these, or any other diamonds could ever sparkle," he told her. "I knew from the beginning that you were the woman who would change my life and encourage me to reach greater heights. I knew that you were the one who made me feel emotions I've never experienced before in my life. I'm whole with you. I'm complete with you. I just want you to feel safe and secure, whole and complete with me as well forever. I can't take back any of the things that have happened Kai, but I dedicate my whole life to making sure that you never shed another tear."

He reached for her left hand and she didn't protest as she held the single rose in her right hand. Quinn positioned himself cattycornered to them to get the perfect angle of DeWayne's proposal.

"Kai Davis, I love you beyond measure," DeWayne stated. "Will you do me the honor of marrying me all over again and rededicating yourself to the life we've created?"

The tears threatened to ruin her makeup, but Kai didn't care. It was the proposal of her dreams. When they'd first gotten married years ago everything had been so rushed. One day he was asking for her hand abruptly, the next day they were exchanging I-do's at the courthouse, and then she was whisked away to another country to begin a new life as his wife. They'd never had the chance to actually create a storybook moment such as this, or enjoy being engaged before getting married. Now they had the opportunity to do it all over again and it was only fitting since they were making an effort to try to strengthen their marriage and rid themselves of the hurt from the past.

Kai removed her hand from his grip and touched his face gently. "Yes," she said softly.

DeWayne took a noticeable breath before removing the ring from the box and placing it on her ring finger. Quinn caught the moment in several snaps. DeWayne smiled up at her before putting her hand to his lips. He kissed her ring and then the back of her hand several times. “I won’t disappoint you,” he promised. “I will never disappoint you again.”

He rose to stand on both feet and pulled her into a loving embrace. The bystanders gave them a round of applause as their lips meshed and Quinn continued to photograph the memory. It was beautiful and Kai knew that she’d never forget the moment that she sincerely fell in love with her husband all over again.

As their lips parted and they looked into one another’s eyes, Kai spoke to him in a whisper. “DeWayne?”

“Hmmm?”

“Who the hell’s gonna get all these roses back to the car?”

Their laughter carried them into yet another passionate kiss. Kai felt that her happily-ever-after had finally made its way to her and it astonished her that DeWayne had turned out to be her Prince Charming after all.

~ CHAPTER 19 ~

CURRENT DAY

Kai walked along the sand with Sissy holding her hand tightly. The gorgeous white gown hung from her body perfectly. DeWayne had even gotten her size correct. The sun was beginning to set and the moment she'd been waiting for was just moments away. The smell of the salty ocean air was refreshing as she took a deep breath in and a long exhale.

"I have a confession," Sissy stated.

Kai eyed her suspiciously. "What?"

"Do you remember when I told you that maybe I was wrong about the two of you…that maybe it was best for you two to part ways and you needed to do what was best for you?"

Kai remembered it. It was the day that Sissy had told her all about Chico. She nodded her head. "Yeah. Why?"

"Girl, I was lying," Sissy stated. "I never thought for one second that I was wrong. I thought I'd use a little reverse psychology on you and maybe you'd start looking at your situation from a different angle. I really figured that if I could find love, me of all people that you two could definitely manage to salvage the spark that burned between you." She squeezed Kai's hand. "See how right I was?"

Kai couldn't dispute it. There they were docked and now prancing along the shoreline at a premiere resort in the heart of the Bahamas where somewhere down the beach DeWayne was waiting for her to commence their recommitment ceremony. They'd come so far from where they'd been that it was amazing. It was far more magical than a fairytale and way more incredible than any other love-story she'd ever heard. Decades from now she knew that their grandchildren would never believe the hurdles they'd crossed in order to become a more solid, stable union. But none of it mattered. All that mattered was this moment.

As they approached the area where the wedding was scheduled to take place, Kai was approached by a member of the resort staff handing her the bouquet of lilies that DeWayne had handpicked. "This is where you stop," the woman said politely with a smile before carefully placing a blindfold over Kai's eyes.

"What in the world?" Kai questioned. Each step of this journey amazed her due to the fine details he'd so carefully planned out.

"Shhh," Sissy hissed. She retrieved her bouquet as the Maid of Honor from the woman and gave her friend one final hug. "Congratulations sis. You deserve this." She walked away from Kai and waited for her cue to walk the path leading to the open space where the nuptials would take place.

Everything was timed. As the sun kissed the horizon on its way to slumber, the sound of a strong voice belting out Kevin Edmund's '24/7' greeted Kai's ears. A firm hand slid into hers and slowly guided her forward. The hand squeezed hers and a feeling of familiarity overcame her.

"Dad?" She whispered.

Another hand touched her right arm and guided it through a stronger arm. Kai was confused. After a moment they stopped moving and while the vocalist crooned about always being together the blindfold was removed from her eyes. As her vision became clear Kai nearly fainted.

"How? I mean, when did?" She looked around her and was completely astonished. "Why didn't? How did he?" None of her questions came out in complete sentences. She looked to her left and into the eyes of her father whom she'd known was beside her by the way he'd held her hand. "Dad, how…"

"That husband of yours thought of everything," Tony replied, smiling at his daughter. "Come on," he said, urging her to move forward down the small aisle of chairs filled with the people who were most important to her in the world.

She locked eyes with her mother who simply smiled and Grandma Lucy who gave her a reassuring head nod. Her siblings, the Literary Ladies of the ATL, Nikki Love, Raquel, and her children all held champagne colored candle sticks which were lit as they sat in two rows on either side of the aisle that was lined with rose petals along the sand. Kai looked to her right at Big Tony whose smile was as big as his heart.

"Did you know all this time?" Kai asked him.

Big Tony squeezed her hand. "We've been rooting for you," he whispered over the music. "I knew that boy had it in him and with a little help he did the damn thing."

Kai was overjoyed as her eyes fell upon the man that had turned their lives around for the better. His eyes were glazed over with tears in the dimmed light that remained at this final moment of daylight. Once the singer finished the final note of his ballad, the officiate inquired as to who was giving away the bride. Together Big Tony and Tony Jr. reoffered their pride and joy the man they fully trusted to love, honor, and protect her. Kai handed Sissy her bouquet and took hold of DeWayne's hand. He couldn't wait to press his lips against hers and quickly stole a kiss before the officiate could utter his next words. Their family went wild with applause and cheers at the display of his affection.

Their vows were exchanged traditionally, but upon the exchanging of their rings Kai's evening grew even more magical. Overhead, a loud hissing sound occurred, followed by a blast, and a clap as colors burst in the sky showering them with a rainbow of bright hues. Kai's mouth dropped in awe of the wonder of it all.

"I now pronounce you, husband and wife…again!" The officiate stated. "Now, you may kiss your bride."

DeWayne pulled Kai into his arms and held her closer and tighter than he ever had before. Their tongues danced against one another as the vocalist burst into song once more and the fireworks continued to boom and flare above them. The family rose to their feet applauding once more, each member sincerely moved by the restoration of a union set forth and governed by the God they all believed in.

DeWayne pulled his face away from Kai's slightly, but continued to hold her as he stared into her eyes in the multicolored light given off by the fireworks. "I love you, Kai Davis."

Kai took an uneasy breath and then relaxed in his arms. She felt as if she'd stepped into a new life. They truly had a fresh start and she had every intentions of making this time count. She stared into her husband's eyes with a heightened appreciation for the man that he was and everything they'd both endured up to this point. Looking at him and being held by him in that moment as everyone cheered on their love and the flares danced in the sky in their honor, Kai felt as if she'd been resuscitated. The feeling of completion that overcame her was like a breath of fresh air.

"I love you too," she whispered before leaning forward to kiss him once more. Her eyes closed as she savored the taste of his lips and the moment of their bliss. Thank you Lord for my happily ever after, she prayed as she gave herself over to the man that was meant for her.

THE END

I FLATLINED & I LIVED

I recall both times not one more than the other
I felt like the walls were closing in or I was being smothered
I could hear my heart racing and hear it beating like an overly loud bass drum
A constant and perfect rhythm bum BUM BUM BUM BUM
People seem to think your life flashes before your eyes, that's far from true
You are observing the commotion not realizing the star of the show is you
Slowly fading away as the room is turning black
You start to give up because you are overwhelmed, thinking there is no turning back
I knew it was over I thought It was my time
I could hear no sound just seeing movement like a mime
He wasn't ready for me yet, God sent me back to my boys
Their mom not being here would create a void that could never be filled not even with decoys
I have been humbled from that day on; I appreciate life just a little bit more
Thanking God for small things which I never did before
I now understand I am blessed, I don't need to be angry anymore
I no longer have to fight alone in this daily war
Almost doesn't count now let's be clear

FLATLINED 2

I live my life one day at a time with no fear
I was RESUSCITATED and given just a little bit more time
Living everyday like it's my last isn't a crime
Life is short enjoy your time while you are here
Walk in faith and not in fear
Tomorrow isn't promised not to you or to me.
But the fact that I FLATLINED and LIVED set me free!

I also want to take time to acknowledge my

LUPIE FIGHTERS

Akielah K. Conway
Portia Corbin
Kisha Johnson McRae
Kristin T Barney
Annette Boynes-McCray
Tia Frazier
JeaNida Luckie-Weatherall
Tawanna Hill
Rosalind Robinson
Kelley M. King
Francine D. Watkins
Tiffany Morrisson
Tiyunna Thompson
Angelina Conception
Ranada Turner
Sonya Stegall
Russell "Rusty" Weaver
Jocelyn Lora-Andrews
Regina Boston-Dixon
La Sonya Tujuan Thomas
Alexandria Rogers
Sandria Carter
Yvonne Lawson
Veronica Adway
Ellen Sade
Sherita Walton
San Dixon
The Princess of Poetry

Flatlined 2

Morticia Gray
Angel Barrino
Francine Watkins

ABOUT THE AUTHOR

K.S. Oliver is an author, poet, public speaker, model and business owner who was born in New York and raised in Georgia. She is blazing a trail that many have been inspired by. The oldest of eleven children, K.S. graduated from Georgia Medical Institute with a diploma in Medical Billing and Coding in 2005 as well as Colorado Technical College in 2011 with an a degree in Business (while minoring in Criminal Justice). Since then, she's been moving forward with building a unique and touching legacy.

On May 20, 2010, following the birth of her youngest child, K.S. was diagnosed with SLE, also known as Lupus. Subsequently, she was also diagnosed with Discoid Lupus (Skin Lupus), Fibromyalgia, Pulmonary Fibrosis, Hypotension, Hypothyroids, Cricoarytenoiditis (Lupus in her voice box), and severe depression. With a myriad of health issues staring her in the face at the age of 25, K.S. had to make a decision on whether she would allow it to consume her or fight for the life she and her family deserved to enjoy. The choice soon turned into a mantra commonly used when discussing her life: "I have Lupus. Lupus doesn't have me."

Taking her life story and using it to inspire others, K.S. has penned two poetry books dedicated to building a connection from one Lupie to another and helping others to understand the emotions and trials that a Lupus patient may endure. Still Standing and Affectionately 360 are poetic gems that are touching for patients of any kind, but also speak to the hearts of every individual who reads them. In 2013, K.S. was awarded as Poet of the Year for her outstanding contributions to the field of poetry.

In 2014 K.S. released her first novel, FLATLINED: Almost Doesn't Count, which was inspired by her truth. FLATLINED was ceremoniously released on the four (4) year anniversary of her diagnosis. She decided to take a leap and let the world read her rhymes of reason due to several people suggesting that she share her complete story after experiencing fragments of her memories via her poetry.

Despite the plethora of times that she's been cut, poked, jabbed, hospitalized, and operated on K.S. is not only still standing, but she is constantly thriving. In 2011 she created her first business entity, Events by Ebonee, which prides itself on cultivating quality, memorable events at affordable rates throughout the Atlanta area. True to her literary passion and experience, in 2014 K.S. started her own publishing company, Diamante Publications, in which her star only began to shine brighter within the literary community.

With all of her success and accomplishments, K.S.'s greatest achievement is centered on her two sons, Sha'Kwan and K'Shaun. Through everything she does, she incorporates the children including her literary ventures. In 2013 the boys released their first book Through Our Eyes, a glimpse into the life of a Lupie kid.

With each year that passes, K.S. finds more innovative ways to reach and touch the masses with her powerful story of strength and overcoming. Via interviews, book signings, meet and greets, modeling opportunities, and simply networking, she is able to increase awareness and expand her love for helping others. God's amazing grace has spared her from death more times than any one person deserves and even still she is here continuing to walk in his glory.

ORDER FORM
DIAMANTE' PUBLICATIONS, LLC
P.O. BOX 1034
Stone Mountain, GA 30086

Name (please print):______________________

Address:________________________________

City/State: ______________________________

Zip: ____________________________________

QTY	TITLES	PRICE

ORDER FORM
DIAMANTE' PUBLICATIONS, LLC
P.O. BOX 1034
Stone Mountain, GA 30086

Name (please print):______________________

Address:______________________________

City/State: ____________________________

Zip: _________________________________

QTY	TITLES	PRICE
	Flatlined 1	$20
	Kharma's Child	$15
	Kharma Deadly Demise	$15
	Ma'Dam by Night, Secretary by Day	$20

Shipping and handling: add $3.00 for 1st book. Then $1.00 for each additional book.

Please allow 2-4 weeks for delivery.

Stay Tuned as Diamante' Publications has plenty more heat for you

Join our mailing list
diamantepublications@gmail.com

To see what's releasing next, read a sneak peek or win great prizes

YOU CAN ALSO VISIT US AT
www.authoresssksoliver.com
www.diamantepublications.com

Stay Tuned Diamante' Publications has plenty more heat for you

STAY CONNECTED

FB: Ebonee' Oliver

IG: authoresks

TWITTER: authoressks

FACEBOOK

www.facebook.com/authoressksoliver

Happy 5 Year Anniversary Lupus

Im still Winning

May 20, 2015

Made in United States
Orlando, FL
06 March 2023